The Grey Witch of the North

The Grey Witch of the North

THE MID-WORLD OF THE TRUCE

BOOK THREE

STEVE DOUGLAS

ISBN: 978-1-7778868-2-0

The Grey Witch of the North is a work of fiction. The names, characters, businesses, places, events, locales, and incidents are either products of my imagination or used in a fictitious manner. Any resemblance to actual persons, living or dead, or actual events are coincidental.

Illustration and cover design by Thea Magerand
Typesetting by C'est Beau Designs

For our grandchildren: Kaela, Nathalie, Kai, and Benjamin,
who brought a second wave of joy into our lives,
while also fighting so hard against the Darkness
as characters in 'Grey Witch'.

Contents

ONE SIDE OF

The Game of

THE MAN AT ARMS

THE MID-WORLD SPY

THE ILLUSION

THE APPRENTICE

THE CHARMED KNIGHT

THE PRINCESS

THE TALISMAN

THE WEB OF FATE

THE GREY COUNCILLOR

THE MAGI

THE ARMED HOST

THE GREAT SPELL

THE WIZARD

THE MASTER

the Masters

THE
APPRENTICE

THE
CHARMED
KNIGHT

THE
ILLUSION

THE
MID-WORLD
SPY

THE MAN
AT ARMS

...CIAN

THE
CAPTAIN

THE
SENDING

THE
MID-WORLD
WEAPON

THE
ARCHERS

THE
MID-WORLD
POWER

THE
ANCIENT
SECRET

THE
SORCERER

THE
FORTRESS

N
W
E
S
Gravesend
The Ruins of Dahlak
The Mirage of Rainbows
City of the Truce
Gangean Range
Mt. Evergrey
(Vale of Whispers)
River Saugaram
Cloudland Plateau
River Zor
Rigal
Rivermeet
River Asaram
Hestari
Narsis
River Saugus
Durian
Stone Mountain
Isles of the Sorcerers
Gravengate

Chapter One

A Storm Over Gravengate

THEY WERE RIDING IN a fury toward the great fortress of Gravengate. It was night and mostly overcast, but Julian's enchanted staff blazed with bright light, shining over the ground so that his mare, Bluescent, could race safely through the darkness. But Bluescent was beginning to tire; traces of foam were beginning to form on her lips.

Above them, dark shapes were surging through the night sky, also heading for Gravengate — but these wanted to destroy Gravengate, not defend it.

Rafir stared up at the shapes that were streaming toward the fortress. The fox was riding on Julian's left shoulder, struggling to hold on. Rafir was Julian's second Familiar, a young, fox with red fur with the ability to turn completely invisible, a quality that helped him not at all as he bounced through the darkness, trying to avoid being thrown to the ground.

Rafir heard wings flapping, then he felt a *thump* as the winged Sebastian landed on Julian's right shoulder. Sebastian was Julian's first Familiar, and he had the body of a brown-furred monkey, but the greyish wings of a hawk extended from his shoulders — and Sebastian could fly.

"What are those things overhead?" Rafir called to Sebastian.

"Ghosts," Sebastian panted, "floating bear shaped ghosts with eyes of fire. They're on their way to Gravengate — and they're going to reach it much sooner than we will."

"Ghosts with eyes of fire," Rafir repeated, staring up into the night. He could see only dark blurs. If Sebastian lacked Rafir's ability to become completely invisible, Sebastian could see and sense matters of magic much more clearly than the fox.

Bluescent pounded on, racing over soft grasses, following the path of light made by Julian's staff, as she kept carefully on the horse track leading to the fortress. All the ghosts streaming overhead were so quiet that only the pounding hooves of Bluescent broke the silence of the night. Rafir focused his eyes on the gleaming horse track, but after a time he raised his head, finally seeing the distant glow given off by the watchfires of Gravengate.

"Fortress lights ahead," the fox murmured. "What comes next?"

"Some Power wants to destroy Balardi," Julian said, leaning forward, urging Bluescent forward. His left hand held the reins, while in his right hand, his staff beamed light on the path in front of them. Coils of his raven dark hair fluttered behind Julian. "The Wizard is defending Gravengate from his peak tower, and we should be fighting beside him."

"As usual, we're on our way to help the Wizards," Sebastian muttered. "Do they ever thank you for your aid or recognize your strength? Why they keep calling you an Apprentice is something I will never understand. You should have been raised to Adept level long ago."

Rafir carefully kept his fox's tongue quiet. If anything could make the normally calm Sebastian angry, it was the Wizards' treatment of Julian the Apprentice. To Rafir, the Wizards were always remote and mysterious, though Balardi was more approachable than Thorian at Stone Mountain or Merlin at Sea's Edge. But Sebastian's annoyance with the Wizards seemed to be growing stronger every day. Rafir shook his head in worry. *Keep your mouth shut and your eyes open, you silly fox.*

Suddenly, Rafir's eyes were able to see much more than the dim glow of distant watchfires: flashes of light were leaping out from Gravengate's topmost tower. A second later they could hear echoes from the blasts, rolling across dark skies.

"The Wizard should be using lightning against ghosts," Sebastian muttered, as they pounded toward the fortress gates. "Shocks of electricity would probably work better than blasts of power."

In the last thousand paces of their race, Bluescent increased her speed. With all the jostling and pounding, Rafir hunched down and held on grimly. Then Bluescent slowed as they finally reached the fortress gates.

Gravengate was named after its enormous gates, barriers made of huge oak beams strengthened by bands of steel, with complex inscriptions and images carved in the door's wood. Now, those gates were wide open, waiting for Julian and his small allies to enter. They rode quickly through and were met by the Captain of the Guard.

"Hail, Julian!" the Captain called out. "You are *most* welcome. The Wizard wants you in his conjuring tower — but on the third floor of the tower only. He doesn't want you at the top, in his Conjuring Chamber, at least not yet."

"What?!?" Sebastian muttered, unable to keep quiet. "You mean we nearly killed ourselves and Bluescent too, just so we could wait while the Wizard fights his battle without us?"

The Captain, embarrassed, looked away. "You should speak with Balardi," he said quietly. "I am only the Wizard's messenger." The Captain then lowered his voice even further. "But there is talk of needing to protect Julian, that powerful forces are trying to destroy the Apprentice. Guard yourselves carefully."

The Captain mounted his own horse and led them swiftly through the inner fortress toward Balardi's great conjuring tower. Watchfires were always lit throughout the fortress, though most of the night watch was still asleep. At the peak of the tower, floating, ghostly bear shapes were pressing closer, while Balardi was struggling to drive them back with his own strong magic — and the floating dark forms were fighting back with their own sorcerous powers.

"It's a Sending," Julian murmured. "Some Dark God has launched a powerful force of sorcery against Balardi, and I should be fighting beside him." Sebastian shook his head, but this time he, too, forced himself to keep silent.

They reached the tower and let an exhausted Bluescent be led away to the stables by the Captain of the Guard. As they scrambled up the long staircase to the third floor, they could feel the stone of the fortress tremble, shaken by the forces of magic that fought at the tower's peak.

Four floors above them, Balardi, the Master of Gravengate, was standing in his Conjuring chamber. Spell words were racing from the Wizard's lips while magic burst from the chamber and dark shadows swirled overhead outside the tower.

Julian took a deep breath and tried to shake the fatigue from his mind. From their chamber window, the three could see some of the struggles outside. The night was dark, with only a few pale stars blinking through the overcast sky. The air was filled with tension and surges of dark sorcery.

"Are we winning?" Rafir asked in a hushed voice, and Julian shook his head: no. He stood, holding his staff with one hand, eyes glancing at the ceiling overhead. Julian could feel the Wizard above him on the top floor of the fortress, struggling with some strange form of dark sorcery. The Apprentice tensed, pushing coils of raven dark hair back from his face.

On Julian's shoulder, Sebastian's greyish brown hawk wings fluttered anxiously. The Familiar could feel magic overhead, wild, swirling magic.

"Let's go now," Sebastian whispered. "We'll tell the Wizard that his instructions were too confusing to follow."

"He wouldn't believe us for a minute," Julian muttered, "but we're not going to wait much longer." He grasped his staff with both hands, ready to race up to the topmost tower.

The stone of Gravengate's tallest tower began to tremble. On the floor beside Julian, Rafir paced nervously, red tail thrashing over dusty stone floors. The fox glanced up to the ceiling, then back to the faces of Julian and Sebastian. *Why is everything so complicated? All I want is something to sneak up on. Something with magic that I can steal — then Sebastian and I can be heroes again, really, really, wonderful, and charming little heroes!*

It was then that the first explosion shook the tower.

WHAM!!

Dark magic smashed at Gravengate, shaking the stone peak of the great fortress. Bits of mortar like small, jagged pebbles rattled down over Julian and his two Familiars. Dust swirled through every chamber of the tower. Huge stones from the upper ramparts of the fortress trembled, threatening to topple to the ground.

Sebastian flew up toward the ceiling, while Julian planted his feet, holding his staff with both hands. On the chamber's floor, Rafir vanished, turning invisible so that even the most powerful magic sniffer couldn't sense him.

WHAM!!

A second concussion shook the tower, and all the inner torchlights of Gravengate were blown out. In the darkness, Julian stepped quickly toward the tower window — it was a gap in the fortress walls, surrounded by the tower's stone, without curtains, so it was only a gateway into the night. As

Julian stood in front of the window's dim light, Sebastian stayed on his right shoulder, while Rafir scrambled catlike up to his left. Both Familiars were coughing from the dust.

The three peered out. Shadows twisted through the night sky, showing faint streaks of light. Julian could feel the shadows' rage — an anger focused on the Wizard in his conjuring chamber. Magic was blurring the night sky so that it was now dark with all the stars of the night hidden.

Suddenly, lightning flashed from the tower. Dark shadowy shapes were blasted back, moaning in pain, but then they struggled forward through the night sky toward the highest tower, challenging the Wizard with even greater strength. His voice shaking with anger, the Wizard Balardi called out more spell words. Jagged bolts of lightning flashed through the night. Again, dark shadows were blasted back, though now there seemed to be more of them, cloudy forms pulsing with rage, determined to destroy the Wizard.

"I was sure that lightning would really hurt those things," Sebastian said in his smallest voice, "and I was wrong."

"I didn't ask before," Rafir said, "but what exactly are those 'things?'"

"Some grim, Dark God is attacking Balardi," Sebastian said, "with an unusually powerful Sending in the form of bear shaped ghosts."

Julian stepped back from their window and sent a thought into Balardi's mind: *Hold on, my Wizard Master, we are on our way.* Then Julian threw open the chamber door and raced up the stairs, taking them three at a time, with both Familiars following quickly behind him. But then Balardi's mental message stopped him halfway up the next flight.

Stay below. Help is coming, aid from Thorian.

Julian stood frozen in the darkness for a moment, feeling magic surging through the night. The tower trembled again. Julian took a deep breath. Help was coming, help from the Wizard, Thorian. If Merlin was the most powerful of Wizards, Thorian was next in power, a step or two ahead of Julian's master, Balardi. The three Wizards formed the Wizards' League, an alliance that ruled — or tried to rule — the Southern portion of Alantéa. Though now some powerful being calling itself a God was trying to destroy Balardi.

"This isn't right," Julian said, shaking his head, "we should be at the Wizard's side."

"Back to the chamber window," Sebastian said quietly into the darkness. "At least there we can see some of what's happening." Julian's staff flashed bright light, and the three retreated down the stairs and back into the lower chamber. Once again, they stared out its window.

Dark clouds surrounded the tower, so Rafir's eyes could see little except the faint lines of light swirling around them, with sudden bright bolts of jagged lightning blasting from Balardi's staff. But the eyes of Sebastian, sensitive to magic, were following events much more clearly.

"Those huge, floating bear shapes are crowding the tower," Sebastian explained to the fox in low tones. "Grey and black bear shapes, with eyes of fire." Lightning flashed again, driving bear shapes back a short distance, though their eyes seemed to flash a brighter red, with anger — and with hunger.

The fox looked away from the faint lights, staring off into the distance. The night sky was losing its blurry shadows. Far away, pale, distant stars were partly hidden by the glow of magic forces that battled all through the night sky. Rafir wanted to see more, much more. *Eyes of fire — maybe one day I can learn to see magic as clearly as Sebastian. Maybe...but then I might have to give up my own power that lets me completely vanish. It's a force so strong that not even Merlin can see me when I don't want to be seen.*

More lightning flashed from Balardi's staff.

"These things don't like lightning," Julian said softly, "but it's not really — wait, now Balardi is trying fire this time." Flames surged from the tower, shining a pale red light over the faces of the Apprentice and his two Familiars.

"Fire drives the bear shapes back," Julian continued, "but those creatures are too strong. Now comes the Wizard's magic of icy, chilled frost — their floating bear shapes are starting to sink downward. Ice is forming on their bodies, and they grow heavier. But wait — their eyes of fire grow brighter, and the ice around them melts. They are rising, again, back to the battle, and they don't seem at all afraid of the Wizard."

Julian took a deep breath. "These bear shaped Sendings are too strong. Where is the aid promised to Balardi? I'm only going to wait a minute longer...wait, now the Wizard is using much greater magic. He is trying to *transform* them, to change them into — into bat creatures, things that can be blasted or burned or frozen in midair. The bear shapes are shaking under the pressure of Balardi's spell, but they aren't changing. I should be at Balardi's side! They're getting weaker, and a blast of fire or a surge of cold from my own staff might drive these things far from Gravengate. Why are we watching four floors away from the battle?"

Sebastian shook his head and muttered, "The Wizards are still trying to protect us from harm. You would think that Balardi, at least, would know better —" Sebastian's wings began flapping in excitement. More magic was surging through the darkness. It was a different magic, coming from another Wizard. Now from the northeast other ghostly shapes came raging out of the night.

Thorian's counter spell took the form of a great Sending, ghostly hounds — white as stars and blue as a clear skies — racing through the air. The Wizard's hounds were far smaller than the bear shapes, but they were fierce, and the night sky was filled with them. Howling with menace, floating hound forms fell from the upper skies, landing on bear shapes, jaws snapping at necks and paws and unprotected bear backs.

"Ghosts are fighting each other in the night skies," Sebastian whispered to Rafir. "Our ghosts are smaller hound shapes, but there are a lot more of them, and the bear shaped ghosts are taking wounds, wounds they can't heal."

Now the bear shapes found their voices and they, too, began to howl in pain, so that noise filled the battlements of the great fortress. The second and third night watches were finally called out. Throughout the fortress, armed guards raced up its inner staircases to the fortress walls, then ran over Gravengate's upper ramparts. Flame arrows surged into the night, some of them falling back onto the tower walls.

"Move back," Julian murmured. "We're in more danger from those arrows than from those bear shaped creatures." Confident in his own defenses, Julian had little concern for stray arrows, but Sebastian and Rafir were in danger.

They stepped back from the windows, able to see only traces of fire as flaming arrows sped through the night sky. If they could no longer watch they were still able to hear: drums began pounding as the night watches rallied for battle. Julian closed his eyes, letting the Sight inside him reach out to the struggle.

"This Dark God's Sending — in its form of many bear shapes," Julian whispered, "isn't damaged much by fire or sharp metal. But somehow, they don't like the pounding sounds of the drummers, and now they're being ripped apart by the hounds sent by Thorian. Bear shapes are gathering in a circle, surrounded by packs of hounds, cringing at the pounding of the drummers. I can see Balardi's face now. He's angry but more intent. He's going to —"

Lightning surged from the upper chamber. Power blasted into the cluster of bear shapes. This time it was lightning without light — huge, black, jagged bolts raced through the night and exploded. Thunder rumbled through the fortress. Arrows stopped racing through the sky. Drums of the night watch stopped pounding. All was silent. The sense that magic was fighting magic in the night sky was gone.

Cautiously, the three returned to the window. Torchlights on the fortress walls were dying down as the night watch returned to their posts or to their beds. Overhead, the night sky was losing its haze of magic, and pale stars were returning slowly to their places in the sky.

"Balardi's going to speak with us in the morning," Julian said, after a pause. "Later tonight the Wizards are going to try to find which Dark God was responsible for this attack."

Sebastian tried hard to bite his tongue — saying anything more could only make things worse. *Probably Balardi doesn't want to face Julian. After all we've done for them, the Wizards are going to try to send us away, to protect us from danger. It's really not right — they shouldn't keep Julian at the lowest level, as an Apprentice. At the middle level are Adepts and Magicians. At the top level of Magicians are those nasty Sorcerers, while the Wizards are probably more than a little stronger than Sorcerers. Julian the Adept seems more accurate than Julian the Apprentice, but the Wizards don't seem willing to recognize his knowledge and strength.*

The three kept silent as they left Gravengate's conjuring tower. As they walked slowly through the stone courtyards of the great fortress, all the inner torchlights were being relit by the night watch, so that chamber windows glowed again in the night.

Whenever they stayed at Gravengate, Julian and his two Familiars were housed in a southern section of the fortress, near its huge oak doors. Their sleeping chamber was plain: one small bed was set into a dark corner, with a small nightstand beside it. Tapestries, woven from wool, hung on the chamber walls, showing images of the night skies that lay above Alantéa the Forerunner. Unlike the windows in the conjuring tower, the windows of this chamber were heavily curtained, so when its curtains were pulled, the room became pitch black.

In this chamber the three slept, Sebastian in a fold of blanket at the foot of Julian's bed, while Rafir slept on the floor, on a carpet of animal hide that the fox imagined to be that of a shaggy bear. So, in his dreams, Rafir became a night hound, like those sent by Thorian, leaping at bear shapes in dark skies.

Julian's dreams were very different. The Gift within him — the source of his strength of magic — sometimes took him on night visits to distant places, both imagined and real. On this night Julian was visiting with his parents, two people he had been separated from since he was five years old. Many years ago, his family and two other refugees had been traveling south to the lines of the Wizards' League and had been attacked at a river crossing. Julian and his grandmother, and three others had escaped, while the rest of their party, including his parents, had been captured at the crossing by forces opposing the Wizards' League. Through Merlin and Balardi, Julian had learned that his parents still lived, that they were not in pain, though they were unlikely ever to be freed to join their son in the service of the Wizards.

"*I never know,*" Julian was saying, "*whether my mind has invented you, or whether we are really sharing the same night vision. Either way, my heart leaps to see you, to be with you, even in dreams.*"

His mother nodded, face shining with love. "*I think that sometimes you dream of us, and other times, we are able to slip free from our jealous master, whom we are unable to name, and join you to share your night visions.*"

"*This is one of those nights when we* have *slipped free,*" his father added, "*though we are left with only a little time.*" They were both older and greyer than Julian remembered them as a child, though they still seemed at full strength, not yet touched deeply by the passage of time. So, this was one of his *real meetings with them — they were really beside him! His heart leaped inside his sleeping body.*

His mother smiled, then leaned forward, face intent. *"The Sight is strong within me, Julian, yet a haze is gathering around your future. The Wizards will send you north, in part to deal with a serious matter, in part to keep you far from danger. They fear that some jealous Dark God is launching a new assault on the League — and they also see the haze that gathers around your future, so that they fear you might be destroyed in the coming struggles."*

"Swiftly, now, swiftly," his father added, *and Julian could see that the forms of his parents were beginning to fade, with grey wisps slipping from the edges of their images. He was losing contact with them, and he knew that their time together on this night would be brief.*

"Julian," his mother continued, *"the haze surrounding your future is a clear sign that there is more danger for you to the north than there is to the south. I think you should obey Merlin and go north but be very, very cautious. You know how the Gods of the Mid-World love their games, love to toy with all the humans of the land..."* Then the link with his parents was broken, and for the rest of the night, the Gift allowed Julian only a dreamless sleep.

·)(·

Morning brought a message from Balardi, a whisper into Julian's mind that was so faint that Sebastian sensed none of it. They met the Wizard on the eastern fortifications of Gravengate, with the rising sun beaming down on them. The Wizard smiled at them, though the effect was a little troubling: one of Balardi's eyebrows had been burned black during the night struggle at his conjuring tower's peak, and the Wizard had failed to notice or correct it. The black fringe above his eye contrasted with his gold beard, and its grey edges.

Balardi met their eyes — if only briefly — but then the Wizard looked away.

"I could sense your unhappiness and your disappointment even before we met together," the Wizard said softly. "You have fought valiantly for the Wizards and their League, so in a sense, I can almost, but just almost, agree with your unhappiness. Therefore, I have left this matter to Merlin. He is our leader, and these are his words." Julian took a slip of parchment from Balardi's hand, and for the sake of Sebastian and Rafir, read its words aloud:

"From the hand of Merlin at Sea's Edge:

Julian, would that we had time to train you further and reward you for your most excellent service to the League. However, events stir on our northern border, and some strange Power intrudes upon our lands. Go then and discover what manner of being we are dealing with. If this is a lesser intrusion, deal with it yourself. Otherwise, report back to Balardi and we, the Wizards, will together discover ways to counter this trespass.
This intruder calls herself The Grey Witch of the North."

Chapter Two

Journey to the North

IT WAS THE MIDDLE of the morning when they set out, with the sun still climbing higher, shining a brilliant, bright light over Gravengate and their passage to the north. It was early fall, and Julian hoped that their journey would continue in good weather. In case the cold rains came, the Apprentice led a packhorse with a cart for their provisions, including a small tent for the three of them.

The Wizards' League included both large and small cities. However, most people in the League lived in small farms and villages, places that usually looked forward to visits from the Wizards' emissaries, like Julian. So, where possible, they would look for a welcoming village to stay in; otherwise, their small tent would be comfortable enough.

The great roadway of the League, known as the Greenway, ran east and west, linking Sea's Edge, Merlin's place of power with Gravengate, and Gravengate with Stone Mountain, where Thorian ruled. North and south roads were often no more than simple horse tracks, unable to handle much more than four wheeled carts; and even cartwheels tended to be slowed by the rains of late autumn.

On this morning, Rafir ran beside their horse track. Green leaves were turning yellow, orange, and red; as they fell, drifting over the horse track, the fox made a game of skipping over the leaves, touching only green grasses. In his game, Rafir was always the hero, telling the story of his adventures to himself as he raced over damp grasses:

Swifter than a Wizard's thought, the unseen fox slipped past powerful guards, deeper into the Dark God's most secret and hidden place of power. As he neared the throne room, the air grew heavier, thick with the smell of burning incense. Inside the chamber, the Dark God seemed huge, seated on an even larger throne, protected by powerful servants who were armed with magic weapons. But none of them sensed the invisible Mid-World Spy as the fox slipped through the dark, foggy air of the chamber.

Sebastian's wings flapped, and he glided from branch to branch, enjoying Rafir's game with a slight smile on his face. Only a few trees grew along the early section of the horse track leading north, so Sebastian had to fly farther before he could rest on a tree branch. His slight wings had to work harder and the Familiar grew quickly tired of flight. Then he settled on Julian's shoulder and watched, like as sentry, while Julian's mare carried them north from Gravengate.

Bluescent was completely happy to be free from the great fortress: Gravengate was dark inside, with tall walls that cast shadows over its courtyards. It had few green pastures, and all its many streams had been buried underground so that some of the streams' water could be captured by the deep wells of the fortress. Now, not far from Gravengate, Bluescent could graze on long grasses, tail sweeping back and forth at the few remaining flies of early fall.

"Julian, relax," Sebastian murmured down at the Apprentice. "The sun is shining. We're off on another adventure, and the Wizards will just have to look after themselves for a while. Long ago, they should have promoted you to Adept level — but maybe after we've chased off this Grey Witch creature, they will decide to do the right thing. Now, would you look at what the fox is up to? He will be so tired tonight that he'll probably snore and keep us all awake."

Julian smiled. Sebastian was better, more even tempered when he was away from the Wizards. The Apprentice watched Rafir for a moment, the powerful Sight within him reaching out, barely able to pick up traces of Rafir's fantasy adventure:

And in the far corner of the Dark God's chamber lay the magic ring. It sat on a pillow of Royal Purple, glowing in the dark. Quick as a wink, Rafir closed his mouth over it. Yikes! It was hot! And the sentries saw it vanish! The invisible fox needed to run for his life — again!

Julian laughed quietly, but then the Sight, its range extended, brought another vision: riders were coming from the west, traveling hard to intercept him as he traveled north. One of them was a being of magic or carried a thing of magic. Julian grasped his staff. His shoulder lifted — a signal for Sebastian to rise, and the little Familiar flapped his wings, flying hard, reaching a height of a few hundred feet, but so far to the west that Julian could barely see him.

Moments later, Sebastian was back, still breathing hard. "It's Galad," Sebastian panted. "You can set aside your staff." Julian halted, releasing Bluescent and their pack horse to graze in peace. Rafir raced back to Julian: Galad was an ally, a powerful ally, and a close friend. They waited.

Galad came into view. He was riding Molise, his charger. Behind him followed a dozen well-armed knights; half were spearmen, half were archers on horseback. Behind those riders, pack horses carried large wicker shields as well as Galad's heavy armor.

"No more easy riding through the League for me," Galad called out to Julian. "The Wizards fear ambushes, and so now I have an armed escort!" Moments later, when Galad reached Julian, he dismounted and embraced the Apprentice.

"Worry, worry, worry, like old washerwomen," the warrior muttered. "The Wizards worry about you, and they send you away. They worry about me and surround me with guards." Galad turned to the small company of horsemen assigned to protect him, and called out, "Not that you lads aren't doing a fine job, each one of you. But the Apprentice and I are going to have a brief lunch together on this fine sunny day. So, you might want to set a watch, guard both of us, to make certain that no Demon or Dragon or Creature of the Darkness creeps up on us. Half of you can stand guard, while the other half brews tea for lunch. Our wine should wait until we reach Gravengate."

Galad lowered his voice. "They *are* doing a good job, except for the curly haired one on the far left — he thinks *he* should be wielding the Tarnished Sword and telling the Wizards how to manage their League. It would be interesting to meet his parents, maybe find out how he became so certain of his own brilliance. Good luck to him."

Galad knelt in the grass and embraced Sebastian and Rafir. "You're lucky, Julian," he said quietly, "because the only guards you need to deal with are these two heroes. Did you know that the children of the villages say very little about the distant Wizards, but they tell endless tales of these two small heroes, Sebastian and Rafir?" Rafir's eyes gleamed with interest, while Sebastian shook his head doubtfully.

"No, really, it's true," Galad said, then he stood. The broad-shouldered warrior stood almost a full head taller than Julian. His chestnut brown hair was cut evenly over his forehead, trimmed carefully so that his battle helmet fit solidly. At his side was the Tarnished Sword, one of the great magical weapons of Alantéa: in battle, the Sword would harvest metal weapons and armor, and the flesh within the armor, as though they were wheat.

"So, really, why *are* they sending you away on this silly quest?" Galad asked more seriously. "No one, not Kalanin the Great Captain, or Galad of the Tarnished Sword, was as much of a force in our last struggles as you, Julian, the Humble Apprentice."

Julian smiled and offered Galad a mock bow. "This 'Humble Apprentice' is very glad to be at your side again. As for our 'quest,' Balardi asked Merlin to send me a note. You should read it." He pulled the note from a side pouch and handed it to Galad.

"Ha!" the warrior scoffed, after scanning the note, then he nodded thoughtfully. "Still, it's a Wizard's business to see bits and pieces of the future. Something very dangerous must be headed toward Gravengate, perhaps some power that's focussed on the death of a lone Apprentice. And this Grey Witch of the North sounds so vague and mysterious. The Wizards must have probed her from a distance and failed to find what they needed. They probably sent the eagle, the Eye of Merlin, to check on this creature. Or maybe they know that there's no real challenge, but they want to get you far from Gravengate. Being mysterious goes along with being a Wizard. It's definitely *not* what I need on a battlefield."

"You mentioned lunch," Julian said, "maybe just to get your armed escorts out of earshot. But it's a good idea, so let's eat while the horses graze." They pulled provisions from their saddlebags, with Galad and Julian adding cured meats to pieces of fresh baked bread.

To celebrate their gathering, Galad drank deeply from a flagon of ale, adding quietly, "Note that I warned the guards about wine, though I said nothing about ale. I wonder if they're smart enough to understand that themselves."

Sebastian picked at fresh fruits and nuts, while Rafir ate his usual meal of vegetables and fruits; fresh small carrots and newly ripened tomatoes had been packed for him.

Galad raised his flagon of ale in a toast. "Here's to the mysterious Wizards and your equally strange errand! And here's to the vegetarian fox!

Every day, mothers throughout the Wizards' League are saying to their small ones, 'You know, if you want to become invisible like Rafir, you have to eat your vegetables.'"

"Now, *that*, you made up," Sebastian noted.

"I cheerfully confess that I did," Galad said. "After you three leave, I'm going to be trapped with grim, unsmiling Wizards and the even more humorless eagle, the Eye of Merlin, so you have to allow me some small bits of wit."

Julian laughed, then grew serious. "The last time we spoke, you were going to seek the lore masters, to find out more about the world to the north of our League, where the Gods of the Mid-World of the Truce rule, surrounded by many thousands of magical creatures. Did you learn anything from those lore masters?"

"First, I told Merlin that the ignorance of his servants was extremely unhelpful," Galad said cheerfully. "I said to him, 'So there I am on the battlefield, smashing away. The Tarnished Sword is moaning, carving up metal and flesh as though it was slashing bits of grass. Then suddenly, some unknown magical creature pops up, and I don't know whether to pet it, kiss it, or kill it.' Then, of course, Merlin noted that this knowledge seemed unlikely to do me much good, that I should probably just keep slashing away with the magic sword."

"But he didn't tell you *not* to search for knowledge," Julian noted.

"Ha! That's what I thought," Galad continued, "and so between training scouts and the organization of war parties, I've had more than a few conversations with the keepers of records."

Julian nodded. "Good. Since you were surprised by references to the Grey Witch of the North, I will assume the Witch's name was never discussed. What about these jealous Dark Gods?"

Galad looked skyward for a second, then lowered his voice. "It seems that all Gods are jealous," he said quietly. "To speak the name of a God seems too often to attract that Power's attention, and so most of my conversations — lacking a shielding of magic from the Wizards — took place in regions underground where the rush of surrounding streams made the reach of magic less and our voices difficult to hear."

Julian nodded, then he spoke soft but powerful *words*, calling upon the magic that lingered always at the edges of the Gift inside him. Then the afternoon sounds around them seemed to grow quieter, so that even nearby songbirds could be heard only faintly, and the insects that buzzed and hummed through the surrounding meadows and woodlands became completely silent, as the four sealed themselves in a *cone of silence*.

Galad glanced around, north, east, south, and west before speaking. "First of all, could the Wizards enter your *cone*, and hear our words?"

"They could certainly overcome my magic," Julian replied, "but I would then be aware of their intrusion and wave all of you to silence."

"Then first, let's speak about the Wizards," Galad lowered his voice. "We all talk of the heroic survival of the Wizards and their League, but essentially, we were monumentally deceived, duped into a civil war."

Sebastian shook his grave face one that was wiser than any monkey's. "Given the forces gathered against us, how could we have avoided that trap?"

"Still, some portions of the League covered themselves with great credit, even glory," Galad said. His manner was normally playful, but now he spoke with utmost seriousness. "And while we do not rebuke or chastise them, other cities and regions are still recovering from shock and shame. So, as our League recovers, the less said about our previous trials, the better. Let us drag your *cone of silence* over the League's past struggles."

The Apprentice and his Familiars glanced together and nodded. "Wise counsel, for we do need time to heal," Julian murmured. "Now, tell us what you learned about our potential enemies."

Galad shook his head. "Not just yet, for there's one other, minor matter. I don't know what to call it, but two days ago, a thought reached out to me, and it was not from one of the Wizards. I could identify a Wizard's thought."

"We call that unnamed reaching, a *whisper*," Julian said. "It's an unusual moment to have a reaching sent to a Charmed Knight like you. What did this *whisper* have to say?"

"Simply a suggestion that the Mistress of Illusions might be willing to provide further aid. You recall that she sent a partial tier of three hundred archers in support of the League. So, my question for you is this: should I leave this *whisper* with you, or pass it on to Merlin?"

"And my answer for you is simple," Julian replied. That *whisper* goes to Merlin. Now, what of those Great Dark Gods that you have carefully avoided discussing so far?"

"All of that Ancient History makes my head ache," Galad muttered, taking a deep breath before continuing. "So, famous among the Great Dark Gods are Set, Ahriman, Kali, Moloch, Mallegro, Arioch, Hecate, and Bael. Others exist, perhaps equally powerful, but those are the names known to our lore masters. You might think that if the Great Dark Gods wanted to destroy our League, that they would band together, and with their combined power the League would be overcome almost instantly in a surge of black magic."

"The Truce of the Gods seems to prevent them from banding together," Julian added. "Even if their goals were the same and they could set aside their differences, the Great Dark Gods don't seem to be able to make alliances."

"But what about those 'good' Gods?" Rafir blurted out. "If all the evil ones are out to destroy us, why aren't the 'good' ones trying to save us?"

Galad laughed darkly, shaking his head. "Just because some Gods are called 'good' doesn't mean they have any love for the Wizards and their League."

Julian nodded. "Still, the Truce seems to shield us against an alliance of Dark Gods — or even of the ones Rafir calls 'good'."

"We've only ever worried about the Dark Gods," Galad said, "and the strength of the Wizards might be just enough to hold off one, but only one, Great Dark God. So, what have we learned?"

"One Great Dark God seems to be testing the League's defenses," Julian said. "Is that Power of the Mid-World getting ready to attack us?"

"The Wizards seem to think so," Galad replied. "At the same time that a Dark God tests us, some lesser force is probing at the northern borders of the League."

"Are these two events related?" Julian asked. "And from our discussions, I can answer that question myself: we have no idea, nor have the Wizards. That the Wizards are sending us north means that they have tried to test this 'Witch' through the reach of their own strong magic but have not been successful."

"Do you really think," Sebastian asked, "that some time ago they sent the eagle north, and that the Eye of Merlin learned nothing?" As Merlin's Familiar, the eagle was greatly admired by Sebastian and Rafir.

"It seems likely to me," Galad said, nodding his head, "but the ways of the Familiars are strange to me. None of the Wizards every showed me a 'Warrior's Guide to Weird and Wonderful Familiars'."

Julian laughed. "There is no such Guide, even for Apprentices. But Merlin once told me in a hushed voice that a Familiar might be a strong magical ally, or an assistant, or a nightguard, or even a spy. What was most important was that the Familiar acted as a companion, because the business of magic was often lonely."

"Here's a question," Rafir said, "that I've asked in the past, but never got a real answer: where are the Familiars for Thorian and Balardi?"

Galad shook his head. "Years ago, when I started to ask that question, Orlan, a Charmed Knight senior to me, waved me to silence, and told me later that this question was one they all avoided — a sore point with those two Wizards."

"Images come to me in dreams," Julian said. "I think that several Familiars of the League have died in battle or passed into decay and madness. One or more may have actually betrayed their masters, so the Wizards do not wish to discuss those unhappy moments."

"One more question," Galad said, "then I'm on my way back to Gravengate. Julian, I know that Magicians like their secrets, but will your hidden serpent ally still come when called?"

Julian only smiled and nodded to Sebastian.

"Sometimes at nightfall," the little Familiar said, "I see this long, forked tongue dart out from nowhere, and I know that Kath is testing for any threat to Julian."

"I see it sometimes, too," Rafir added, "then I disappear with a blink. Usually, I can control that vanishing thing, but Kath is so big, powerful, and more than a little scary. I may be brave, but to Kath, I would just be an accidental snack."

"Still, I'm glad that he's there," Galad said, nodding thoughtfully. "You probably need all the allies you can get."

They were quiet for a moment, then Galad stood and finished his ale. "Back to matters at hand. You know that it is entirely possible that this 'Grey Witch' is no more than a distraction, that Merlin is sending you north to protect you from the hatred of some Great Dark God. The next time we meet, we will know a great deal more — and hopefully, we'll be laughing at our own confusion while toasting the great wisdom of the Wizards. Hopefully."

Galad embraced them, gathered his bored horse troop, and set off for Gravengate, while the afternoon sun still shone down on the warrior and his followers. Julian, Sebastian, and Rafir watched them ride south until they reached a bend in the horse track and passed from view.

"It's too bad," Sebastian said quietly, "that the Wizards couldn't send Galad north with us."

"It *is* too bad," Julian said. *It's too bad that they couldn't send the whole force of the League to deal with this matter, including the standing armies of Gravengate and Stone Mountain, together with all three Wizards, supported by one kindly disposed Great God, ready to leap to our aid. Instead, it's just Julian the Humble Apprentice and his two Familiars. At least Sebastian and Rafir are managing to be friends now and don't quarrel the way they once did.*

· ✗ ·

Not long after lunch, they reached the banks of the Saugus, the great river that ran along the northern borders of the League. Then near Tuvan, the Saugus turned sharply south and finally emptied out to the sea.

All the stone bridges across the Saugus had been destroyed during the League's past struggles, but recently, wooden beams had been hammered into the riverbed and then supported by blocks of stone. Over this foundation, a temporary wooden bridge had been built, though it didn't feel as though it would hold up much longer. Julian led their horses and cart on foot over the creaking, shaking wooden planks, and they were all glad when they reached the other side safely.

"That thing won't last," Rafir muttered, staring back at the bridge.

"After the first winter storms," Sebastian added, "all those timbers will be headed south, out to the ocean."

Julian was silent for a moment, then he said, "I agree. I am sending a thought to Balardi. Maybe next spring, a real bridge could be started."

They continued north through the long afternoon. Sometimes their passage was quiet, as they watched streaks of clouds slipping over blue skies, and sometimes their eyes were drawn to brightly colored leaves as they drifted down from nearby trees. At other times they spoke together, recounting stories of old adventures together with plans for a future time of peace when they could visit the great cities of the League: Khiva, Tuvan, Amalric, and Narsis. Sebastian was older than Rafir, and he had visited Amalric, while Rafir had only been to the fortresses of the Wizards.

Sebastian had never been a powerful flyer, but he knew that he had to keep up the strength of his wings for any emergency. So, in the late afternoon, he lifted into the air, flapping, and gliding for hundreds of feet, hoping to stay in the air for more than a few minutes. As always, though, he had to watch out for the crows; and from the top of nearby woodlands, they rose to harass Sebastian, cawing their challenges.

The little Familiar flapped higher, then darted down. As he flew, Sebastian reached into a hidden pouch at his side and tossed a handful of dust backward. Crows flew into the dust then choked and sneezed, crying out in alarm. Finally, the flock of crows dropped down and hid in the upper branches of nearby trees.

Sebastian laughed quietly, but he was getting tired. He floated back down to Julian's shoulder. Flying was hard; it was much easier to watch the fox and his little games from a safe perch on Julian's shoulder.

Rafir had discovered a new trick: effortlessly, he would vanish, then reappear suddenly beside flocks of birds feeding on seeds and small insects a little distance from their horse track. As the fox suddenly appeared, flocks of birds always squawked and fled. After a time, though, all Rafir's running and leaping over clumps of tall grasses left him tired. Then he would scramble up onto the cart drawn by their packhorse and sleep until the next deep rut in their grassy roadway jostled him awake.

In the late afternoon, as the sun began slipping downward, Julian launched Sebastian into the air to search for safe places for a night's rest.

"A farmhouse is fine," Julian called up to him, "but maybe a small village — where no one has ever heard of us — would be even better. Let's avoid anything too large, because they tend to keep us up all night, asking for stories about the League."

Sebastian had watched it happen too many times. Everyone would talk happily, then sometime after midnight they would start asking Julian to use magic to dig their wells deeper or ask Julian to persuade the Wizards to widen their roads, work that they might have easily done themselves.

The little Familiar flew higher, eyes scanning the distant meadows and woodlands. At this time of year, fires were being lit to cook evening meals and to warm houses, so Sebastian could judge the size of a human settlement by the number of smoke columns in the village: one or two and it was usually a farmhouse, while twenty or so meant a small village. If there were many more than twenty columns of smoke, it was a larger village or a town. He flapped higher. It would be dark soon. Now he could see half a dozen widely spaced smoke columns: farmhouses. Staying at a farm was sometimes awkward — their hosts often felt uncomfortable, without the right food or shelter to entertain visitors.

Sebastian's wings flapped higher, eyes glancing at the setting sun. Just a few hundred paces along the north horse track lay a small town, with columns of smoke rising from forty to fifty chimneys. If they stayed there, they would be up all night, talking! But just to their left, a much smaller village had only sixteen or so smoke columns. They would have to backtrack, but the delay might save them hours of endless talking later in the evening. He fluttered back to Julian's shoulder.

"Just a short way back," he panted, "then a little to the west, there's a small village."

They backtracked, turning west off their roadway onto a rough pathway that led through a wooded area. Julian could see that carts had been pulled over this path, though only small carts. After a few hundred paces, they could see columns of smoke rising from the village and the smell of a goodly number of separate dinners being cooked.

As Bluescent led them into the village, the sun was setting before them, bathing the Apprentice and his Familiars with a red glow. A woman of midyears was the first to meet them. Her mouth opened in surprise, and she dropped the bundle of sticks she had been carrying.

"Greetings from the Wizards and their League," Julian said, and he held both palms out, showing that he carried no weapon. "We are seeking only shelter for the night and can offer silver if it's needed."

From a doorway, another villager, a young man, peered out then raced to the woman's side. "Mum, Mum, it's the Apprentice!" he exclaimed. "He's the one who saved the League!"

"We are just travelers," Julian said, shaking his head, "heading north on Wizards' business. Legends make every story so much larger."

"No Mum, I was there!" the young villager said, his voice growing louder with excitement. More people were emerging from houses. "I held a pike for the League, in the line with hundreds and hundreds of other men, while Julian and Galad battled this huge monster. A Creature of the Darkness! And they beat it! We didn't think they had a chance, but they fought it, then killed it dead!"

More people were gathering. Some were staring at Sebastian and Rafir and beginning to whisper to one another. Before the young soldier could continue his tales of their battles, Julian dismounted and drew him aside.

"Softly, softly," Julian said. "We serve the Wizards and have been sent to deal with an intrusion in the north. But we need to pass quietly through your village, without warning our foes."

Eyes wide, face flushed with excitement, the youth nodded then turned to his mother. "Mum, sorry, Mum, I shouldn't have blurted all that battle stuff out. We need to get the Elders." As the two departed, more people crowded around Julian, many peering at the Familiars.

"Is that really them?" one asked.

"Is that Sebastian?" another said, "and Rafir?" One elderly man reached out cautiously, as though to poke the two to make certain they weren't stuffed toys. Rafir vanished, while Sebastian's wings lifted him into the air, and the old man drew his finger back quickly as though it had been burned.

The three were saved by the intervention of the Elders. Two men and one woman came bustling forward, murmuring, "Back, back, everyone back."

To Julian, the older woman said, "What's your wish? Everyone will want to be with you, to speak with you, but if you must have quiet, you can come with me."

"No," Julian said quietly, "that's one of our tasks, as emissaries of the League, to greet people. Can we assemble after the dinner hour, in some common area? Is there a chance of a small bonfire?" The Elder nodded.

After a brief, mostly quiet meal with the Elders, they were led to the village's central square. There the people had gathered, nearly sixty of them, elderly, midyears, younglings, and children, crowding the small village square, firelight flaring over their tanned faces. Overhead, hundreds of moths were fluttering, drawn by the bonfire, and other torches that blazed in the night.

"First," said the older woman, chief among the Elders, raising her voice, "we need to send our great thanks to the Wizards for their League. Other peoples of Alantéa survive only at the whims of the Powers of the Mid-World. But the Wizards have been our shields, and our swords when it comes to our defense. So, there's little we can do to express our thanks, except when an emissary of the Wizards travels through, we can ask them to thank the Wizards."

Murmurs of approval rose from the villagers, and Julian stepped closer to the fire.

"When danger arises," he said, "you have willingly sent your young men to bear swords or pikes in the Wizards' service. So, the League thanks you. We all belong to the League, yet so few of you will ever get to see even one of its great cities, or view, from afar, one of its great Wizards. But tonight, parts of the League will come to visit you."

He raised his staff, calling out soft *words*. An image appeared, hovering overhead, showing a substantial city, with great deep-sea vessels sailing into its port, while surrounding ocean waves foamed white in the distance.

"Here is Khiva and the Coast, some distance to the south and west of your village." Julian said, "The trade of Khiva creates a goodly portion of the League's wealth." Slight gasps came from the villagers. Julian let the image linger for a moment, then waved the image of Khiva away, to be replaced by a city resting on a hillside, heavily fortified by great walls at its outer limits.

"Here is Tuvan, to the east of you," Julian continued. "Tuvan is a citadel, a fortress, ready to repel any armed incursion." The image lingered, then faded, to be replaced by a long series of halls beside a rocky, overcast coastline, where a shortish Wizard ambled distractedly, sometimes staring out to sea.

"Behold Merlin, master of Sea's Edge." The image glowed briefly as though sunlight had broken through the clouds, then it, too, faded, and was replaced by a tall fortress, built upon a mountaintop, gleaming in the sunlight. At its highest battlement, a tall, silver haired Wizard gazed out to an ocean that rippled with foamy caps.

"Thorian rules Stone Mountain, the most challenging of citadels. What force could possibly destroy, or even reach, the ramparts of that fortress?" Moments later, the last image emerged: a huge complex of walls, with inner towers and ramparts. On its topmost tower, a third Wizard leaned out studying the sky: Balardi, with his golden beard, lacking its current grey fringe, as Julian had chosen to overlook that change.

"And here is Balardi at Gravengate, built on the lush Plain of Gravengate, filled with orchards and vineyards. Gravengate lies to the south of you, and when danger threatens, it is to Balardi you call for help, and to Balardi you send your young men to defend the League."

Applause filled with wonder broke out. Stories about the Wizards and their League were filled with references to great magic, and yet few had ever seen real magic before. Julian chose not to explain that creating illusions was the simplest act of sorcery. Instead, he bowed and continued.

"Now, we are going to expose one of the League's greatest secrets," he motioned to Sebastian and Rafir. "These two seem to be nothing more than a secret fox creature, and a winged monkey. You may have heard of their adventures. Now we will show you their true shapes." Again, Julian spoke *words*, and the magic of illusion slipped over his two Familiars.

Rafir became an extremely small Dragon, but a confused, distracted creature, scratching his ear while emitting puffs of green smoke. Sebastian became an equally confused Wizard, even smaller than the Dragon, examining a tiny wand as though he had only just found that it had magic properties.

Wizard and Dragon discovered each other, and each jumped back. The villagers began to stifle laughter. The Dragon, fluffing itself in anger, breathed a small stream of fire at the Wizard — who fell backward, howling in pain, flapping at his smoking cloak. Then the Wizard pointed its tiny wand and sent tiny bolts of lightning surging at the Dragon, which caused the Dragon to flop and twitch before rising to continue the battle.

Now, Dragon and Wizard conjured up Sendings, small, puffy green and yellow beings made of cloudy smoke that snarled and raged at one another, before settling down and playing at dice, using the bonfire to light their game.

As Dragon and Wizard continued their comic battle, the villagers began to laugh openly. Round and around the bonfire the two pretended to fight, mocking the true strength of the Wizards of the League, and the enormous power of the ancient Dragons. In the end, both images lay heaped together in ruin, tongues hanging out in defeat.

Applause brought them back to life, and back to their true forms. Sebastian and Rafir rose to stand beside Julian, and all three bowed to the villagers. The Elders, still clapping, drew Julian away from the bonfire, to a small guest cabin where the three could spend the night.

"Thank you, Apprentice," the old woman said softly. "Had anyone told me this morning that this event would take place tonight, I would have called them mad or overcome by wine. Yet it is interesting that the Wizards don't object to such mockery."

"Hopefully, they will never learn of it," Julian said, "and if they do, they are too focussed on their own challenges to pay much attention to my small magic."

"The pity is," noted the soft-spoken woman Elder, "that we can't record this event, somehow, for our children's children, and the future people of our Village."

"But why not?" Julian asked. "Others have asked me the same question, and I always make the same suggestion: Why not create a small book, perhaps with pictures to mark this event? Not every detail would need to be included, but you could tell the story of Julian the Apprentice and his Familiars, how they came and entertained the village with illusions. Perhaps on days when the winter rains come down heavily, it would be a good story to read to your little ones."

The woman Elder shook her head. "Then that's twice the pity. Our Scribe was also skilled at images in ink. It's sad that he has withdrawn, feeling that death calls to him."

Julian took a deep breath. "Sometimes not even a Wizard can turn aside death. Yet I have some skill as a healer, so I should at least have a look at your Scribe."

At the edge of the village were a few abandoned cottages, small, grim places, where the ill and the dying lay, waiting either for death or a return to health. In the first lay an old woman who was clearly in the last stages of her life, beyond a healer's reach. Julian touched her thin, boney hand, straining to hear the last whispers of her dying mind:

Remember this! Do not forget these words! Choose your husbands, choose your wives wisely, for you can never completely unmake those first choices. And you must not plant the same field two years in a row with the same crop, or you will wear down the soils....

Julian pulled back. She was struggling to pass a few last bits of advice to her children and grandchildren. Where were those people? Hopefully, they had come and gone while she was still able to speak with them. He wove a healer's sleep over the dying woman so that all her troubles slipped away from her into forever dreams.

In the next small cottage, the village Scribe lay in a soft bed, breathing hard, face damp with a sweaty fever, as his body struggled with hordes of tiny intruders, causing his lungs to fill with fluid. Julian leaned over him, speaking soft *words*. Fluids slipped gradually from his lungs, and his breathing became steadier. Moment by moment, his fever lessened. Within his body, guardians of the Scribe's blood stream rallied and began to expel the tiny intruders.

Finally, Julian mixed a potion of Heart's Ease with water, and held the Scribe's head up, so he could slowly sip the potion.

"I told my people," the Scribe whispered hoarsely, "that I did not fear death — and I do not. But it would be good to hold on for a few more years, to watch my grandchildren grow wiser and to tell them stories when the snows begin to fall."

"The village also has a task for you," Julian said, "though only if you are willing." Then the Apprentice sent images of the evening's entertainment into the Scribe's mind, showing mostly the duel between Sebastian and Rafir. The Scribe laughed, coughed, and laughed again.

"A short book," he wheezed out, "might be entertaining."

Julian stood. One more villager lay sick in a third cottage, and then he would be done for the night. He opened the Scribe's door and stared out into the darkness. A pale moonlight hung over that third cottage. That cottage glowed, too, with more than moonlight — a sense of wrongness hung over its doors, with danger hidden inside.

Julian turned back to the Scribe. "What can you tell me," he whispered, "about the patient in this third cottage?"

"Mostly I was lost in feverish dreams," the Scribe whispered back hoarsely, "yet I think they found someone — a person who was not from the village — lying in the street, stiff but still breathing. That was perhaps... two days ago, I think."

Julian found a rough cane lying beside the bed and passed it to the Scribe. "Guard yourself, as much as you are able." Then he sent a message into Sebastian and Rafir's minds: *Trouble was waiting for us when we rode into this place. Be careful!*

He left the Scribe's cottage and stood outside in the moonlight. The Sight within him brought images to his mind — if he opened the door of the third cottage, a dagger would be waiting for him.

As Julian stood uncertainly in the moonlight, the cottage door burst open. A dagger was hurled through the moonlight. Julian leaped aside, and the dagger only tugged at the edge of his cloak. Carrying a second, longer knife, a large man burst out, leaping toward Julian.

The Apprentice held his left palm out, speaking a single *word*.

The explosion blew the assassin backward. Still gripping his long knife, the assassin lay on the ground, staring with menace at the Apprentice.

"They told me," the man muttered, "to finish you before you could point your staff at me. But you didn't even need your staff, did you?" Suddenly the man shifted, transforming himself in one split second. Gone was the shape of a human; instead, something shaped like a huge brownish grey hyena sprang away from the Apprentice, racing into the night with a high-pitched hyena's shriek.

Julian joined Sebastian and Rafir in the guest cabin assigned to them for the night. Their visit to the village had gone well, but the presence of the assassin told them of a danger that couldn't be ignored.

"Rafir, someone, maybe several people, have been watching us very closely," Julian said quietly. "It would be very nice to know just what kind of spies are studying us, and how many of them are still out there."

Rafir vanished and was out into the moonlit night in seconds.

"They even knew that we would stay in this village," Julian continued in low tones. "Merlin tells me that the Sight is strong inside me. But I had no idea at the beginning of this day where events would take us. So, some very powerful force has been watching one lowly Apprentice and his two Familiars very carefully. Did *you* have any sense of being watched?"

But Sebastian, at the end of a long day, was already asleep.

Chapter Three

The Fight in the Forest

"THERE WERE LOTS OF creatures hunting through the moonlight," Rafir was saying, "and they were either sneaking around or trying to hide, except for this particular Badger, who was staring at the village without even blinking. That was one clue that the Badger was a spy, but when it didn't even look at the nearby rabbits, that made it pretty certain — most of the time, Badgers find those adorable little bunnies very tasty."

They had left the village and were again heading north, Bluescent in the lead, pack horse, and cart to the rear. As they rode through bright sunlight, with falling leaves of many colors drifting over their horse track of green grass, Rafir was telling the others about his nighttime explorations.

"Let's count the Badger as one spy," Julian said. "Was there anything else?"

"I'm just starting," the fox replied. "What are those birds called, 'night' something or other?"

"Night-Ravens," Sebastian said.

"Right, Night-Ravens were watching from the trees," Rafir continued. "Three of them were hidden by darkness and tangles of branches. They made not a single sound, just watched, staring silently, heads bobbing around so they could peer through leaves and branches from different angles. I think they were as interested in the Badger as they were in the village."

"So, then, two sets of spies," Julian said thoughtfully.

"That's not all," the fox continued. "I really couldn't be quite as certain, but a large hawk flew overhead, high up, circling, staring down at the village, and the Badger and the Night-Ravens. Moths were fluttering in the moonlight, and bats were out gobbling up moths, but all this hawk did was circle, floating in the sky for more than an hour, staring down at the village."

"Three sets of spies!" Sebastian muttered. "Why were all these things watching us?"

"Actually," the fox said, pleased with himself, "there was a fourth spy, and this one was very, very difficult to see. It was some sort of Goblin creature, and it seemed to drag a small cloud of shadows with it wherever it went. I couldn't even sense it when it kept to the forest, so it was only when it moved closer to the Badger and had to pass through bright moonlight, that I could see that the thing was dragging a grey cloud around itself. Otherwise, the Goblin was almost as difficult to see as Rafir, the Incredible Invisible Fox."

"Ha!" Sebastian scoffed. "So, what if there were spies around us? Nothing was as dangerous as that Assassin. Julian, was it some strange kind of werewolf? You said it changed into some four-legged furry creature, leaving its clothes and dagger behind, so it must have been some sort of werewolf."

"It certainly seemed like a werewolf," Julian said quietly, then he spoke *words,* drawing a *cone of silence* around the three, and then he continued: "In truth, I believe it was a Carag, a creature not seen in League lands for many, many years. Werewolves are powerful beings with supernatural strength, but to me, Carags are even more dangerous. A werewolf can take only two shapes, one, a single human form, and the other a lone wolf form, while Carags can change shape, to become your friend, your neighbor, even your sister. The lore masters tell me that Carags once overran the League, a plague of assassins, each of them able to change shape in a split second."

Sebastian looked sideways at Rafir. "You have always seemed a little strange to me. Maybe now we know why."

Julian laughed. "Don't worry! Carags can change their shapes, but not their sizes. To be the same size as children or small creatures like you and Rafir, they would need to bring Carag infants to their game of terror, something that the Carags never seemed willing, or able, to do."

"If I had been there, I would have smelled that Carag Assassin," Rafir muttered.

"And Sebastian is sensitive to magic," Julian added quickly, "so he would have known something was wrong. Anyway, now all three of us are prepared."

The two Familiars had become somewhat unhappy with each other, so Rafir slipped to the ground, to play his new game with flocks of birds, while Sebastian lifted into the morning skies to study the roadway to the north and the cloud patterns overhead.

Julian watched the two with a slight smile on his face. *This is my family, though right now it's just a little unhappy. Sebastian is the older child, while Rafir is the younger one. They argue from time to time — though much less than they once did, and they care for each other deeply. I can't imagine not loving them and having them always at my side.*

The day passed swiftly, with the two Familiars avoiding each other, while Julian searched the sky for intruders. Only a shift in cloud patterns could be seen, with masses of clouds pushing south, bringing a touch of dampness, and overcast skies. The land grew hillier and more forested, with fewer farms and villages. After meeting a Carag Assassin the night before,

Julian thought that a night in the woodlands might even be less dangerous than in a village.

Toward evening Julian called a halt to their journey, shifting away from their horse track, passing deeper into the forest. Horses were set to graze, though the surrounding forest blocked bright sunlight, and grasses were harder to find. The three had a brief, quiet supper, with the Familiars glancing away from each other, unwilling to talk, while Julian was lost in his own thoughts. In the last light of day, Julian set up their canvas tent while Sebastian watched on in some unhappiness.

"I don't have the furry skin for this weather," Sebastian muttered. Rafir put one small paw to his mouth and yawned.

"Canvas tents and bearskin cloths," Julian said, "can cover both Sebastian and this soft-spoken Apprentice, while Rafir can nap beside us or creep around outside. Now, listen to me. You two are doing better, much, much better than you did a year ago — you only argue every few hours, and you no longer snarl and bicker and fight afterward. I made a mistake last evening. Rafir, you are my nearby spy, while Sebastian is my distant magic sniffer. Go, each of you, and find out what kinds of things are trying to track us."

Rafir vanished, while Sebastian studied the night sky uneasily. "Don't worry," Julian said softly, "I will be watching. No hawk or flying creature will bother you while I'm on guard."

Sebastian flapped his wings hesitantly, then flew to the top of the highest surrounding tree. From this peak, Sebastian launched himself, flapping higher into the night sky. Julian stared upward, just as a few pale stars began gleaming over the wings of his slight Familiar. A half moon shone dimly through a ragged patch of clouds. Rain was coming.

Julian closed his eyes and *reached*. The night forest was busy. Small, nervous deer were nibbling leaves. Owls floated silently through the darkness. On the forest floor, glow worms hunted snails. As for reports of nearby magic, he needed to wait for Sebastian and Rafir.

Sebastian returned twenty minutes later, breathing heavily. "Nothing will ever surprise me again," the little Familiar panted, shivering from the cold. "About two thousand paces north, there's —"

"Let's wait for Rafir," Julian interrupted quietly. "You can tell your story first, then Rafir can list all the nearby spies. First, let's get you warm. With all the creatures watching us, I'm afraid that making a fire is a bad idea, but we can at least cover you." Julian pulled out a heavy blanket from their tent and wrapped it around Sebastian, who gradually stopped shivering from the cold. The two sat, waiting quietly, expecting Rafir at any moment.

But it was close to an hour before Rafir returned, blinking back to visibility not two feet from them. "The count is now up to five," the fox said. "In addition to —"

"I asked Sebastian to speak first," Julian interrupted, "but I'm very interested in the number of creatures and things watching our travels. Sebastian?"

In his excitement, the little Familiar pushed the blanket away. "'Thing' is the right word for it. About two thousand paces north of us, there's a 'Thing' walking through the forest. It's more than three times as tall as Julian and it must weigh ten times as much. It looks like a greenish scaled lizard, but it walks on two feet, and it has a sword belted to one side and a staff on the other. Why would it bother wearing a cloak with a hood over its green lizard's head? It certainly wouldn't fool anyone into thinking it was human."

Sebastian shivered, then pulled his blanket back over his shoulders. "It definitely didn't fool the wolfpack, although they probably wish they had never seen it. There were more than twenty wolves in the pack — with those numbers, they made the mistake of attacking the creature. But instead of just ripping the wolves apart, this *'Thing'* drew a staff from its side and blasted the wolves into smoking pieces of dead fur and flesh."

Julian stood, facing north, and he drew his own staff. "A monster with magic," he said softly, "and no doubt it's headed toward us."

Sebastian shook his head. "No, that's the funny thing. It was traveling north and west, as though heading toward North Haven. But maybe it was circling around."

Julian stared into the distance for a moment, then sat back on the forest floor. "It's very unusual to have a powerful invader in the middle of the Wizards' League, and it can't be good news for us. Rafir, tell us about the watchers."

"I think I listed four sets of spies before," Rafir said. Sebastian's story seemed to have made him lose a little of his enthusiasm. "The Badger is still with us, as well as Night Ravens, and that distant hawk. That Goblin creature is now followed by a glowing blue and gold butterfly, who seems interested both in our camp and in that pool-of-darkness Goblin. What in the name of all the Nine Billion Gods is going on?"

"I have no idea," Julian said softly, "though maybe we shouldn't talk about the Nine Billion, because it's a nasty reference among humans about the huge numbers of beings calling themselves Gods, and how it's so hard to keep track of all of them, much less satisfy their different commands. Sebastian, what does it feel like to you? Can we at least have a few hours of sleep in safety?"

Sebastian glanced around, shifting north, south, east, and west before nodding slowly. "Rain may be coming soon, but trouble will wait at least a few hours."

Sleep came only after the first drops of a soft rain came sliding over their canvas shelter. Then the three of them were glad to be inside, glad to be beside each other, and gradually drifted off to sleep, Julian first, then Sebastian, and lastly, the restless Rafir.

·)(·

And Julian dreamed, again, of being in a dark and lonely tower, seated across from his parents. This time he knew right away that they weren't truly beside him because they seemed much younger, and so his mind was remembering them as they had once been, not as they were today.

"It is always good," Julian said, *"to share dreams with the two of you, even when you can't really be beside me, and I have to imagine you."*

"You know that we would be with you," the image of his mother said, *"if we could."*

"And these dreams are useful," his father added, *"because you can explore your own thoughts — finding things that you almost know, but do not really completely understand."*

"So, my wonderful son," his mother said, shining love upon Julian, *"what sort of creature, or being is stomping through the forests of your League?"*

"A giant creature, completely inhuman, armed with magic," Julian said, hesitating, *"who might sometimes be described as a Creature of the Darkness."*

"Monsters that existed before the Birth of the Gods," his father added. *"Yes, some were armed with weapons and all of them had some force of magic."*

"But none wore cloaks with hoods," Julian's mother noted. *"Most were ragged beings, rough evil beings. Many could not even speak simple words."*

"Also, the creature described by Sebastian seemed more polished," Julian said, *"with the cloak and hood representing a kind of clothing."*

"As though it belonged in a court," his father prompted, *"perhaps serving one of the Mid-World Powers."*

"So, an Emissary of the Gods is passing through the League," Julian said quietly, "a chief servant of some Dark God who does not wish any good thing for our people. Armed with an Adept's power, we would need a Wizard to overcome it."

Julian's mother nodded thoughtfully. "Let us just say that a Wizard could cast it from the League, another Adept, one serving the League, could counter it and not be himself destroyed. Let me also say that the Sight has grown within you, Julian, and you can now see as far and as deep into the magic of the Mid-World as Balardi or even Thorian. You have sensed another event, something you barely understand."

"When Sebastian told me about the Emissary," Julian said, hesitating, "I reached out and sensed its presence. But it wasn't alone — there was a second being following the first Emissary as it passed through the League. With your help, I now understand that a second Emissary of the Gods has entered the Wizards' League."

His father nodded gravely. "So, there are two Emissaries, perhaps willing to challenge your journey to the north."

"And I'm not strong enough for even one of them," Julian murmured.

"Recall that the Truce does not permit them to work together," his mother said. "Also, deep within yourself, I think you understand that you now have an Adept's strength. You wish always to seem no more than a low-level Apprentice, yet you have gained power while fighting for the Wizards and their League."

"That is a thought," Julian said, "that I have tried hard not to think. I would still prefer to appear as the young, frail, low-level Apprentice."

"Battle is coming," his father said, "a fight in the forest. Be ready for that battle and be careful that the small ones do not get injured."

"We see Sebastian and Rafir through your eyes," his mother added. "Because you have such great love for them, we share that love, so they almost *seem like our own grandchildren, though we are separated by time and space, and can visit them only through the Dreamways."*

Both his parents stood; Julian rose too. "I think you understand," his father said, *"that it is time for you to wake and to protect your camp."*

Julian woke. In the darkness, he could hear soft rains pelting the sides of their canvas shelter. Otherwise, the night was silent. He stood, carefully hunched over, so that he didn't bump into their tent's roof and wake Sebastian and Rafir. Out in the night, it had become pitch black, without a hint of moon or starlight. Raindrops dripped over the tangles of Julian's curly black hair as his eyes adjusted to the darkness.

Staff in hand, Julian walked quietly about two dozen paces from their tent and began a quiet chant. His staff glowed with power, but for a few moments, nothing seemed to happen. Then came the sounds of many wings flapping through the night. Flocks of birds gathered to him as he continued to chant his summoning spell.

Then he wove a Healer's Sleep over the several flocks so that hundreds of small, winged creatures — sparrows and mourning doves and emerald jays — came to rest quietly on the forest floor surrounding their canvas shelter. If anything stalked the three of them in their canvas shelter, hundreds of small guardians would wake and alert him that danger was near.

Julian slipped back into his shelter and slowly drifted back into sleep. This time his parents no longer entered his dreams; instead, he dreamt that two enormous beings were following him through a dark forest and that he had somehow lost his staff, while his legs seemed weighted down so that it was impossible to race away into the darkness.

·)(·

And Julian woke to the sounds of hundreds of birds crying out in fear. Danger was near. He grasped his staff and slipped quickly through the tent's opening. In the darkness, the enormous hand of a lizard was reaching for him. He jumped to one side, rolled, and pointed his staff, calling out *words*. A jagged bolt of force blasted the huge hand aside.

A great howling sound burst over the night forest.

"Sebastian! Rafir!" Julian called. "Out, now!" He leaped again, rolling behind a tree, just as the Emissary in lizard form blasted at him with its own staff. The tree, three times Julian's thickness, shuddered, cracked, and began to topple. Julian leaped back, hurling more jagged lightning at the Emissary.

Then he ran toward Sebastian and Rafir, who had stumbled from the tent — but they could only stare, frozen, blinking in astonishment at the enormous Emissary. Julian grabbed them, launching Sebastian into the night sky with one hand while gathering Rafir with the other. A second blast from the Emissary blew apart their tent.

Rafir scrambled away from Julian's arm, dropped to the forest floor, and vanished. Sebastian had flown to the highest nearby tree. Julian, face grim with anger, turned to confront his adversary, a powerful Emissary of the Gods.

Then suddenly, from out of the night, an even larger Emissary smashed at the great, green lizard creature. The second Emissary also wore a cloak, but beyond that, it was completely unlike the first: it was tall, spindly, dark as night, more like an insect, with powerful legs, and two sets of arms. With all its strength, it grasped the huge lizard being and bit down. But the lizard's skin was thick and could not be broken. In frustration, the insect-like Emissary hurled the gigantic lizard form into the night forest.

More cries of pain echoed through the forest as the lizard-being bellowed in agony — and hearing those cries, its insect-like opponent chirped in triumph.

Rafir blinked back into view. "I can lead you to the horses," Rafir panted. "Let's get out of here."

"Let's find someplace safer," Julian said, "but I need to watch these things. Why are they fighting? Is the winner still going to come after us?" As they spoke, Sebastian fluttered down to Julian's shoulder.

"Our tent is gone," the little Familiar said quietly, "and we need to be gone, too." As they left the struggle the lizard-being had recovered its staff and was hurling blasts of power at the insect Emissary. Now it was the turn of the second Emissary to cry out in pain — high shrieking and clicking noises, just at the edge of Julian's hearing, though Sebastian and Rafir needed to stop up their ears.

They slipped and slid over damp forest ground, but they found Bluescent and their pack horse with its cart just a few hundred paces to the north. Then they rode to a small hilltop where they could look down on the battle raging between the two huge beings. Overhead, the cloud cover had broken, and a ragged moonlight poured over the fight in the forest.

Julian watched closely, trying to learn if the intruders had any weaknesses. If the insect Emissary was larger than the lizard Emissary, the lizard-being seemed more powerful in its sorcery, with dark magic surging back and forth between them, followed by smashing and shattering sounds as the two grappled together, sliding over the damp forest floor, crushing nearby small and large trees. Then the two would separate, and hurl more dark magic at each other from a distance, filling the night with blasts of power, dark lightning, cries of pain and the cracking sounds of shattered trees.

Julian shook his head; neither of these two mighty beings had any obvious weakness.

"They are so evenly matched, but what's the point?" Sebastian asked. "Why would they continue to fight if neither of them can destroy the other?"

"The Great Dark Gods," Julian murmured, "are not kind, considerate beings, and if their Emissaries fail, their masters will not be pleased. We should be glad that we serve the Wizards and not Dark Gods, although I know that Sebastian isn't happy with them. Balardi might stare at us sadly if we didn't do well, maybe even shake his head in disappointment, but he wouldn't make us feel great pain or transform us into things unliving. I'm afraid that a failed Emissary might find — wait, wait. Can this night get any stranger? Something else is coming, some being of great power."

The three stared skyward, watching as lights flared in the night sky, radiating blue and gold over the forest. Then the lights faded as the being flapped its huge wings downward and descended into the forest.

"I can't see," Rafir said, voice rising in excitement. "I know you two can. Tell me what's happening!"

"I can see, or sense, only part of it," Julian said quietly, "but it's a thing of magic, a powerful Sending, shaped like a huge Firedrake, a bright force of magic with the wings of a Dragon, and powerful talons. Instead of flames, the Firedrake is breathing out clouds of vapor, trying to stun the two creatures rather than destroying them. The Sending breathes its numbing force over the two Emissaries, and they become slower, stooping things, beginning to sag to the ground — but wait! No, it's not going to be that simple. The two Emissaries are calling up counter spells and so they will not be stopped so easily."

Julian took a deep breath, then continued. "I was hoping to find some weaknesses in those two Emissaries, but I've learned nothing. Really, I understand less about our adventure than I did when I started. Nothing we've met seems to have anything to do with that Grey Witch of the North."

"Let's go," Sebastian said, "there's no reason to stay here if there's nothing left to learn. We should follow this horse track to the north, do as Merlin asked until the Wizard comes to his senses and calls us back."

Julian nodded in fatigue, but Rafir blurted, "Wait, please wait. I don't understand what's happening in this three-way battle, but it's one of the most interesting things I've ever heard about. You two will be able to watch some of it with your magic, but I won't know how it turns out. Can you at least tell me what's happening as we ride?"

"I can try," Julian murmured — he would need to watch the battle with his Sight anyway. They began their slow journey to the north, Julian using his staff to shine a pale light over their forest path. A light mist drifted overhead, and gradually the sounds of smashing and blasting and the cries of pain grew less; finally, they could hear only the soft clopping sounds of their horses and misty rain dripping from the forest's upper branches.

"Here are images that the Sight brings me," Julian said quietly. "Three beings of magic are fighting on the damp forest floor. Moonlight peers through from time to time, but most of the light comes from the blue and gold shining of the Firedrake Sending, together with flashes from the magic of the two Emissaries. The Firedrake seems to be the great enemy of both Emissaries, and they blast it back, hurling power with magic aimed at its gleaming body.

"The Firedrake slumps; it has taken wounds, and sags to the forest floor. A light rain begins to fall softly around it. Now the two Emissaries stare at each other as though surprised at finding the other still standing. They explode in rage, calling on each other to withdraw in defeat. Neither will give way. Their battle starts again — there will be only one winner!

"They begin to damage each other. The lizard-being has one leg that will no longer leap, while the insect-creature has lost a part of an arm, though it began the fight with four arms and two massive legs.

"But wait! The Firedrake is recovering! It breathes heavy smoke. Fire surges from its mouth. Instead of waiting for its enemies to destroy each other, it rises to battle. Now it showers the Emissaries with fire! Parts of their bodies are on fire! Emissaries throw themselves into the leaves and bushes of the damp forest and roll and roll again until the flames die down. Now they rise and if they no longer burn, their skins still smoke.

"Now each of the three creatures has been wounded, and they are becoming much more cautious. The lizard-being and the insect-thing are looking for larger trees to protect themselves so that they can peer out behind tree trunks and blast their opponents with their staffs. Twice, the Firedrake Sending lifts to the skies and seems to draw some strength from the mists of the forest heights. Then it slips cautiously through the forest and tries to breathe a thin stream of fire at its enemies. It does not seem to want flames to spread to the forest's upper branches.

"The two Emissaries blast the Firedrake back, and the Drake circles around them in a wide path. Whenever the Firedrake falls back, the two Emissaries blast away at each other, though as the fight in the forest dies down, they are beginning to moan with pain and to look into the night sky and into the depths of the forest for some way to escape."

As the battle between the three beings of magic became less heated, the interest of Sebastian and Rafir seemed to fade. Julian stopped relating the story of the struggle and glanced at his two Familiars: Sebastian was sagging on his shoulder and was fast asleep, as was Rafir, lying just in front of Julian's saddle. Very carefully, Julian brought Bluescent to a halt, then gently gathered the two Familiars and covered them with a blanket in their cart.

With no shelter for himself, and with daylight coming soon, Julian continued their journey. As sunrise brought a dim grey light from the east, Julian also continued his tale of the battle, speaking quietly to himself as though comforting a child who needed to be lulled to sleep:

"The rain overhead has stopped, and mists are lifting. Trees, large and small, for hundreds of paces, lie smashed on the forest floor, blasted by magic or broken by these huge Emissaries, while more than a few tree trunks have been blackened by the Firedrake. All three creatures lie defeated on the forest floor, though now the two Emissaries are starting to twitch and shiver.

"They wake and struggle to rise, yet they cannot. Each Emissary carefully ignores the other, crawling in a different direction so they won't have to fight again. The insect-being is left with two arms and one leg still working, while neither of the lizard-thing's legs can support it, and so it has to drag its huge legs as it pulls itself forward with its arms. Both Emissaries have been burned by fire — sections of the lizard-being's green skin are now black, while the insect-Emissary has great gaps in its armored skin.

"The two crawl deeper into the forest making soft moaning sounds. In front of each of them, separate Portals emerge, magic gateways to their Dark Gods' kingdoms. Both beings crawl through, heads bowed in defeat — and in fear. I feel something like pity for them because they will never receive justice at their masters' hands.

"The Firedrake Sending lies still, dead or dying. No, wait! It glows one last time, blue and gold, and then something forms on its forehead — a blue and gold butterfly. Was that the spy-thing discovered by Rafir? A glowing butterfly lifts from the Sending, flapping higher, and disappears into the forest. The Firedrake Sending fades, becomes mist, then it, too, is gone. Now, all that's left of the fight in the forest is a tangle of broken tree limbs and dying trees."

Julian rode on, staring into the misty path that led them north, and finally, he repeated Rafir's question, "Now what in the Name of all the Nine Billion Gods is going on?"

Chapter Four
The Old Man of the Woods

"**N**OT A SINGLE ONE of these creatures — spies, assassins who turn out to be Carags, Emissaries of the Gods, Firedrake Sendings," Sebastian complained, "has anything to do with this Grey Witch of the North."

"It's like someone sits down to read you a story," Rafir added, "and the title of the story is 'Voyage to the Lost Isle.' But when the story begins, the heroes are stuck in a desert, stung by scorpions, chased by lions, with buzzards always circling around them because they're expected to die any moment, and they can't seem to get out of the desert. It may all be very entertaining, but where is the ship that they're supposed to 'voyage' on, and where is that Lost Isle?"

"The next time we see the Eye of Merlin," Julian said dryly, "I'll ask him to take your complaints to Merlin."

"Oh no," the fox said quickly, "don't say anything to the eagle!"

"And I certainly won't complain anymore," Sebastian added. "Just imagine the nasty look and the long lecture from the Eye if he heard that we were being difficult." Merlin's Familiar was a powerful flyer that the Wizard used for long distance communications, and to watch over remote areas of the League. The eagle was no diplomat, however, and from time to time he even argued openly with Thorian or Balardi. Sebastian and Rafir also saw the Eye as the greatest of Familiars, so the eagle's approval was important to them.

"Now that you mention it," Sebastian said after a pause, "why didn't Merlin send the Eye out to investigate this Witch?"

"Galad and I wondered the same thing," Julian replied. "We thought that Merlin did send the eagle out — and guess what the great Eye of Merlin discovered about the Witch?"

"Very little," said Sebastian.

"Or nothing," Rafir added. "Still, if we succeed where the Eye failed, I'm not going to tell him about it."

All three were tired from the night before, and so after a time, all their conversation died down. The afternoon brought a brief rain shower, but later the sun began peering out. The sun's warmth seemed to make Rafir and Sebastian even sleepier, so Julian again cleared a space for them in their cart, and the two Familiars slept underneath a canvas covering. With the loss of their tent, there was more than enough space for them.

Julian led them forward, with the afternoon sun beginning to slide lower to the west, slipping in and out of clouds as the *clump, clump, clump* of Bluescent's hooves led them slowly to the north.

Suddenly, from the corner of his eyes, Julian caught sight of an old man, walking slowly through the woods.

Julian turned quickly. Nothing. No old man could be seen, only woodlands, with falling leaves drifting slowly to the ground. Was he overtired, was he drifting off to sleep like his Familiars? Julian whispered a *waking* spell over himself to counter his own lack of sleep and became suddenly alert.

There! Was that the same old man shuffling through the woods to his right?

Julian turned suddenly, but once again the image was gone. Very quietly he brought their small caravan to a halt, taking care not to wake his two Familiars. Then he turned, *reaching*, searching carefully in all directions.

No one, not any living being could be sensed, not a hint of the Old Man of the Woods. Both Emissaries had completely vanished as had the Firedrake Sending. All the spies following them were hidden, though that should have not been surprising — spies were taught to stay out of sight, even to avoid magical sight.

But to the east came the same sense of twisted bodies seen in dark moonlight — a sense of Carags! But even these were being followed by other creatures, four-footed, brutal beast warriors — Vorrs! Vorrs and Carags!

And from the north came the first whisper of laughter from the Grey Witch of the North, the laughter of a leopard playing with a tiny mouse....

Julian pulled himself back from his trance and again, now to his left, from out of the corner of his eyes, he could see an old man, walking through the woodlands. This time Julian forced himself *not* to turn; instead, he tried to stare ahead and see what he could from the corner of his eye — an old, grey-haired, bearded man, was walking through the woodlands, almost drifting, as though he really had no place to go. His clothes were dark and ragged, while his head was bowed, studying the ground — what was he doing, searching for mushrooms?

When Julian turned to look, all he could see was the setting sun. He was tempted to call again upon the Nine Billion Gods, but this time he clamped his mouth shut.

At nightfall, the two Familiars woke and stretched, muttering about the lack of padding in the cart. Julian smiled but didn't remind them of the Eye of Merlin's ability to ignore discomfort. They made their camp in a small, grassy clearing, with a low hanging moon overhead. With bedding for the three placed under the cart and a sheet of canvas covering their bedroll, Julian knelt beside them and again called upon his *cone of silence.*

Both Sebastian and Rafir became quickly alert.

"Listen," Julian said in a hushed voice, "when you search tonight, I need you to look for an old, grey-haired man. He seems to be walking through the woodlands without any destination, but I saw him out of the corner of my eye at least three times, and yet he vanished as quickly as Rafir when I turned to look at him. We need to look carefully for him — as well as all the other Emissaries and spies."

"Could it have been a fairy?" Rafir asked. "Don't they just vanish when humans stumble on them?"

Julian shook his head. "Not when Adepts or even Apprentices are looking for them." Rafir blinked out of sight and was gone. Sebastian lifted into the night skies, this time without hesitation. Julian watched Sebastian carefully as the winged Familiar flapped higher. The Sight within Julian was troubled, as though some conflict was taking place high overhead.

I should have checked the skies. I was concentrating on the Old Man. But something was happening overhead.

Suddenly, a cry of great pain came from the upper skies. Sebastian dropped downward in alarm, then straightened. The little Familiar then flew higher in his searches, sweeping through the night sky in wider circles. Sebastian found nothing, and moments later he returned to Julian, breathing hard and looking frightened.

"Let's wait for Rafir," Julian said quietly, eyes studying first the skies, then the grasses and the surrounding woodlands.

As before, the fox returned later than expected, but this time, instead of being excited, Rafir also seemed alarmed.

"Sebastian?" Julian prompted.

"This time I looked for the hawk," the winged Familiar said. "I thought Julian would protect me if trouble came, and I was interested in what kind of Raptor was following us — it seemed too large to be an Osprey or Sparrow Hawk. But before I could get close enough, it disappeared into a cloud, so I turned away, trying to look for Emissaries, or Old Men or anything strange. Not long after that, I heard sounds of a struggle overhead, followed by that horrible cry, and I couldn't actually see it, but something heavy and crippled tumbled out of the skies. I didn't see anything else. I'm sorry Julian, but I couldn't find your Old Man of the Woods."

"I didn't like what I heard," Rafir muttered, "but I especially didn't like what I found. That hawk is dead, the largest hawk I've ever seen, bigger even than the Eye of Merlin, but now it's lying crumpled on the ground, ready to be chewed up by weasels or Night Ravens. It was huge, fierce and horrible looking and now it's dead."

"The Eye of Merlin," Julian said grimly, "never had any love for spies with wings that soared over League lands. Maybe they clashed. What else?"

"Before the hawk dropped out of the skies," Rafir continued, "that blue and gold butterfly seemed lost in the woodlands, drifting far away from us, and now it's gone. After the hawk crashed to earth, the Badger began to dig like a crazy thing, and I think it's still digging its way to the center of the world, while the ravens began to fly away as though a windstorm was blowing them out to sea."

The fox brightened a little. "As for the invisible Goblin, first it tried to dig — and found that too hard, then it tried to melt into a pile of brambles. Then when it seemed to figure out that magic sniffers would catch it, finally the Goblin began to run north, dragging its magic cloud stuff behind it."

"And what of the Old Man of the Woods?" Julian asked.

"Nothing," the fox said, "not even a hint. Everything happened very quickly after that hawk creature fell, and I wanted to rush back to you, but

I made myself wait, scout around, look for that Old Man, but there was nothing."

Julian reached out to touch each of them. "Good work both of you — though I have to tell you that I saw that Old Man again and again, so he wasn't just an image from a very tired young mind. So, if that Old Man of the Woods has something to say to us, he'll find us, instead of us finding him."

It was clear out, though they protected themselves from rains that tended to come late at night by camping beneath their cart. As he had done the night before, Julian called bird flocks to himself, then wove sleep over them, so that the three were surrounded by hundreds of small, cooing creatures, as they themselves reached for sleep.

"It's a good thing," the fox whispered, "that I'm not a real fox, because my stomach would be very quickly filled with cooing little songbirds."

"Maybe one songbird," Julian whispered back, "because the rest of them would be awake quickly — that's the idea, anyway." Julian turned, glancing at the stars that lay to the west of their wagon, and willed himself to sleep, hoping to find guidance in dreams from his real parents, not just the images created by his sleeping mind.

· ✕ ·

Once asleep, Julian found himself back in the dark tower again, seated across from his parents and he knew immediately that it wasn't going to work, that he was only imagining them, because they were young, the parents of his childhood. He forced a smile to his face, but instead of smiling back, his mother and father looked away, as though a voice was calling to them from a faraway room.

"Julian!" A faint voice reached to him from a great distance. *Those whispered sounds came from his mother's real voice. He turned his head,*

reaching for the sounds. "Julian, I can only touch your mind for a few brief seconds. From your thoughts, I have watched this Old Man of the Woods, and you are dealing with power beyond that of an Emissary of the Gods, or a Sorcerer, or even a Wizard. Watch yourself!"

"Then I am dealing with a God," Julian murmured into the night, *and suddenly the tower was gone, as was his mother's voice, and Julian found himself standing alone in the moonlight. When he glanced beneath the cart, he could see his own sleeping form beside Sebastian's and Rafir's. All three were sleeping soundly, surrounded by hundreds of birds.*

He looked up, and across the grassy clearing, the Old Man of the Woods was smiling at him. Grey-bearded, cloaked in black, the woodlands seemed motionless around him. And the moonlight surrounding the Old Man was so bright, it seemed almost as clear as day.

Julian bowed. His mouth struggled to form words, but finally, he murmured, *"Greetings, Lord."*

"Greetings, Apprentice," the Old Man of the Woods said. *"Come away from your sleeping self and your small friends. Let us walk together in the moonlight for just a few moments." Julian stepped cautiously away from his sleeping Familiars, taking care not to disturb any of the cooing birds surrounding him — though his own body seemed so light that it almost floated over the ground, and it seemed unlikely that his dreaming body had the power to disturb any part of the real world of Alantéa the Forerunner.*

They walked in silence for a few moments, as Julian searched for words. Finally, the Apprentice murmured, *"Lord, I wish the Wizards were here to properly greet you and acknowledge your wisdom and your power. Anything I say is likely to be the wrong thing, so forgive me."*

"If I wished to speak with a Wizard," the Old Man said, *"I would have called Merlin to a place of my choosing and carefully explained all his errors to*

him in some detail. In truth, I wished to speak with you, Julian. What do you believe is happening in this moonlit meeting?"

The Gift and the Sight sent images and thoughts racing through his mind, and when Julian finally spoke, many things seemed clear. *"Lord, please forgive me if I misspeak, but I believe my dreaming self stands before a God, likely a greater God. At this moment, the Sight brings me many images, including that of an Old Man of the Woods, a device sometimes used by the Great God Wotan to speak with mortals, without forcing them to fall in fear before him."*

The Old Man of the Woods laughed softly, then stared up into the night sky. Everything around them seemed frozen — a moth flapping toward the moon floated in the air with its wings frozen in midflight. And the moonlight surrounding them was brighter, made stronger by the Great God's power.

"I choose this form," the Old Man said, *"so that humans would not need to feel fear. Yet I am also surprised to learn the true thoughts of mortals — they can be so incredibly blind, and they can also be surprisingly wise. For the first question, you were wise. Here is the second: why am I speaking with you?"*

Again, a thousand thoughts raced through Julian's mind — and some of them were better not spoken, and so he said. *"Lord, I truly cannot answer your question."*

"You mean that you have thoughts," Wotan said, *"but you are unwilling to offend me. Fear not! I chose this form so that mortals could respond freely to me, and so I might truly learn the abilities of their small minds. You must know that I have little love for the Wizards and their League. Let us not argue their cause or my claims! But deep within me is a love for justice, for fairness for all beings. And so, when two Great Dark Gods threatened you and your small allies, I felt a need to speak with you so that you might understand matters more clearly.*

"Julian, when you called upon the Nine Billion Gods, you feared offending the Gods. Yet I laughed, and rejoiced — you were quoting the small one, the

fox, who is always so entertaining to watch. When I think of the three of you stumbling into a grim death, a darkness clouds my mind. So, I will at least help you to understand what has happened to you. Let us watch together." They slowed to a stop in the center of an open space where bright moonlight poured down over them, and Wotan waved his hand.

Before them images formed, small on the ground, showing the great Emissary in its lizard form prowling through a dark forest, seeking Julian and his small allies. Some distance behind him followed another Emissary in its giant insect form. When the first Emissary came closer to their canvas shelter, with its surrounding small bird sentries, he stopped, staring at the tent with hatred and an appetite for destruction. But some distance away, the second Emissary watched the tent with an equal amount of hatred.

"So, they both wanted us dead," Julian whispered. "Why did one interfere with the other?"

"And why indeed?" Wotan prompted.

Julian's mind raced. "The first Emissary has been sent by a Dark God who believes that we are nothing but tools of the Wizards," Julian murmured, "tools that should be destroyed as quickly as possible. The second Emissary serves a Dark God who wishes us dead — but only after we reach the Grey Witch of the North and can be destroyed at her hands. Death now or death later — what a terrible choice!"

"A grim choice," the Old Man agreed. "Here, now are images of the Sending, a force sent to counter the two Emissaries." As Julian watched, images formed in the moonlight — small images, but carefully portrayed, showing the Firedrake descending to give battle.

As they watched the struggle between the two Emissaries, and then between the Firedrake and the Emissaries, the Old Man asked, "So, Apprentice, who sent this Firedrake, and what was its purpose?"

"*Lord,*" Julian said hesitantly, "*Firstly, I do not believe that it was your Sending.*"

"*Ha!*" the Old Man scoffed. "*Had I sent a force to deal with those two clumsy Emissaries, they would have been instantly transformed into things unliving and cast back to the courts of their masters in broken pieces. No, the Firedrake was Merlin's magic — surprisingly powerful for a mortal magician. So, the Sending came from Merlin. What was its purpose?*"

"*At first,*" Julian said, hesitating, "*the Firedrake struggled to overcome both Emissaries without damaging them — it only hurled fire at them when they could not be turned aside.*" Julian took a deep breath, his mind racing. "*Merlin must have sent the Firedrake to remind the Dark Gods that they could not interfere with League matters without being challenged, although Merlin would not want either Emissary to be destroyed. The death of an Emissary might well create further conflict.*"

The Old Man laughed. "*You do know your Wizard! When those Emissaries departed, neither of them would wish to return to your League — though of course their demented Masters might heal them and force them to return.*"

"*Lord,*" Julian said quietly, "*I believe that I now understand all three sides of that struggle in the forest last night. Is there anything that you can tell me — or show me — about this Grey Witch of the North?*"

The Old Man shook his head sombrely. "*If she danced upon a balcony at a tower's peak, the eagle, or the Wizards could tell you much about her. Instead, she remains hidden, deep underground, in a fortress of stone covered by such a great weight of earth that even I cannot reach her.*"

Julian nodded. As they began to walk again through the moonlight, Julian glanced up to the moth frozen in midflight — except that the moth had managed to complete one full flap of its wings and was now drawing back for a second flap.

"*Time has slowed for us*" the Old Man explained quietly, "*though it has not completely stopped. Now, Julian, you understand the story of the two Emissaries and the Wizard's Sending. But why would two grim Dark Gods be so interested in destroying one lone Apprentice?*"

"*I have been told before,*" Julian said softly, "*that my presence creates uncertainty. I have no idea why this should be.*"

"*Even I cannot foretell your future,*" the Old Man said. "*A haze gathers about you, like that pool of darkness dragged around by that sneaky thief of a Goblin — who has just now been drawn to the kingdom of his most unhappy Master. Did you know that the Goblin served a Creature Indomitable, a being you call a monster, a Creature of the Darkness? Do you realize that you are the only mortal alive to have destroyed a Creature Indomitable? It is no wonder that they follow your progress through their spies and their magic.*

"*Julian, some Doom or Destiny awaits you. I fear for you, and I am uncertain even for my own kingdom. Even now — look at your own form, how it begins to fade!*" Julian looked down at his sleeping form, and it had become so thin that moonlight was shining through it.

"*Some other Power seeks to interfere,*" the Old Man said in a deep, dark voice. "*I will not permit this intrusion.*" The Old Man's palms flashed in the moonlight, and Julian's fading form was suddenly restored.

The Old Man stared up into the moonlight before continuing. "*I intended to send you back into your innocent sleep. Yet since the Mid-Word is interfering, I must teach you more about the Mid-World of the Truce.*"

On the ground before him, formed an image of the continent, Alantéa. Then, the Kingdoms of the Gods began to appear — palaces formed of magic, surrounded by large lakes and rivers, or dark regions filled with pain. Layer after layer of them built higher, spreading up into the sky, farther than Julian's eyes could reach.

"*Incredible,*" Julian whispered in a hushed voice, "*amazing, and astounding.*"

The Old Man nodded. "*All that and more. The Wizards have seen portions of the Kingdoms of the Gods, but not one of them has seen the many kingdoms that I have shown to you, Apprentice.*"

The Old Man waved the images away, and they vanished. "*Many pieces of wisdom have been passed to you, but at this moment I must tell you something that will make you far less happy: Apprentice, you will not remember the events of this night.*

"*You will keep your understanding of the Emissaries and the Sending that assailed them. You will understand more clearly that you have a destiny, and that this Grey Witch is beyond the reach of many Powers. You will understand the Mid-World better than the Wizards. You will know that the Creatures Indomitable follow your progress. Yet you will not remember the Old Man of the Woods. When the name 'Wotan' arises, you will seem puzzled — 'Wotan, why would that powerful God involve himself with the League?'*

"*And so, Apprentice with an Adept's power, why would I strip your mind, and the memories of your Familiars, of these thoughts?*"

Surprise and anger raced through Julian's mind — but then he tried to clear his mind and reconsider his thinking. Was this another test? "Lord," he, said, very slowly, "*let us say that you have helped many mortals over the centuries — helped them to counter other Gods. If your interventions became known, then a substantial number of the other Gods would try to oppose you. They could not defeat you perhaps, but they could make your life far more difficult.*"

The Old Man leaned back and laughed. "*Wisdom! In one so young! Who might have guessed?*" Wotan became more serious, staring carefully at Julian. "*Other humans have exploded in anger when they were told they would not remember their moments in the bright moonlight. I did not punish those humans*

— had they voiced anger at me before the Throne of Wotan, they would have been dead things. This form was created so mortals could speak to a God as though they spoke to another human, so to punish them would not be just.

"So, Apprentice, though I watch over you, I cannot —"

Suddenly, a low rumbling sound echoed through the night, and the sky trembled. Reddish black lines crept overhead, like spiderwebs linking the stars. From the south, three pale lights began to shine dimly, where the southern sky met the soil of Alantéa. While to the north a single glowing force surged, carnival orange and deep purple. Other lights blinked dimly with pinkish hues like coals from a dying fire.

Wotan took a deep breath and stared at Julian. "What have you done, Apprentice, to attract such attention? You are away for only a few seconds, and what happens?" Wotan peered overhead. "Two Dark Gods shake the skies in their search for you, while at Stone Mountain, and Gravengate and Sea's Edge, three Wizards are struggling to find you with pale lights. Those flickering pinkish hues come from the Creatures Indomitable and their need to know your location. But, Apprentice, you should concentrate on the lights summoning you to the north."

Julian turned, watching dim lights glowing with carnival orange and dark purple.

"Watch the glow of the Witch as she reaches for you," Wotan murmured. *"Are you facing only a Witch, or is this a Queen of Witches? Certainly, she is much stronger than you, much stronger than the Wizards ever guessed."*

Wotan sighed. "Rarely am I forced to take steps such as I take now, yet you face a power that I believe is beyond your strength. For that reason, I will grant you further aid. If you accept my gift, help will come to you when you face defeat and death — and it will be aid that you recognize, immediate, practical assistance. Will it be enough? I fear that it may not, though perhaps it will give you a fighting chance.

"You must accept this aid on the same terms as the knowledge I have given you — for you will never know the source of this gift, and no one else will realize that Wotan blessed a young Apprentice with a gift of power. Do you accept these terms?"

Julian bowed. "Lord, I have come to trust you. Of course, I accept, but how will I know what kind of help —"

Suddenly, Julian found himself standing alone in the moonlight, not fifty steps away from their cart. He was just outside their circle of nesting birds that both cooed and purred as they slept. How had he ever slipped past them without waking a whole flock? He looked around in all directions, completely confused. Then images and understanding flooded his mind: of the Emissaries both staring at Julian with a desire to destroy him, that the Firedrake Sending came from Merlin to counter those Emissaries, that Creatures of the Darkness had an unhealthy interest in him, and that the Grey Witch of the North was likely to be much more powerful than the Wizards expected.

"Some force has tried to help me," Julian whispered into the night. "I don't know why it did, but now I understand the aims of the two Emissaries and the Sending, and I'm beginning to understand that this Grey Witch of the North is a Power, not some lost and lonely ghostly spirit."

Chapter Five

Carags, Vorrs, and Wolves

"THIS ADVENTURE DOESN'T SOUND like much fun," Rafir complained. "Either we get killed in the next few days, or this Grey Witch of the North gets hold of us and crushes us to death a few days later. Heroes are supposed to do better than that, much, much better." Julian had explained to his Familiars why the two Emissaries had fought, and how Merlin had used his great Firedrake Sending to deal with them. As they traveled north, Sebastian and Rafir were trying to make sense of what was happening to them, and why. Rafir was younger, and full of questions, while Sebastian had been serving the League for years.

"I remember," Sebastian said, "that Galad used to quote that old warrior, what was his name?"

"Orlan," Julian said. "In addition to an Apprentice or Adept, the Wizards have always had at least one champion, a warrior knight. Orlan was before my time, but then came Kalanin, who was joined by Galad, and the two of them journeyed together for years. Now we have only Galad, but he's easily the deadliest of them all because he wields the Tarnished Sword."

"Anyway," Sebastian said, "when things looked grim, Galad always used to quote Orlan: 'It is better to be dead tomorrow than dead today.'

Think about that, Rafir. Wouldn't you rather be dead tomorrow, and at least have today?"

"Dead anytime doesn't sound like fun," Rafir sputtered. "Why not live to be old and cranky? I — oh no, talk about bad timing. Here comes the Eye of Merlin. Forget I said anything." The sharp eyes of the fox had caught a glimpse of a rapidly moving speck that raced over blue skies, circling from the west, then dropping swiftly downward.

Merlin's Familiar landed so heavily that the eagle made a thumping sound on the grass roadway before them. Julian brought Bluescent to a halt, while the Eye studied them for a moment.

"Well met," the eagle said, shifting so he could study each of them from different angles. "Some matter of hidden magic took place last night when my Wizard Master Merlin was searching for you, Julian. What can you tell me about that, Apprentice?"

Julian nodded and climbed down from Bluescent. "I remember nothing, though when I woke, I understood things that had confused me the evening before — that the Firedrake Sending was Merlin's creation, that one Emissary wished us dead now, while the other wished us destroyed sometime later by the Grey Witch, and so the two fought. My understanding comes from a third source, and so you should ask Merlin this: is it possible that one of the Great Gods has intervened on our behalf?"

The eagle was silent as he sent thoughts to his Wizard Master. After a pause, the eagle said, "Merlin fears that some Power or Force has crept inside your mind. He wonders if that particular God now secretly influences you, or even controls you."

Julian's eyes flared with a dim blue fire, though he kept calm, and he knelt so that he and the eagle were almost at the same eye level. "If I feel anything," Julian said, "it is a sense of having spent time with a wise elder."

Sebastian flapped down to stand beside Julian as he confronted the Eye of Merlin. "I'm linked to Julian's mind," the Familiar said, "and if there was anything wrong with him, I would be the first to know."

Rafir was already on the ground, but he shifted to face the eagle. "I don't have Sebastian's magic, but if someone tried to control Julian, he would fight back, and the struggle inside himself would make him very, very angry. Now, he's just worried, worried about us, and worried about this Grey Witch of the North."

The eagle stared at the Apprentice and his two Familiars, forces that he could usually dominate. "And how this worm has turned," the Eye of Merlin muttered.

"Hear me," Julian said softly. "You are our ally and our friend. Merlin was wise to send you north to ask about our misadventures. We are alive and not wounded — either in our bodies or our minds. We will continue to investigate this Grey Witch of the North until the Wizards need us for other tasks."

The eagle stared at them with fierce, unblinking eyes, then finally looked away. "You were always a truthteller, Apprentice, and so I will carry back to the Wizards this judgment: that you are strong, determined, and resourceful, though lacking strength for the task set for you.

"Know this," the Eye of Merlin continued, "you three see only the task before you, yet you must also see the world through the eyes of Merlin: fleets of warships stir off the coast of the League, and all our strength has been drawn south. Still, this fight in the forest begun by two Dark Gods and the intervention of a third Power of the Mid-World, a God, shows the importance of your mission. We need to find some way to aid you. In fact, I will *insist* that aid should be sent, but do not be surprised if this help comes from *outside* the League, for we are committed to battle on the coast."

The Eye was silent for a moment, studying the skies overhead. Above them everything was blue and clear, though the eagle could feel the earth slowly turn away from the sun, leading into the chilly rains of late autumn and then into the snows of winter.

When the eagle finally spoke, he seemed to struggle to find words: "I must also speak to you about the hawk creature that confronted me last night. On two separate evenings, I warned that creature to depart from our League — yet it would not leave. Finally, the thing challenged me, and I realized that it had been sent to destroy me. It was larger and swifter than I was and had been sent as an assassin to sweep me from the skies."

"It should have known better," Julian said. "Eagles are attacked by smaller birds that use their flying ability to dart and jab the larger fliers, while you have always had your *surge,* an ability to leap in midair, and strike before the lesser creatures attack."

"That hawk creature also had a *surge,*" the eagle muttered, "but it was not nearly enough when life and death fought together in the upper skies in the darkest night. Now, my friends and allies, farewell! May confusion and disaster fall upon all the enemies of the Wizards and their League!" The eagle hopped up to their cart's surface, flapped his huge wings, lifted into the clear skies of morning, and was gone.

"I never thought I would live to see this day," Sebastian murmured.

"Did the eagle almost apologize?" Rafir asked.

Julian laughed. "The Eye of Merlin would never really 'apologize.' He might speak a few soft words, or stare into the distance until someone else changed the subject."

· X ·

They made good progress throughout the rest of the day. No villages could be seen, but every few thousand paces, the forest around them cleared and clusters of farmhouses could be seen on either side of their grassy horse track. Sometimes farmers would wave to them, or grazing cows might study the travelers with dull eyes that understood very little.

Loud afternoon sounds came from crows disturbed from feeding on newly mown fields. As always, whenever Sebastian took flight, crows tried to drive him from the skies, and as always, Sebastian defended himself easily with handfuls of sneezing powder.

Rafir laughed as the crows sneezed, coughed, and fled. "We should get Sebastian an itching powder, too," he said to Julian. Then the fox slipped down from Bluescent and went to nap on their cart.

Once they saw in the distance jagged lines of stone walls with a broken tower rising from its center. The old fortress was grey with age, overgrown with vines and inhabited only by hundreds of birds — rock doves, crows, and starlings.

"Don't ask me," Julian told Sebastian. "I have no idea what that old castle was defending or who made it. That's one of the League's problems — we don't keep histories very well. Large cities like Tuvan and Amalric keep records, but I don't think either city could tell us much about this old fortress. That's why I always suggest that village scribes keep a record of —" Julian stopped suddenly and brought Bluescent to a halt. The sea-grey eyes of the Apprentice flashed with blue fire.

"*Things* are out there in the fields and forests," Julian said quietly, "and they are not human."

"I should be able to sense an Emissary," Sebastian muttered, "but I can't." Rafir blinked out, ready to investigate.

"No, wait," Julian murmured. "Don't go — they are too far away. It's not another Emissary; it's at least two bands of very different creatures ahead of us. But you each have a much stronger sense of smell than I do. What can you smell in the upper and lower air? Even from a distance, you might be able to sense something." Rafir lifted his nose skyward, while Sebastian rose into the air, sniffing. Moments later, the three gathered together on the ground.

"Two strange scents," Sebastian murmured, "very different from each other. One smell is like a beast of the darkest forests, harsh and powerful. The other comes from strange beings, ones that might even be creatures touched by magic."

"And there's a third scent — wolves!" Rafir added. "It smells like all the wolves in Alantéa are heading toward us."

"I sensed Carags and Vorrs before," Julian said quietly. "These creatures are monstrosities created by Dark Lords to plague humans. Now they're returning to League lands, something that hasn't happened for many, many years. Carags are shapeshifters and very dangerous. They can appear as human, with the faces of any human that they choose. But when they cast aside human form, they become beasts, like large, grey hyenas. Those are your 'creatures of magic.'

"As for the other creatures, a Vorr with its thick, brown fur, has roughly twice the strength of a large wolf, making it a large and fierce killing machine, with a body about the size of a lean bear. That's what you sense when you smell creatures of the darkest forest."

"What about those wolves?" Sebastian asked, "If they're only half the size of the Vorrs, wouldn't they just move out of danger instead of racing toward the Vorrs?"

"I thought they would hide in the hills," Julian said thoughtfully, "but instead they seem to be gathering to give battle. Will the wolf packs rule the night? Or will the Vorrs? And how will the winners of that struggle deal with the Carag Assassins?"

"So, Merlin thought he would keep us safe by sending us off to a soft little errand, did he?" Rafir muttered. "This has certainly turned into a nice little picnic in the park."

"Some 'picnic'," Sebastian added, "but you know the eagle has excellent hearing, in addition to his distant, enchanted eyesight." Glancing at the skies, Rafir was suddenly silent.

The blue skies above them were completely cloudless as they rode north through the afternoon sunlight. Everything seemed peaceful, though Julian could sense the movement of distant enemies as Vorrs raced through forests and Carags, in their hyena forms, sped through sunlit meadows.

In late afternoon, messengers on horseback came riding hard from the north, three of them, all showing signs of panic. When they were almost a hundred paces away, Julian raised his staff and sent a jagged bolt of force into the upper skies. A small explosion echoed over the nearby woodlands, and the messengers came to a confused halt.

"Carags?" whispered Sebastian. Rafir vanished and raced forward, carefully circling to the right of the messengers.

"Stay where you are!" Julian called to the riders, then to Sebastian he whispered, "You can see that they're riding farm horses — the smell of Carag would make any farm animal very difficult to control, so I guess that they are farmers."

Moments later, Rafir blinked back into view. "I can only smell humans and horses," he panted, "nothing like those shapeshifters."

Still cautious, Julian nudged Bluescent forward until they stood twenty paces from the messengers.

"Many raiders have come to our lands," Julian called to them. "They are coming after me, and when I leave, they will probably depart too. Carags have come, shapeshifting killers. Vorrs have come, with their thick brown fur, as large as lean bears, both swift and powerful. Lock yourselves and your farm animals away behind strong doors. When you speak to a friend or neighbor, ask them questions only that person would know — prove to yourselves that the person before you is not a shapeshifting Carag."

"What are the Wizards doing to stop this?" one messenger called out.

"War is coming to the south," Julian said. "Wizards have gathered men and metal and magic to guard our southern shores. As far as I know, only small bands of enemies have entered from the north. I will destroy any of those beings or people that will not leave League lands, but I need all our people nearby to protect themselves. Stay behind strong doors, make certain your neighbor is really your neighbor, and keep your livestock safe."

"We have weapons, Apprentice," another messenger said. "We can protect ourselves."

Julian leaned forward, shaking his head. "Carags and Vorrs are too great an enemy. Against a trained force of many men armed with bows and spears and swords, Vorrs and Carags can be defeated, but against farmers and villagers, these creatures are too strong."

Julian took a deep breath. "Listen to me: I am peaceful by nature, but if these creatures do not depart, I will destroy them. Tell your villagers and neighbors to protect themselves, and to pass my warning on to those nearby. Do not throw your lives away! Messengers should ride only during daylight. Look above you! Nightfall can bring death to travelers!"

All three messengers stared at the sky, seeing that evening was coming. They glanced nervously at each other then turned to ride back to the north. One rider stared back at Julian with a sour, unhappy face: so, this was the famous Apprentice — what a disappointment!

"Yes," Julian said quietly as the messengers returned to the north, "I'm not very happy myself. The Wizards should have sent two powerful Magicians armed with magic weapons, leading five hundred well-armed men. Instead, they could spare only one poorly prepared Apprentice."

And two Familiars who are not really very clever, Sebastian's mind added.

Rafir bit his tongue and instead of traveling with Julian or napping on the cart, he vanished and raced ahead, scattering grasshoppers that were feasting on tall grasses. After a few hundred feet, the fox found himself panting. *Foxes chased by hounds can run for hours. But I'm tired in minutes. I spend too much time talking. Run instead of babbling, you silly fox! Otherwise....*

The fox trailed off. Just ahead and to the right, four farmers were walking quickly from northeastern fields toward the horse track. Their hands held farm tools — but as they neared Rafir, the fox could see that the tools were simple, thin clubs, not hoes or rakes.

And when the fox sniffed the air, he smelled Carags. Rafir raced back more swiftly than he had come. Julian was watching the approaching farmers carefully and had already drawn his staff.

"Carags!" Rafir hissed, as he blinked back into view. Julian slipped down from Bluescent, staff in hand, a blue fire racing over his sea-grey eyes. Four creatures in human disguise began running toward Julian.

"Apprentice!" one cried. "Help us! Help us!"

"They are coming!" another cried. "Help us stop them!"

"Back!" Julian called out. "Get back or die!" A blast overhead made the Carags hunch down, but instead of turning back, they sped up, trying to overrun the Apprentice before his magic could strike them.

Julian called out *words*. A wall of fire rolled toward the Carags, twice the height of a man and thirty paces wide. Grasses along the horse track smoked and nearby fields began to burn.

"Get behind me," Julian said quickly to Sebastian and Rafir. When they hesitated, he cried, "Move — now!"

Carags pushed through the flames. Their clothes burned, and their human faces seemed to be melting. Metal flashed from their hands, and a dozen small daggers leaped toward Sebastian and Rafir.

Julian's left hand flashed with power, and the daggers were blown down, dropping to the ground. The staff in his right hand surged with magic — jagged black bolts of lightning struck first one Carag, then a second. Both fell dead.

The other two Carags changed from their human forms, slipped out of their loose clothing, and burst back through the wall of fire. Fur smoking, their hyena voices shrieking in pain, they rolled and rolled through damp fields until their fur stopped burning. Then they raced away into nearby forests, still calling out in pain and rage.

"It's too bad," Rafir said softly, "that those three unhappy messengers missed this battle."

"Our battle has just started," Julian said grimly. "What we need is two different spies — one hidden by magic, the other by leafy forest branches — to tell me what the Carags and Vorrs are up to. Did you see that they tried to kill you both? So be careful, be *very* careful!"

Julian watched Sebastian as he flew into the distance, then he walked toward the dead Carags and studied them closely. Their clothing had old bloodstains on the backs of their shirts — so the Carag assassins had already stabbed farmers or villagers just to get clothing for their disguises. Shaking his head, Julian sat, waiting in fields near the horse track as their horses grazed in fading daylight, and the sun crept lower. Stars were beginning to shine when a very tired Sebastian returned. By the time Rafir blinked back into view, the day had grown dark.

"Rafir was probably closer," Sebastian said, "so he should go first."

"It was too dangerous to get close," Rafir said, "and it was getting dark. Anyway, there was a fight, Carags against Vorrs. Carags in human form had bows and arrows — and spears. Did they bring those weapons, or did they steal them? I couldn't tell, but Vorrs were powerful and deadly. The Carags only stopped them because there were more of them, and they had weapons.

By the time the Vorrs retreated, there were three dead Vorrs and seven dead Carags."

"I saw the same thing," Sebastian added, "but I was too far away, and it was getting darker, so I couldn't count the numbers of dead creatures. But why would Carags and Vorrs fight? When they invaded League lands long ago, didn't they work together?"

"They were allies," Julian replied, "very close allies."

Sudden understanding raced through Rafir's mind like a flash of lightning. "Here's what I think," Rafir said. "Let's say there are two groups: one of them is the 'Kill Them Now' group, and the other is the 'Kill Them Later' group."

Julian nodded. "Just like the two Emissaries, two Dark Gods have sent different forces with different instructions."

"So, the Carags," Sebastian added, "are probably the 'Kill Them Now' force."

"And the Vorrs," Julian finished, "are on the 'Kill Them Later' side. I think you've got it, between the two of you. Here's our Wizards' League, with all its magic, and its fortresses and armed hosts. Right now, we're counting on a pack of Vorr killing machines — who want us dead later — to protect us from Carag assassins, who want us dead now. Very, very nice."

They traveled only a short distance farther before they found a clearing in the woodlands where they could make camp. The sky was filled with stars as Julian called bird flocks to their camp and wove a Healer's Sleep over them. Surrounded by hundreds of birds doing duty as sentries, the three tried to sleep. Julian wanted badly to reach out to his parents in dreams, but Rafir was restless, while Sebastian's mind turned and twisted as he thought about Carags and Vorrs.

So, all three of them were awake when the wolves began to howl.

At first, only a few howls could be heard from a distance, then others added their voices, and the noises grew louder. Then came louder cries as Vorrs howled in rage and pain. Under starlit skies, wolves and Vorrs were fighting to see which beasts would rule the night.

"The wolves are defending their hunting grounds," Sebastian whispered. "You said they were going to fight, rather than hiding in the hills."

Howling and shrieking sounds went on for some time, while the three listened in silence. It was impossible to know which side was winning. Hours later the noises died down. The Gift brought Julian images of fallen beasts, grey wolves and Vorrs with thick brown fur leaking red blood while lying dead under peaceful starlit skies. With half the night gone, Julian finally turned his mind from the struggle, and finally, he slept.

· X ·

In dreams once again, Julian found himself seated across from his parents. A few small candles flickered a dim light over their faces. As before, he could tell immediately that they were not really his parents; they were only images from his own mind. Yet they no longer smiled at him blankly. Instead, they stared to a place at Julian's right, to the farthest end of a long table, and their faces were frozen in horror.

At the table's far end sat the Grey Witch of the North.

"My Sweet Little One," she whispered to Julian, "how wonderful to finally meet you! But I fear we will see each other only here in Dreamland, for you will never reach me, not without much more help." She shook her head with regret, watching Julian with a soft, sad smile.

Julian stared: The Grey Witch of the North called herself the Grey Witch because her skin was as grey as slate or granite. She looked as though she had been dead for more than a year before being brought back to life by the darkest of Black Magics. And while her face was smiling its soft sad smile, her eyes were filled with hunger.

"You lovely, sweet little boy," the Witch continued, "I have done everything I could to help you, but sad to say, the Great Dark God aiding me has lost interest in our cause. Let me show you what has happened."

She waved her hand, and Julian's dreaming mind saw himself floating in the darkness over a nighttime forest lit by pale moonlight. Below Julian more than twenty wolves lay dead, dribbling blood into the roots of white birch trees. Seven Vorrs also lay dead, most of them lying on their backs, staring up into night skies with blank eyes that saw nothing.

Some distance away, a pack of fifteen or more Vorrs was racing through the forest. Their brown fur was smeared with the redness of their own blood — mixed with the blood of many wolves.

In his dreams, Julian followed the Vorrs as they raced through the forest. When the pack came into a clearing, the Vorrs halted at the edge of an armed camp, where manlike figures stood with spears. There, the pack snarled in low, deep voices, while their bodies were hunched down, waiting.

More manlike figures emerged from the camp, spears extended. Behind them, hyena shapes followed. As the Carags appeared, they spoke with the Vorrs in a language Julian could hear clearly if faintly, though he couldn't understand a single word of their dark speech. Finally, the manlike figures put down their spears.

Then the images grew faint, as Julian's dreaming mind was led away from the forest.

"So, you can see," whispered the Grey Witch, "that the force you called 'Kill Them Later,' has joined the 'Kill Them Now,' group, and so you will never reach me, you poor, sad, sorry little Apprentice."

Chapter Six

The Archers

"THIS GREY WITCH," JULIAN said quietly, "doesn't think we have a chance to even reach her. When she pushed her way into my dreams last night, she seemed almost sorry that she wouldn't have the chance to kill us herself — but she also wanted to gloat that we were all going to be dead soon." Sebastian shook his head, but he was too shocked to speak.

"You're sure," Rafir asked, "that the 'Kill Them Laters' have joined with the 'Kill Them Nows'?"

"I saw them meet," Julian replied. "Some sort of agreement was reached. If I were watching magic images made by the Witch, I would have known. Think about it: to be a God is to live almost forever, to spend a short time watching millions of stars move through the skies, and then when you turn your thoughts back to Alantéa, you find that hundreds of years have passed. So, whether we live for a day or two more, it can't be that important to the Dark God that's guiding the 'Kill Them Later' group. So, some sort of 'trade' or 'deal' must have been reached."

As before, they were riding north, with morning light from the east slanting down over meadows and forests. All the nearby fields had been recently harvested so the soil was brown, with bits of wheat grain on the soil's surface; while the forests of early fall were still changing color, from green to a mixture of red, yellow, and orange. Julian watched for farmers and herders, but none could be seen, and Julian hoped that his advice to stay inside had reached everyone nearby.

He glanced back to Sebastian and Rafir: both of his Familiars seemed stunned by events and surprised by the Witch's power. As they rode north, Julian whispered soft words, calling on a *cone of silence*, to surround them, magic that shielded them from the prying ears of others. Inside their cone, they could speak openly.

"Don't lose hope!" Julian said quietly. "When I spoke earlier, I knew that the Witch could hear our words. Be careful when you speak outside our *cone* because the Witch is listening, she used your names for our enemies, calling them 'Kill Them Now' beings and 'Kill Them Later' creatures. But Sebastian, think about Merlin at Sea's Edge. Has he given up on us? Does he think we are doomed?" Inside the *cone*, all their voices were dim, as though they were speaking through heavy cloths. On the other hand, all the sounds outside the *cone* were also much quieter.

The little Familiar shook his head. "Merlin is so wise — the Wizard can play two or three complicated games all at once, while at the same time another part of his mind is thinking about something completely different."

"You mean he's tricky," Rafir said.

"Very, very tricky," Sebastian replied.

"I can even see Merlin's next move," Julian added. "Remember how the eagle spoke of help coming from 'outside' the League. Rafir, what was the only force that came out of the Mid-World during our last struggle?"

Rafir's tail wagged back and forth in excitement. "Out of the Mid-World — you mean the Mistress of Illusions! The Sorceress might come!"

"She wouldn't come herself," Sebastian corrected. "Remember that she didn't come before. What she did was to send about three hundred archers, female archers, and dangerous fighters. A force of archers would be very, very nice. But how would she reach us?"

"When you belong to the Mid-World, like the Mistress of Illusions," Julian said, "you can use magic gateways. I think you both have seen Portals form before. Anyway, help is coming, but right now...right now, I think two very cautious spies need to tell us what's going on just over that hill. When our *cone of silence* ends, be sure to watch what you say."

Julian nodded, pointing to a small, thickly forested hill that rose just to the left of their horse track. The hill was overgrown with fir and pine trees — evergreens that kept their green needles through both fall and winter. Sebastian peered into the hill's forest, but he could see nothing but dark shadows, with almost all light blocked out by layers of upper branches.

Rafir blinked out of view. Sebastian began flying cautiously to the hill's peak, staring down into the tangle of forest — waves of bright sunlight were reaching only the highest of the evergreen branches, leaving the forest floor filled with dark shadows.

Suddenly, the Sight within Julian sent a shot of alarm through his mind.

"Back!" he cried. "Get back — Carags and Vorrs. It's a trap!" As Sebastian turned in the sky, arrows sprang up after him. Julian's left hand curled, then flashed open. Power surged from his palm and the arrows veered away.

Face grim with anger, the Apprentice then gripped his staff with both hands. But music and magic were stirring on the other side of their horse track. Dense forest lay to the left of their roadway, while to the right, an archway was forming over green fields — an enchanted Portal, a gateway from the Mid-World. From the archway came the music of women singing, and beyond the arched Portal, a cloud of fine silvery dust seemed to spin in the air.

A thin smile formed on Julian's face. *They are coming just as our need is greatest. Prompted by the eagle, the Mistress of Illusions sends a force of archers to our aid.*

From the forested hillside, a pack of Vorrs appeared, snarling first at Julian, then at the three riders emerging from the Portal to the right of their horse track. Three woman warriors drew bows as the Vorrs snarled; the two forces were only fifty paces apart. Then behind the riders, other women appeared from the mists, armed with bows and spears, all of them moving in tight formation, looking well trained and deadly. Julian counted three on horseback, with thirty-six archers or spear carriers following them.

The smile on Julian's face vanished: he had hoped for at least twice the number of archers.

Vorrs turned and vanished back into the hillside and its dark forest. Then from the forest came a volley of arrows — Carags in human form shooting arrows at the women warriors. Shields were raised; three arrows struck shields while the rest fell harmlessly into the fields beyond.

Six arrows lashed back into the forest: Vorrs howled and Carags shrieked. Then came silence, but Julian could sense motion in the hillside as Vorrs and Carags retreated deeper into the forest. The three leading riders turned away from the forest and rode back toward Julian. As with all the women serving the Mistress of Illusions, they were tall, with long dark hair, strong, and mostly grim. They would be beautiful, Julian thought, if they ever let themselves smile, and the three seemed so young — barely more than teenagers.

"Hail, Apprentice," the leading rider called out, "and greetings from the Mistress of Illusions."

"As always," Julian said, "Our League thanks you, and it's good to see you again. I remember how we had to exchange information so very carefully before the battle at Gravengate."

"Your Captain, Dargas, never approved of us," Kayal said, "so we avoided him whenever we could."

"Dargas was smart," Julian said, shaking his head, "though maybe he spent too much time in the field, and too much time muttering at night over his goblet of wine. Anyway, you are most welcome, and if Vorrs and Carags come too close, you will fill them with arrows."

"We have also brought our own pike force, Apprentice," Issah added. "Even at the edge of death, Vorrs have the strength for one last leap. They will come down on the sharp metal points of pikes and impale themselves. They will be dead before they even reach the ground."

"But first come the arrows," Naith said, holding her bow up — it was made from white bone, strengthened by dark, treated wood. "Always we lash out first with arrows, shot either from horseback or on foot."

Julian's smile vanished. "But watch for Carags. Otherwise, one you know and trust, might be something completely different — an enemy, a monster."

"We are prepared," Kayal said, "though we may turn to you for guidance with things magical. Still, have we not already pushed past the force opposing you, Apprentice? Our goal is to get you to your destination — some Witch creature intrudes on League lands, and we are to help you reach this Grey Witch, but not fight her with our own forces. How much of your journey remains, Apprentice? Have we perhaps a day and a half, then we are done?

"Do not put aside your bows," Julian said grimly, "and keep your pike forces ready. I'm afraid that our fight has only just begun."

· X ·

Kayal, Naith, and Issah led on horseback with half their force in the front. Julian rode Bluescent next, leading their horse cart, while a rear guard of mixed archers and pike followed. Julian and his two small allies were protected from danger before them, and from ambush behind them.

Issah looked up into the afternoon sun and spoke quietly under her breath: "It's good to see Julian again, but I was hoping he'd be a little taller, and wearing a couple of medals after that battle."

"But think of that curled, dark hair, and those grey eyes," Naith said dreamily. "He's still very handsome and even more mysterious." Issah looked away, and Kayal rolled her eyes: Naith was at a stage where she found a wide range of men "handsome."

"First," Kayal said, "we should speak openly only when we can see the fox. The Mistress of Illusions says that when Rafir wishes to be unseen, he is completely invisible. Secondly, it seems likely that we'll never know if the reputation of the Apprentice is deserved or not. In two more days, we should be done with him, having delivered him to this Grey Witch creature. This mission seems only half an adventure, barely worth our time."

"Careful!" Issah hissed.

"Not now, Benja!" Naith muttered as a hint of gold flashed in the air.

Some distance behind the leading archers Julian also spoke quietly with his two small allies: "I always liked watching the three sisters," he said. "Like me, they were young, but they were also very dangerous. While those following them — a total of three dozen archers or women wielding pikes, also seem strong and well trained, so they might be enough, just enough, to get us to the Grey —" He then caught a hint of gold flashing in the air above the three riders. "And *that's* what I felt when we first met. There's some strange magic guarding them."

"You mean like a magic talisman," Rafir said, voice filled with excitement. "Like a magic pearl that warns you when trouble is near? So, when you enter a dark cave, the pearl actually speaks." Rafir lowered his voice to its deepest tones. "Do not go there — the Ogres will kill you dead, then gnaw on your bones when the meat is gone!"

"Maybe not exactly like your pearl," Julian said, smiling, "because whatever it is, it feels — alive. On the other hand, it might deliver the same kind of warning."

They made good progress through the afternoon, though Julian saw two farmhouses that had recently been burned down — smoke was still curling from them. Otherwise, the hunters and farmers of this northern part of the League seemed to have concealed themselves from Vorrs and Carags. It was also clear that creatures of the fields and meadows were avoiding the intruders — rabbits, groundhogs, squirrels, and chipmunks had fled or hidden. Flocks of birds that usually fed on leftovers from the harvests had disappeared and only crows followed the Archers from a distance, as though expecting a later feast after battle supplied them with mounds of dead flesh.

They made camp at nightfall in a field just northeast of their horse track. Camp fires were lit, sending smoke and light into a partly clouded night sky. As their archers prepared food, the three sisters gathered around their central fire, warming their hands, glancing up into a night sky that was brightened both by stars and the sparks from their own fire.

"All this light is telling the world exactly where we are," Naith muttered, her dark cloak bathed in firelight."

"The world already knows," Kayal said quietly, "at least the Vorrs and Carags following us know. Will the firewood last the night?"

"Until dawn," Issah answered. "Who has the first watch?"

"I will take the first," Kayal said. She turned and saw that the Apprentice was walking toward them. She lowered her voice. "Here comes the Apprentice. Say nothing of the Benja. Be polite."

"I can be polite," Naith whispered, turning to smile at the Apprentice.

"Hail, Apprentice," Kayal called out as Julian came closer. "So far, this has been a simple walk through fields and forests, with enemies that flee at the first challenge. Who could complain?"

"More Vorrs and Carags have crossed over into the Wizards' League," Julian said grimly. "They have joined the others and they are coming for us — tonight."

·)(·

Each watch lasted three hours, and each watch had one sub-captain on guard, with all that leader's twelve followers pacing through the darkness, weapons ready. Little happened during the first watch, except that more clouds gathered overhead, and the night grew darker. Kayal called for more wood for the fires, and so as the fields around them grew darker, their camp became brighter. With more light around her, Kayal noticed for the first time that the fox was padding around the camp, sliding through the shadows, carefully sniffing each sleeping form for any scent of Carag — so Rafir was keeping watch for the Apprentice. Kayal smiled; it was good to have a Mid-World Spy on their side.

Issah had the second watch. A short time after midnight, she found herself beginning to daydream, and so began walking more quickly from watchfire to watchfire. As she moved from one shadowy area to an outer watchfire, two archers stood up just outside their campground, seeming to appear from nowhere. Both were dark-haired and dressed like the other archers of the Mistress of Illusion. Issah could almost — but not quite — remember their names.

"Passwords!" Issah called, drawing an arrow.

"Wait!" one figure called out, and another, "We come from the Mistress of —"

"Carags!" came Rafir's cry.

"Loose!" Issah called out. Arrows leaped through the night, and the two would be assassins fell dead, changing slowly back into hyena shaped Carags as life left them.

Suddenly Rafir was at Issah's side. "Vorrs are coming!" he panted. "I can smell them!" From the camp's center, Julian rose quickly and lifted his staff into the night sky. A sudden light flashed over their campground, shining down on the gleaming eyes of Vorrs, who had been creeping through the darkness, hugging the ground.

"Eyes!" Naith cried, drawing her bowstring. "Aim for their eyes and hearts!" Arrows lashed through the night; Vorrs grunted in pain, but others began pounding forward. Naith's arrow caught the first Vorr through its eye socket and it fell dead. Arrows from Kayal and Issah dropped the next two with shafts buried in their hearts.

Then Issah set aside her bow. "Pike forces to me!" she called out. Twelve pikes were raised as Vorrs pounded toward them, lashed by sharp arrows. Some of the creatures stumbled, fell, then began crawling forward. Others reached the camp's edge and leaped — arrows sticking from their bodies — at their foes.

Steel pike tips met leaping Vorrs, and they cried aloud, shaking, and shuddering with pain. Behind the pike force, Issah slashed with her sword, killing wounded Vorrs so their jaws became lifeless, dead things. After her third kill, Issah's boots were spattered with blood. Kayal led the archers, calling volley after volley against their foes so that the main force of Vorrs began to give way. As other Vorrs circled around the main battle, Naith raced to the camp's edge and used her bow reinforced with white bones, to kill them, one by one.

Julian stood beside the watchfire watching, waiting, staff in his right hand, left hand coiled with power. As Naith fired, another archer — without a bow — approached her from behind, mouth opened to ask a question, but the archer's left hand held a dagger.

"Naith!" Julian called, "Carag behind you!" Naith leaped away, rolled, and in one motion fired an arrow into the Carag's chest. The creature dropped its dagger, held the slender shaft of the arrow with a look of astonishment on its face, then it died.

Gold colors flashed overhead: one single flash, then it was gone.

"Right, Benja, right," Kayal muttered, then she raised her voice. "Shields, shields, watch for arrows!" Outside the camp, Carags in human form began launching streams of arrows at the archers. Pikes were dropped, and wicker shields were raised to protect the archers. Others huddled behind the wagon, leaning out to launch arrows back at Carags, but the Carag archers were hidden by darkness.

Again, Julian raised his staff, calling out for light, and the Carag archers stood exposed in a night that was suddenly bright. Arrows brought down five, and the rest cast aside their human disguises and fled into the night. The battle was over.

· X ·

Only four of the archers sent by the Mistress of Illusions suffered wounds, and those were all light injuries. As Julian tended to the wounded, the three sisters moved to the camp's edge, and using their cloaked bodies to shield themselves from the rest of the camp, they met with the Benja. As always, Issah, the youngest of the sisters, called up their ally — their hidden, younger, and magical brother.

"Benja," Issah whispered, "good job warning us, and good job staying hidden."

A golden-hued figure slowly appeared before them. "Keeping quiet," the Benja said, "was not easy." The Benja stood less than four feet high, but his body gleamed gold with a force of magic.

"So, what are your thoughts, Benja?" Kayal asked. "What could we have done better?"

"Naith needed two archers to guard her when she left your main force," the Benja said quietly. "Otherwise, you did well."

"Almost a perfect score," Naith said, smiling, then she grew more serious. "You know the Apprentice may be nice to look at, but I was a little disappointed in him. All that light in the sky was good, but I expected blasts of power or magic spells or powerful servants coming to his aid."

"Remember, he's also useful as a healer," Kayal added, thoughtfully, "and perhaps as a person sensitive to magic like the Benja."

"Maybe we don't completely understand him," Issah said, glancing back to their bonfire. "After all, he's supposed to reach this Grey Witch creature, and then he might die. He might just be saving himself for his last battle."

"Ha!" the Benja said, scornfully. "You three are blind to magic. The staff of the Apprentice surges with an Adept's power, while his left hand contains something like a Sorcerer's magic. Did you not wonder why all the arrows of our foes fell short or leaped overhead into the darkness? That was the power of Julian's left hand. As for his Adept's staff, he was holding himself in reserve in case some part of your force suffered losses. And there is something else...." The Benja hesitated. "When evening comes, often a huge tongue leaps out from nothingness, as though to taste the air and make certain that the Apprentice is not in any danger. So, Julian may very well have some hidden ally who will come to his aid only when great danger threatens."

Kayal nodded thoughtfully. "I suppose that the Apprentice has been trained to keep his strength hidden. In a way it's sad that we will be with him for only a few days, then just when we understand him a little, we will never see him again."

"If you three survive," the Benja said quietly, "you may well meet Julian at least one more time in this life."

Naith's mouth dropped open in surprise. "Where?" she asked.

"I do not know," the Benja said, "but somewhere far from here, far from the archers' barracks you call home. For in three month's time, you will be leaving the service of the Mistress of Illusions."

"What!?!" the three sisters muttered together.

· ✠ ·

"The sisters call it 'The Benja'," Rafir said quietly, "and it's some sort of magical being. It shines with a gold light when it talks to them, and it tells them about the magic they can't see." It was only a few hours before daylight. The Apprentice and his two small allies were camping again beneath their cart. Julian wanted to sleep so he could reach for a dream-link with his parents, but Sebastian and Rafir still needed to talk.

"'The Benja'," Rafir continued. "I like that. I wish I were called the 'something or other', not just 'that nosy fox'."

"So, it can see things of magic?" Sebastian asked.

Julian stared back into the bonfire, thinking. "It might also be able to see parts of the future. I can sense it more clearly now — 'The Benja' is a creature of magic, stronger than an imp or a sprite, but that's all I can tell you this late in the night. Now, we need to sleep. Let's keep fresh for tomorrow because our struggle is nowhere near its end." He turned on his side, reaching for wisdom from his parents in the kingdom of dreams.

· X ·

And dreams led him again to a tablet in the tower, where he hoped to find himself seated in front of his parents. Two figures sat before him, but they no longer even looked like his parents: both were straw dummies, scarecrows with painted smiles, dressed in his parents' clothing, or clothing that his mind remembered from his childhood.

Again, down at the end of the table sat the Grey Witch of the North, with her sad eyed smile, and eyes that gleamed with hunger.

"I am learning so much about you, my tasty little one," she murmured. *"You have this little Sorcerer's paw."* She wriggled her left hand in mockery. *"Light blasts from the staff."* Tiny sparks flickered from her right hand. *"What else do you have to show me?"*

Julian studied the Witch in silence.

"Because," the Witch continued, more seriously, *"what you have shown me so far is not enough to defeat your foes. Your archers are better trained and deadlier than the Great Dark God expected. You might even survive his Vorrs and Carags! Who knows? But do you truly believe the Great Dark God opposing you is going to say, 'Well done, Apprentice! Well done!' and then let you pass into my small kingdom?"* The Grey Witch cackled — and the straw dummies in his parents' clothing laughed, making scraping, crackling sounds as the straw bits forming their pretend mouths rubbed together.

"The Great Dark God will challenge you at the end of your journey," the Grey Witch said. *"It will be most entertaining to watch your final moments."*

Then Julian's dreaming mind was released from the dark vision of the Grey Witch, and he drifted into other grim and troubled dreams.

·))(·

"I'm not certain," Issah said softly, "that I'm ready to leave the Mistress of Illusions." It was morning, with clouds gathering from the north and east. The three sisters were riding at the back of their war party, so they could speak quietly together. Their archers and pike force were at the front, the wagon of the Apprentice in the middle, leaving the three sisters to form a rearguard.

"You are the youngest of us," Kayal replied, "with less than four years serving the Mistress of Illusions. I've been with her longer, and during these last years, I've been thinking about leaving. Lately, that desire has become stronger — in the end, most of us tire of the endless training, the countless archery contests, the battle music and the long waiting between tasks. In spite of the beauty of the lakeshore, the forests, the strange creatures of magic in her kingdom, eventually many leave the service of the Mistress of Illusions and seek their futures in the wide world."

Naith thought of finally seeing Rivermeet, where three rivers joined, forming the great Asaram; and of Erivan Forest where the Elf-Lords ruled; and the Mirage of Rainbows where images of the past and future formed in the sky. Finally, she murmured, "I'm ready to go." The three were silent for a moment as they thought about a world outside their barracks, and how they would need to leave the other archers behind.

"If you are leaving, I will leave too," Issah said finally. When a hint of gold flashed in the air, she added quickly, "And the Benja, too."

In the early afternoon, a soft rain began dripping down over them. Cloaks and hoods protected the archers, though the three sisters and Julian rode bareheaded so they could see more clearly in all directions. Later in the afternoon, as the rain grew heavier, Julian and the three sisters became wetter, so that the dark hair of all four grew soaked and stringy.

Sebastian peered out from a tent flap in their horse drawn cart, glancing back and forth between Julian and the three sisters, and for the first time, the Familiar noticed their similarities: *Look at the four of them! They could easily be related — they even have the same sort of well-formed, lean features, dark hair, and speak the same quiet, restrained language. Where could that kinship have come from? Do they share some distant, great, great, grandfather? Or an even more distant grandmother?*

Chapter Seven

The Hunter

K AYAL RODE, DAMP, AND shivering, through the rain with the leading archers. She was relaxed as they passed cleared fields and farms, but when she drew closer to a forested part of their roadway, she became more alert — dense forest made a great cover for an ambush.

Suddenly, gold colors flashed in the corner of her eyes.

"Good, Benja, good," she murmured, then called out, "shields to me! Julian, watch for your horses! They will try to cripple the horses next." Then arrows aimed at horses leaped at them from the treeline. Five arrows were waived aside by Julian, while a sixth and seventh arrow had to be caught by shields. Woman archers searched the treeline for targets, but in the overcast rainy afternoon, no Carags could be seen.

Not even Naith's sharp eyes could catch the motions of Carag archers, but on the opposite side of the horse track, her eyes did find patches of brown fur. She notched an arrow, riding to her right, slowly, carefully, until she sensed that she was nearing dead creatures, not live Vorrs.

Her two sisters and Julian also left the horse track, and the four stared down at a shallow pit filled with several dead Vorrs, lying carefully arranged, just thirty paces from the roadside. Beside them lay a heap of spent arrows

— mostly from the archers sent by the Mistress of Illusions. Someone or some people had been gathering their own arrows for them.

A hint of gold began to flash in the air, and Issah quickly said, "It almost looks like a message, left for us."

"As though they knew," Naith added, "that we would be running out of arrows. Nice, work, invisible helpers." Naith and Issah dismounted, gathered arrows, and began to distribute them to their archers.

Julian closed his eyes, taking a deep breath. "They aren't invisible. Hunters of the League have been at work," he said softly, "old, grizzled hunters who know this land."

"How could they possibly deal with the shapeshifters?" Kayal asked.

"I have no idea," Julian said, shaking his head. "They may be dead even now — that's why I encouraged them to stay inside. Although, in another sense, it's good that the League has arisen to defend itself. One way or another, it will always rise to give battle."

Kayal opened her mouth to speak, but then she heard the Benja whisper into her mind. After a few moments, she dropped back and joined Naith and Issah at the rearguard of their war party.

"It's a trap!" the Benja whispered. "Not a thousand paces away, Vorrs and Carags have dropped trees across your horse track. When you stop to move them, they will kill many!"

"Now we know about them," Naith said quietly. "Instead of our dying, many of those creatures will die instead."

"No, no, no!" the Benja hissed. "Don't go near those fallen trees — or one of you will die and leave me forever!"

"It's time to have a serious talk with the Apprentice," Kayal said. "Come." The sisters rode forward, asked Julian to join them, then rode to the front of their procession. The four riders stopped not seven hundred paces from a blockade of fallen trees that lay across the horse track. Dense forests lay on both sides of their blocked passage. Vorrs and Carags remained carefully hidden, but none of the four doubted that arrows would leap at them and Vorrs would spring out if they went forward.

"Death," Julian murmured. "Death if we use this road, but this is not our journey's end, because somebody else is waiting for us. Rafir?" The fox suddenly popped into view, his slight, pinkish tongue out, panting.

"Rafir, that 'somebody' isn't a Carag, is it?" Julian asked. The fox, still panting, shook his head: no.

Julian turned to the three sisters. "Hold your archers back." Then he raised his voice. "Come out! You are safe with us!"

An old man slid out from behind a thicket of brambles at the forest's edge. Lean, head covered by a cloth cap, one hand was holding a bow, while lashed to his belt was a long dagger. On his shoulder, a canvas pouch held more than a dozen arrows. His grey beard was cut close but was stained black, so he could slide through dark forests without being exposed by the whiteness of his hair. If he was a little stooped with age, he moved quickly, and his eyes were keen.

"Heh-heh-heh," the old man laughed. "The question is: are you safe with me, Apprentice?"

"I am safe, we are safe," Julian said, smiling. "You left a marker for us — a heap of dead Vorrs, did you not? What are you called?"

"My name matters nothing," the old hunter said, glancing at the sisters and at the other archers. "But what are you doing with such a small force so close to your northern border?"

"Please ask Merlin that question when you meet him at Sea's Edge," Julian said. "I would also love to know the answer to your riddle. How are you dealing with the Carag shapeshifters?"

"Heh-heh-heh," the old hunter laughed again, showing a mouth filled with tooth stumps and worn gums. "Let us just say that sometimes we meet an old man in the woods, dressed as a hunter. Does he know the ways of the badger, or which lakes the geese favor in the spring, or the seasons when the trout streams are richest? If not, maybe he should not have left his fireplace. Heh-heh-heh." And the old hunter's hand slipped to the dagger that was lashed to his side.

By all the Nine Billion Gods! Sebastian thought. *This new "friend" has the most evil laugh I've ever heard. And if you can't answer his questions, he and the other hunters just stab you to death and walk away!*

"Now," the old hunter continued, "let's talk about your own choices. You can go forward and die, or you can return to your masters, or you can follow me on a side path, one that takes you far from that blockade of fallen trees. Then I will lead you back to the road north, and you can continue your quest. But you will lose your carts and your comforts. What do you say?"

Julian turned to the three sisters. "Once past this barrier, we are one long afternoon, and one long morning, from our destination. What are your thoughts?"

"Horses have been useful," Kayal said, "both yours and ours."

"We can walk your horses through the forest trails," the old hunter said, "together with whatever provision you can carry in sacks or saddlebags. But you will need to leave your carts behind."

· ⟩⟨ ·

Led by the old hunter, they made good progress through the forest, though insects owned the floor of the dark, damp forest. The first frosts of fall had not yet come, and mosquitoes and gnats drew blood with every step deeper into the forest. As a rearguard, Issah and Naith led their horses on foot, but they spent more time slapping insects than watching for Carags and Vorrs. The tails of their horses flapped, and flapped again, as they struggled to keep insects from their flanks.

"'Heh-heh-heh,'" Issah said, practicing the old hunter's evil laugh. "This hunter is a real hero of the League. I guess no Healer came this far north to help him with his teeth."

"Good laugh," Naith said, smiling. "But don't use it in front of the Mistress of Illusions. You know they always taught us that border people led rough lives, but I never thought it was this grim."

Issah slapped another mosquito, then wiped the red blood from her palm. "Border, you say? That means we are almost at the end." Naith nodded, waving a swirl of gnats from her eyes.

At the front of their column, Kayal was walking beside Julian, just a few paces behind the old hunter. She found it useful being beside the Apprentice — with just the slightest use of small magic, Julian had confused the senses of mosquitoes and gnats, so they avoided him, and those nearby.

"I like your hunter ally," Kayal was saying, "though he does create a problem for us — when you and Rafir and Sebastian are not around, how will we tell which hunters are human, and which are Carags?"

"You have been so careful to keep your ally hidden," Julian said quietly, "and so we will not speak of this again. But I believe that when danger threatens, 'the Benja' will warn you." Kayal nodded, hiding her surprise, and looked away. Out of their sight, far in the forest's upper branches, a gold light flashed.

The Benja gleamed with delight: *The Apprentice, the secret and mysterious Apprentice, knows about me!*

From the corner of his eyes, Sebastian saw the flash of gold in the upper forest, and he smiled — only he and the Benja were free from the dampness and darkness of the lower forest. Flying through its upper branches, Sebastian could see leaves turning, while all the evergreen branches were wet with rain. Flocks of birds raced away from him, speeding over the treetops. Overhead, rain clouds were clearing, while to the west, the sun was peering out, with rays of light sparkling through the dampness of the upper forest. The little Familiar took a deep breath; it was good to be alive.

Slowly, the forest thinned, and when Kayal came to a meadow at the forest's edge, she remounted her horse and rode back to join her sisters. The western sun was sinking lower as they curled around, heading back toward their horse track. When Kayal reached their rearguard, she dismounted to walk beside her sisters.

"It looks," Naith said, "as though you missed all the fun." She held out a palm smeared with her own blood and with crushed mosquitoes.

"Enough!" Issah muttered, waving at a small cloud of gnats.

"I did miss the insects," Kayal said, "thanks to Julian. Now, hear me: we still need to be so careful, but the Apprentice does know about the Benja."

"It must have been that sneaky thief of a fox," Naith said.

"Maybe," Issah added, "but it could also have been his *Sight*. I think Julian can see things, just as the Benja can."

"He knows about me!" the Benja said excitedly, gleaming gold in the air above the meadow.

"Benja, be calm," Kayal said. "But since we are all here, perhaps a council of war should come next. Benja, what lies before us?"

"Tonight, a fire will race across the skies," the Benja said. "Tomorrow, just before you reach your goal, battle will come, but what sort of struggle, and where, is not clear."

"Usually," Kayal said quietly, "you can see more than that, Benja. What could be blocking your Sight?"

"Dark clouds are hiding so much," the Benja murmured. "I can see only a few shapes and figures fighting in the mists. But here is what I imagine: maybe there are two Great Dark Gods, sitting on their dark thrones in their dark throne rooms, watching down over us. They are not certain what they will do, and so clouds cover many different futures."

Kayal shook her head and sighed. "Not just one, but two Great Dark Gods."

"But after tomorrow," Issah asked, "are we done?"

"We are done," the Benja said. "What will become of us after?"

"I have begun to dream," Naith said, hesitating, "of living in a small city protected by its own small band of archers."

"A City Guard," Kayal added.

"A City Guard," Naith agreed, "but not one that rules our lives. I've been dreaming of racing swiftly and leaping through the air — as we do in battle, though in my dreams I hold no weapons, I only...dance."

Kayal nodded and was silent for a moment. "A City Guard could use our skills. If I could choose, most of my time would be spent studying all the creatures of Alantéa — both creatures magical, and those of the natural world."

"I will join your Guard," Issah said, "and when off duty, I will become a mistress of lore and a teller of tales— if I have that talent."

"You already have much of that ability," Kayal said, then she added hesitantly, "We are so young now, but later there might also be husbands and even children."

"Husbands and children for each of us," Naith added, "with cousins playing together, watched over by the Benja."

"Uncle Benja," Issah said, smiling.

Above them, a flash of gold light gleamed in the air.

· 𝕏 ·

The sun was setting as they returned to the horse track leading north. Their side journey had lengthened their travel time by only a few hours, and it had saved many lives.

"That's it," the old hunter said. "Now it's back to hunting Vorrs for me." When Julian offered his hand, the hunter shook it with some reluctance and seemed relieved when Julian released it. The old man walked a few paces from Julian, then turned back to face the Apprentice.

"Just to put your mind at ease, Apprentice," he said quietly, "all the ones we daggered turned out to be Carags. Heh-heh-heh. Wouldn't want you staying awake at nights, young one, worrying about the innocent old men of your League lying dead in the forest." With one last "heh-heh-heh," the old hunter walked swiftly through a tangle of roadside brush and disappeared into a stand of trees.

The three sisters had ridden up to say farewell to the old hunter, but he had left so quickly that they had no chance to thank him.

"The League should make him an ambassador," Kayal said with a smile, "because he was so charming and well spoken."

Naith added, "Heh-heh-heh."

"In fairness, he didn't smell too badly," Issah said, "for an old man of the woods. But why did he want to be nameless?"

"He was just what we needed," Julian said. "About being nameless, I can offer this guess: Let's say that you were once a thief, or an outlaw — or even a pirate, and you retired to live peacefully in the League. If you didn't want to use your real name, you might hesitate to give an Apprentice a false name, as even a lesser Adept might know when you were lying."

The three sisters glanced at each other with raised eyebrows: though he was young, the Apprentice had learned a store of wisdom from his Wizard masters. As they rode back to their archers, the Benja whispered excitedly to them:

"I can see the hunter; I can see him as he was years ago! Back then he was a pirate, an old water buccaneer, raiding far from the League, off the coasts of Nemesis and Varaj! Now he's fighting in the forest! A pirate, a real live pirate, and the four of us have never even seen the ocean...."

Chapter Eight

Where the Fates Meet

THEY TRAVELED ON THROUGH sunset and dusk until the coming of night brought them to a halt. Sebastian camped out beside Julian, wrapped in the spare cloak of the Apprentice, but Rafir was restless, and prowled through the night, searching for signs of Vorrs or Carags. Nothing was moving except moths fluttering in the moonlight and Rafir was drawn back to the warmth of their central watchfire. Toward the end of the first watch, Rafir had settled down to sleep beside Julian and Sebastian.

·))(·

As before, Julian used his dreaming sleep time to reconnect with his parents, but once again he found himself seated in a tower across from the straw dummies that the Grey Witch had used to mock his parents. But now both dummies lay slumped in their chairs, and at the far end of the table, the Grey Witch had left her seat, and was nowhere to be seen. Julian could hear her voice, though: she was muttering in some nearby room, as though having a conversation with herself.

"All my planning," she was saying, voice choked with anger, *"all this time and all that magic is coming to nothing! Nothing, nothing! And why? Because one Dark God has a hatred greater than a second Dark God's hatred."* Julian rose silently and tiptoed cautiously toward the voice of the Grey Witch.

The tower around Julian had been copied from his own dream world. Somehow, the Witch had rebuilt it as part of her own place of power inside her underground kingdom. The tower was a strange mixture of real matter mixed with magic. The floor beneath his dreaming spirit was real. As he drifted past the pictures on the tower walls, he could see that they were made of rainbow mists — the magic of illusions. None of the books on the bookshelves had real writing on them, just markings that looked like titles from a distance — so these were also nothing more than illusions.

This chamber was filled with false things, and yet there was magic, real magic, hidden somewhere in the room. Why would the Witch mix real matter, and strong magic with illusions, and what was she doing now?

At the chamber's end stood a door, partly open, and Julian peered through it to a second chamber. Now, his dreaming mind was moving into a portion of the Grey Witch's place of power, and Julian took a deep, silent breath.

The Grey Witch was kneeling before an altar. Before her, a low fire flickered from black and red stones. The walls around her were the grey rock face of an underground tunnel; the kingdom of the Grey Witch was a dark, lost, and lonely place.

"Great Dark One," she was murmuring, *"I beg you to release the Apprentice to me. I need him, I hunger for him, and he will fulfill my destiny, and after, I will help you to become the greatest Power at Time's End."*

That silence, a lack of response, seemed to mean that her prayers were ignored.

"Great One," the Witch whispered, *"at least let your own Emissary heal, for the Great Lizard heals, and is ready for battle."*

As before, her prayers were met by silence, and she began to moan.

The Grey Witch was completely clothed, in a long dark cloak, with grey boots on her feet, and dark gloves covering her hands. With her face of dead grey skin turned away from him, it was hard for Julian to even think of her as human. Julian tiptoed away from the partially open door. Lacking any other dream link to his parents he returned to the table, and touched the straw dummies, reaching for his mother and his father.

Nothing happened for a moment, except that the Grey Witch continued moaning in the background, then came a distant whisper: "Wake, Julian. Death is coming for your friends and allies...."

As the voice trailed off, Julian jerked wide awake. He stood. In the center of their camp, their lone watchfire was blazing. All three sisters stood by the fire, speaking to each other in low tones, almost as though they were arguing. Staff in hand, Julian raced to meet them.

"I've been warned," he said quietly, "and it seems as though you've been warned, too. Tell me what's happening."

"It's the Benja," Kayal whispered. "He can see something coming, but all he can say about it is 'fire in the sky.' What does that mean?"

Julian closed his eyes and reached out into the night. "The Carags have made or brought some sort of...war machine. Fire in the sky! Of course! Get your shields ready. It's —"

At that moment, Carag archers used their war machine to launch flocks of flame arrows into the sky, then another volley, then a third. Hundreds of fire arrows hung in the night sky.

"Shields!" Kayal called out. "Shields if you can but find some covering!"

"Too many," Naith said, staring upward, "and we can't protect our horses."

"We can't protect ourselves either," Issah whispered. "Some of our people will die, and maybe even we will die." She glanced at her sisters and felt a wave of fear and love sweep over her.

"You will *not* die," Julian said, and in his anger, he clenched his staff with both hands. Power raced from the ground into the body of the Apprentice. Lifting his staff into the night sky, he called out spell words into the flame-lit darkness. Winds leaped up, strong, powerful, storm winds choked with rain.

Hundreds of flame arrows dropped toward them, bringing death.

Storm winds met the fire in the sky and blew death and sharp arrows far away into damp, distant forests. Only a few scraps of broken arrows fell harmlessly close to their camp.

Gold light gleamed in the darkness. "I told you the Apprentice had some hidden strength," the Benja whispered to his sisters.

· X ·

"We are nearing the borders of the League," Issah said to Naith, "and the end of our roles in this adventure."

"We did get to know the Apprentice," Naith said, "though I wish we had also talked more with Sebastian and Rafir."

Issah smiled. "You mean the fox you called, 'that sneaky thief'?"

"Well, he was a sneak, but maybe not a thief. It's too late to apologize, anyway."

In early morning, the two sisters rode in bright sunlight, forming a rearguard. When they had to leave their carts, they had lost most of their food and spare clothing, and the saddle pouches carrying supplies were slowly becoming empty. If they got through the last part of their journey, the sisters would be warm, and properly fed — but they would also never see the Apprentice again, and they were already feeling a sense of loss.

As the two sisters thought about the future, they grew silent. Still cautious, the two studied the surrounding fields and forests carefully, though small chickadees and juncos, and larger ones like grouse and the butterflies of the meadows seemed never to have heard about Vorrs or shapeshifting Carags, or even the Grey Witch of the North.

They passed a stretch of mostly evergreen forest, then came to a wide area of meadows, where farmers had raised food years ago, then abandoned the fields to long grasses and brush. As they rode through the meadowlands, the two sisters saw that Kayal was riding toward them, and behind them came Julian. Sebastian was also returning, gliding back down from the north toward the rearguard of Naith and Issah.

Suddenly Rafir blinked into view, causing the sisters' horses to jerk away from the fox.

"It's a council of war," Rafir explained, then he vanished, and amused himself by surprising grasshoppers, who leaped high through tall grasses whenever the fox brushed by them.

When they had gathered together, Julian said quietly, "You have been so careful to hide the Benja, but now, Death is tapping on our doors. Do we let Death inside just so we can keep our secrets? I might see one part of our future, while the Benja might see another, different part. Can we now speak openly together?"

Gold light flickered above the three sisters. The three sisters glanced together, then nodded. Suddenly, the Benja was beside them, less than four feet high, gleaming gold.

"Ha, ha!" he sang out, "it's the Benja to the rescue."

"We all hope so," Julian said, smiling, and he dismounted from Bluescent to kneel on the grass. "Here's what I see." An image formed before them, small on the grass, showing a ruined fortress, with a broken tower beside its gates — just two feet high in Julian's illusion image. Tall trees grew inside the fortress walls, so it was clear that time or some other enemy had reduced the stronghold's strength long ago.

"Yes, yes, yes," the Benja murmured, "they come from behind us, and we move west to this strong place."

"Former strong place," Julian said. "Vorrs chase us to this place, and we create a bonfire." In Julian's small illusion fortress, fires leaped up inside the fortress, and archers gathered around its walls, driving away the first Vorrs.

"But then the Carags come," the Benja whispered.

"They come openly," Julian said, nodding, "without disguise. I can see that now."

"Watch for the main strength of Vorrs!" the Benja muttered. "They come at us here." He pointed to the walls at the far west of the fortress that had crumbled lower than others.

"Where we meet them with arrows and pikes," Julian finished drawing a deep breath. "All right, I can see more clearly now. We might win this battle and survive. Thank you, Benja." Looking tired, Julian remounted Bluescent and began riding north toward the front of their column.

"There's something else you are not saying," Kayal said, riding alongside the Apprentice. "You might not even live to reach this Grey Witch. And if you live, the Grey Witch maims and murders you. What have you done to get yourself into this mess?"

Julian smiled, but it was a strained smile. "Like all messes, it's complicated. Now, after this next battle, are you ready to leave? Your people will have suffered wounds, and so you will need to get back to the Mistress of Illusions quickly."

Kayal pulled an amulet from a side pouch and held it before Julian. "This will call up a Portal to the Mistress of Illusions. We can be gone in moments. Apprentice, guard yourself and your small allies. You should know that we will never forget our time with you."

Julian glanced for a moment into each of their strong, determined faces. *I will never forget you four either. But we are all traveling to a place*

where the Fates meet, where Archers fight Vorrs and Carags, to a place where
two Dark Gods may well decide our fate, while the Grey Witch of the North
reaches out toward me.

Naith, with her sharp eyes, was the first to catch the brown fur of Vorrs
as they raced through the nearby forest. She notched an arrow but could
not be sure of her aim. She dismounted, aimed carefully, and launched. One
Vorr died instantly with an arrow in its eye socket. A second died moments
later as Issah's shaft buried itself in the Vorr's chest.

"I could never match your skill with the bow," Issah said quietly.

"And I could never lead pike forces the way you lead them," Naith said,
"or handle a sword the way you handle one. But watch out now — trouble
is coming our way." Kayal was riding quickly toward them, with a force of
archers and pikes jogging behind her.

"Our way ahead is blocked," Kayal called out. "Julian and the Benja
are looking for another path to that ruined fortress. The rearguard will be
attacked — just about now." Vorrs were coming closer. Kayal, Naith, and
Issah knelt beside one another: as they launched arrows, two of the closest
Vorrs died, while one Carag archer toppled.

Then a force of pikes and archers gathered around them, and they
fought a fighting retreat. As they launched a killing strike at nearby foes,
they would turn and race toward Julian for twenty paces, then turn and
launch arrows again. Twice, Vorrs came so close that pikes had to stop them,
backed by the killing strokes of Issah's sword.

They left the horse track, turning westward, following Julian, and
their main force through a meadow leading to the abandoned fortress. As
they streamed across the meadow, they passed a small thicket of trees. At the
treeline their earlier guide, the old hunter, stood. With one hand he waved
them closer, while his other hand was holding his bow.

"Is this help," Kayal asked, "or something else?"

"It's a Carag!" Rafir called out, popping into view.

One lone arrow from Kayal buried itself in the thing's chest. Both hands gripped the arrow as it stood in bright sunlight, staring at them in disbelief. Then the Carag cursed them in a language no mortal had ever heard, much less understood.

"Do not curse us," Naith snarled. "If you come with a gift of death for us, you will be repaid by death!"

"Instead," Issah called out, "you should curse the Great Dark God who sent you here." And then the Carag turned its face to the skies, calling out prayers and questions to the Dark God it worshipped. Finally, it died, still clutching the arrow, losing human form as it slumped to the ground.

They fought their way through the fall meadowlands, with enemies on three sides. In the distance, they could see the fortress, with archers already on its walls. More archers and pikes were jogging toward them to aid their retreat.

"Almost there," the Benja called, "my sisters, we are almost at the place where the Fates gather."

"The Benja!" Naith cried, launching another shaft, then she turned toward the fortress. As they grew closer to the stronghold, their enemies began to fall back — they had failed to destroy the rear guard, and now they would be forced to attack the fortress itself.

"Hold, now, hold!" Kayal cried. "Save arrows! Kill them only when they come near!" They jogged toward the fortification, so close now that they could see the faces of their allies. Julian stood just outside the ruined gates of the old stronghold, staff in both hands.

"One last stand," Kayal called out. Archers and pike forces turned one last time to face their foes, but Vorrs and Carags no longer pursued them. Turning back, they reached the walls of the ruined fortress and Julian led them through its broken gates. Just inside the gate walls lay a canvas tarp, covering a bundle of dry arrows.

"Just what we needed," Naith said, kneeling and helping herself.

"Wait — what is happening here?" Kayal asked. "Did the hunters of the League leave these for us?"

"Would that it were so," Julian said, shaking his head. "I believe these were left by the Grey Witch of the North. Her kingdom is not far away — perhaps no more than five hundred paces from these ruins, but deep underground."

"And so, she is helping us," Issah said, "just so you can live a little longer and then she can kill you herself? What have you done to get yourself into this mess?"

Julian smiled a soft sad smile. "That's exactly what Kayal asked, and I must give you the same answer: like all big messes, it's very complicated."

Gold gleamed in the air, and the Benja said, "They are coming."

Julian climbed the fortress wall just to the right of the broken gates of the fortress. "This faces north," he said, "so before the Wizards ruled this land, its ancient rulers feared invasion, even then. Now, look at what's coming."

The three sisters had climbed to stand beside Julian, and they could see in the distance that Carag archers in human form were carrying a wooden frame toward the front gates. The wood frame was both a shield against arrows and a partial tower that matched the height of the northern walls of the fortress.

"Their own fortress," Kayal murmured, "a citadel coming at us from the north, while Vorrs leap over the western walls. Benja, how many must we kill before they leave us in peace?'

"More than a hundred," came a voice in midair, with only a hint of gold flashing.

Julian, face grim, held his staff with both hands high over his head and he spoke dark *words*.

Naith looked east, west, north, and south; all she could see was bright sunlight moving over long green grasses — nothing else was moving in response to Julian's use of magic. "What was that about?" she asked.

"The Wizards would not be happy with me," Julian said, "but I have called a hazard of hawks and a vengeance of vipers to challenge the passage of our foes. For too long, they have passed without challenge through League lands."

"That won't stop them," Issah murmured.

"Hawks and vipers may not even come," Julian added.

"Then *we* must stop them," Kayal said, grimly. She climbed down to the ground and paced, studying the inner yard of the fortress, with its western, tumbled walls and long grasses and trees inside.

"Three forces," Kayal called out. "Naith, twelve archers to the north on the walls around these broken gates. Issah, pike forces to the west to meet the Vorrs: twelve pike, supported by six archers, three to each side. I will take the remaining six archers and so we will destroy any that pass through the gates, or past the wall of pike."

"I have held back," Julian said quietly, "but if foes come inside these walls, I will kill those beings dead. Sebastian and Rafir, watch for shapeshifters."

"And the Benja!" came a voice.

"And the Benja will watch, too," Julian added.

The first arrows came floating overhead and fell harmlessly into tall grasses. Moments later the wood frame half tower came closer, halting at two hundred feet from the gates. Archers launched arrows from behind it, but they struck only the stone of the fortress, not the flesh of its defenders.

"Hold back," Naith said softly, "they will come just a little nearer, a little closer." The wooden citadel lurched closer, closer. They could hear Carags in human form grunting with the effort of lifting its beams. Now as they drew closer, they could see small windows in the citadel's wood, where archers could launch arrows while themselves being protected.

"A week's leave in Rivermeet," Naith whispered, "to those bowshots passing through small windows into flesh." The citadel lurched forward. One bowshot struck only wood; other archers laughed darkly. Then first one, then a second arrow surged through an opening that was only hand's width wide. Wild cries of pain and astonishment came from the citadel. A third and a fourth arrow struck home, and the citadel halted, now just fifty feet from the ruined fortress.

"Ha!" Naith murmured. "I may have promised more than I could deliver, but I will make it right. I will —" Wild roaring sounds interrupted Naith, and she turned — Vorrs had leaped over the west walls. Some landed on sharp pikes, but others were free inside the fortress.

Issah's sword stabbed and hacked, spilling red Vorr's blood on green grasses. But then a great brown furred Vorr launched itself at her — it tumbled in midair, falling dead with three arrows in it. Julian, face grim, sent bolts of jagged black lightning into a second, then a third Vorr. Kayal killed another, then the remaining Vorrs fled, leaping back over the walls, howling with rage.

They had held their ruined fortress — for the time being. Julian and the three sisters walked around the borders of the walls, peering outside.

"Destroy a hundred," Issah murmured, "and the rest will go away."

"Benja, what's the count?" Naith asked.

"Five Carags at the gates," came the midair voice, "and twelve Vorrs both within and outside the walls."

"Fewer than twenty," Kayal said, shaking her head.

"You should add," said the voice of the Benja, "four Carags and two Vorrs who lie stricken in the fields, dead from snake venom."

"There's your 'vengeance of vipers,' Apprentice," Kayal said. "Where is your 'hazard of hawks'?"

"Gathering," Julian said, "though they will only distract our foes, not destroy them."

"Fire," Issah murmured, "we have forgotten the fire seen by the Benja and by Julian. Fire will help us guard our backs against Vorrs." Quickly, they gathered fallen branches, then dragged limbs from dead trees to the center of the fortress. As flames surged higher, there were calls from the gates. The wooden citadel was being moved.

"That's what I was afraid of," Kayal said.

"They will come at us from the west," Naith murmured.

"Where the walls are weakest," Issah finished.

"We still need to guard the front gates," Julian said. "Everyone should know that those inside are friends and allies, while those outside are foes — no matter what shape they take. Rafir, can you help make certain no Carag sneaks in?"

When the fox nodded, Julian continued, "And Sebastian, can you take the highest, safest perch and tell us what's happening?" The little Familiar's wings flapped, and Sebastian lifted into the skies of late morning.

Then Vorrs and Carags came at the west walls with their wooden fortification and all their strength in numbers. Vorrs began leaping over walls then running freely through the fortress, attacking archers separated from their main force — though Vorrs avoided their central bonfire. Carags launched flights of arrows down on them from the heights of their wooden citadel; woman archers began to take wounds. Julian bandaged several but was forced to weave a Healer's Sleep over two badly wounded women.

"You will need to get them back to the Mistress of Illusions — quickly," he muttered to Kayal.

"It's fight or die time," Kayal replied, and she buried another arrow in the chest of a Carag Archer.

Naith shook her head grimly. *Maybe it's fight **and** die time.* She caught a Vorr in its midair leap with an arrow to its throat. When it landed, it still crawled toward them, until Issah slashed it, and the Vorr gushed its life's blood onto green grasses.

Gold flashed in the air and the Benja said, "Hawks are coming."

Scores of raptors dropped down on Vorrs and Carags, talons raking at unprotected eyes. The attack on the fortress lessened. Julian looked up from tending the wounded.

"How many, Benja?" the Apprentice whispered into the air.

"More than fifty dead," the Benja said. "You are halfway there. But your venom has done more harm than your hawks — more than fifteen Vorrs and Carags now lie dead or dying from snake venom."

Julian shook his head: the hawks were being driven off, though some lay crippled with broken wings. Julian glanced up at Sebastian who was waving frantically with both hands to the Apprentice.

"What is he saying?" Julian asked. "I can't hear him."

"Something about hunters," the Benja said. And then Julian could sense them at the edge of the meadow: two dozen old men armed with old bows and rusting swords were coming to the League's aid.

"The fools," Julian said, "poor old men, too ready to die."

"The battle hangs in the balance," the Benja said quietly. "Every small bit will help, even the distraction of the hawks and the old men dying in the distance."

"This battle hangs on the edge of disaster," Julian muttered, but then he seemed to come awake. "Fire! We saw fire in our visions! Fire blazing both inside and then outside the fortress!"

"Fire!" Kayal called out. "Wood burns while stone does not!" The three sisters raced to their bonfire, pulling out burning branches, then they raced back to the west wall and hurled fire at the wood of the citadel manned by Carag archers.

Carags raced around to the front, pulling branches from the citadel's smoking wood. Arrows felled only a few.

"Maybe they can stop a natural fire," Julian murmured, "but not a sorcerous fire blazing with magic." Then Julian called down a wall of fire against the citadel. Its wood began to burn. Carags leaped from its walls. Some cast aside their human forms and loped away from the battle. With the fight turning against them, Vorrs began to leap from inside the fortress, racing outside then snarling as they hesitated in the fields.

As the battle hung in the balance, they began to feel a trembling in the earth. The ground was shuddering beneath their feet.

"What is this?" Issah asked. "Are they digging their way toward us?"

Julian shook his head. "I fear that the Grey Witch is reaching towards us."

"One fight at a time!" Kayal cried.

"Death to all Carags!" Naith called out.

"And death to all Vorrs!" Issah added.

The three sisters called out commands. Archers drew bows. With their foes hesitating, pikes were set aside, and more bowstrings sang. Vorrs began loping from the battle. Carags cast aside their human forms and began racing north. In the distance, the ancient hunters of the League called out insults to fleeing Vorrs and Carags.

Kayal killed one last Carag — a being disguised as a wounded archer — then muttered, "Benja, how many was that?"

"One hundred and ten," the Benja said quietly. "Vorrs and Carags are done. Now comes our real test."

"Yes, the Grey Witch of the North," Kayal said. "I can feel the trembling beneath our feet. How can we deal with —"

"*She* is not our real problem," the Benja interrupted. "*There* is our real problem."

Vorrs and Carags lay dead in the bright sunlight, brown and grey bodies leaking red blood into green grasses and wildflowers with the many colors of the meadows.

But outside the fortress gates, in the middle of the meadow, a great Portal was forming. Beyond the Portal stood a tall figure, almost a giant: the Emissary in Green Lizard form. Healed from its injuries, the Emissary slipped through the Portal gates holding its staff with both hands, eyes fixed on Julian.

"It's fight and die time," Kayal muttered. A weight of sorrow stirred inside her: there would never be a civic guard, or a time of great learning, or even children.

Naith's bow slipped to her side. "How are we expected to deal with *that?*"

Gold flashed in the air. "My sisters, my wonderful sisters!" the Benja called. "The Apprentice says this: get everyone behind strong walls or large trees. Move now! I beg of you!"

The great Emissary stared down at the Apprentice and his supporting troop of archers, and he laughed.

"Scurry away, little women," the Emissary said. "You will all be dead soon — and you will be the first to die, Apprentice. Did you truly believe that my Dark Master would permit you to triumph?"

Julian carefully backed through the gates, so that he stood within the broken walls of the fortress. His eyes studied the Emissary as it moved toward him; its lizard's tongue was flicking out as though tasting the meadow's air. Its body had healed, although the skin on its right-hand side was rough and patchy.

Beneath Issah, the ground still trembled, and as she watched the Emissary approach, she muttered, "Benja, what is happening?"

Gold gleamed in the air. "The Apprentice asks through me for two strikes — one to its eyes as a distraction, the other to penetrate its wounded shoulder."

"What about the ground?" Kayal called out.

"That's the Grey Witch," the Benja cried. "But one battle at a time!"

The Emissary raised its staff, hurling power at Julian — who was already diving away. Rolling clear, the Apprentice hurled magic back at the Emissary.

Stung, the Great Emissary cried out in anger, then blasted down the section of walls that protected the Apprentice — who was gone before the stones could topple over him.

"The Apprentice peers into the future!" the Benja called out. "But look, now look! There's the tongue, a great snake's tongue, tasting the air. Now, my sisters, the distraction — have your archers force the Emissary to protect its eyes! But sisters, hold your own arrows — for just a second longer."

Archers sent a dozen, then a second dozen shafts at the Great Emissary's eyes. As Julian had done, the Emissary raised its staff arm, and the arrows were waved away.

But as the Emissary raised its arm, it exposed the burned section of its right side.

"Now, now," the Benja hissed, "into the wound, its burned side!" Three sisters launched three arrows — and they buried themselves in dark green, only partly healed lizard flesh. The Emissary bellowed in pain.

Julian leaped out from behind stone walls, crying, "Now, Kath, now!" Then he blasted at the wrist holding the Emissary's staff. He dove again, rolling, and in one motion he rose, blasting the wrist a second time.

Wounded, and stung, the Emissary's staff dropped to the ground.

From a gap in the meadow's air, Kath poured out — Julian's ally was as long as five tall men, and as thick as a grown man's waist.

As Julian blasted again at the Emissary's wrist, Kath coiled around its left leg and began to tighten. The Emissary cried aloud in agony and tried to grasp Kath's head, but only one arm still worked properly. The other arm flopped around, again exposing its wounded side.

The three sisters struck again at the Emissary's wound — now six arrows were buried deep in its wounded side. Howling in pain, it began to stumble backward.

Julian again blasted at the Emissary's stricken wrist, then he hurled fire at the Emissary's fallen staff — and it burned.

Kath's coils tightened. The Emissary's leg made a great shattering sound, and the lizard creature toppled over, roaring in agony.

· X ·

While the battle raged, Sebastian and Rafir were pulling food packets together, both from Bluescent's saddlebags and from the remaining provisions carried by the archers, dragging them to one clear space not twenty paces from the gates of the fortress.

"What on earth are they doing?" Naith asked

"Getting ready for the next battle," the Benja said quietly.

All around them, the ground was shaking and shuddering so much that the sisters had trouble keeping their balance.

"What *next* battle?" Kayal asked. "This one is far from over." And yet it *was* over. A Portal was opening some distance from the broken Emissary. As the Emissary dragged itself toward its escape hatch, only one arm and one leg worked, and the great lizard creature was moaning in agony.

Kath had released his hold on the Emissary, and now slithered its heavy coils to the west and after a few hundred paces, the great serpent slipped through a pool of darkness on the ground and vanished.

In the distance, a second Portal was opening: a gateway to the Mistress of Illusions. Archers were gathering their wounded and their weapons and pushing forward through the gates, back out into the meadow. They stepped aside to let Julian pass back through the gates, back into the fortress.

"I never called for that Portal," Kayal said.

"There must be something else we can do for him," Issah murmured. The Apprentice was inside the gates, walking slowly toward Sebastian and Rafir. His face was grim.

"Julian!" Naith called out. The Apprentice turned to the three sisters, waved, and offered a brief smile. Then in one harsh and brutal second, all was changed.

Without warning, a great pit opened before the Apprentice and his two Familiars. The three vanished without even time to call aloud. Then just as suddenly, the ground was restored — but Julian, Sebastian, and Rafir were gone.

The three sisters stood frozen. Just fifty paces away, a Portal loomed, a path back to the Mistress of Illusions.

"Swallowed up," Kayal breathed out in a hollow voice.

"By the Grey Witch of the North," Naith murmured, then she asked bitterly, "Why is there no justice in this world? The Apprentice fought like a demigod. And now he's been destroyed in one single moment."

"The Apprentice still lives," the Benja said softly.

"And yet we will never see him again," Issah said, choking back tears. "Never."

"That is not quite true," the Benja said in a low, hushed voice. "If Julian survives, the four of us will meet him again at the Goblin Market on the outskirts of Far Avalon."

Chapter Nine

In the Labyrinth of the Grey Witch

ULIAN FELL, LANDING WITH a *thumping* sound onto soft earth. Rafir, quick as a cat, twisted in midair and landed on his feet, while with two flaps of his wings, Sebastian came to rest beside Julian.

Suddenly, it was dark. Above them, the tunnel's ceiling closed over so that it was pitch black. Clouds of dust choked them, and they began to cough. The three of them lay in the dark struggling to breathe. In the background, they could hear distant, soft laughter: echoes of cackling sounds made by the Grey Witch.

Julian rolled over, coughing out spell words so that their breathing grew stronger. Light flashed from Julian's staff, and they stared through the dust of the Grey Witch's underground kingdom. They lay at the far end of a tunnel that had been dug to reach out underneath the walls of the broken fortress — stretching out to trap Julian and his two Familiars.

The tunnel's surface seemed to be made of only earth mixed with pebbles, but as they watched, root systems were growing, inch by inch over the soil, sealing the tunnel and making it stronger.

"This Grey Witch is very powerful," Sebastian whispered. "Maybe she's really some kind of Sorceress."

"Is there a chance we could be dug out?" Rafir asked softly. "Then the three sisters and the Benja could be down here fighting beside us."

"They had too many wounded," Julian said, standing. "They will need to return to the Mistress of Illusions. My hope is that they will take Bluescent and our pack horses with them, and eventually return them to the League." The tunnel was almost twice his height, and its air was clearing as though the Grey Witch was drawing dust back to her underground kingdom. As they spoke, they could still hear the laughter of the Grey Witch — echoes were bouncing back and forth as her cackling sounds passed through her kingdom's dark underground passages.

"She sounds so weird," Rafir muttered. "It's as though she read a book once — 'How to be a Crazy Old Witch,' and now she's acting the part."

Julian took a deep breath, then touched each of them so he could speak into their minds.

Careful. The Grey Witch may not be exactly what she seems. But somehow, we have things that she needs, and she will want to keep us alive, at least for a while. Let's make sure we have all our food, then see what we can find out about her.

Their belongings had been buried when the tunnel collapsed; so, they had to dig down into soft earth and pull parcels of food out. Pouches and saddlebags filled with dried meats and cereals contained few of Rafir's favorites. The fox stared down at their supplies with an unhappy expression.

"Tell me again," Rafir said, "what that knight Orlan had to say."

"You mean about better being dead tomorrow than today?" Sebastian replied, staring into the dusty tunnel. "It's still true — most of the time."

"Come," Julian whispered. They began walking slowly through the tunnel, as it led downward. Julian carried most of their supplies, leaving only a small packet for each of his two Familiars to carry. As they moved farther down, the air was clearing, and their coughing gradually lessened until it finally stopped. Above them, spidery networks of roots were spreading, and the tunnel itself began to glow with a dull light so that Julian let the light from his staff grow slowly dimmer, then fade out completely.

"You saw into the future that we would be stuck here," Sebastian whispered, "didn't you, Julian?"

"Faint images and hints only," Julian said softly, "but yes, I saw some of it."

"That's why you told us to get the food," Rafir murmured. "You were afraid we might be poisoned."

"Not poisoned, but mixed with potions," Julian said. "We don't want to eat food treated by a force of magic that could cloud our minds."

As they walked, Julian touched Rafir and spoke softly into his mind: *Rafir, vanish as only you can disappear.*

A half second later the fox was gone — but not completely gone: dust still covered the fox, and his fur glowed faintly with the same pale light as the earth of the tunnel. Carefully and in silence, Julian and Sebastian used their fingers to brush the fox's fur until Rafir was again completely invisible.

They walked on in silence through the gloom of the tunnel. After less than an hour, they came to the end of a recently dug section of the tunnel. In front of them was an older, broader, and higher twist of the tunnel, where spiders wove thick webs, and beetles scurried over the tunnel's surface, collecting bits of dead matter that had fallen from the spiders' webs. Some distance ahead, they could hear the flapping sounds of batwings. The light glowing in this tunnel was both brighter and grimmer: they had entered a network of tunnels, the underground kingdom of the Grey Witch of the North.

From the Grey Witch came a great *sigh* of satisfaction. Julian stood straighter, clasping his staff with both hands, face filled with determination.

Sebastian shook his head grimly. *And so, our duel with the Witch has begun. What were the Wizards thinking when they sent us north? Maybe they should have put the eagle in charge, let him make decisions instead of the Wizards.*

"We can be seen," Julian said, "and our voices can be heard. But some things we need to talk about openly: we need a source of water. I can feel water running below us. You two can sense it better than I can though; let's find water first."

The laughter of the Grey Witch faded suddenly, as though the search for underground springs had never been part of her plan.

Rafir raced ahead, and Sebastian followed, flying part of the time, and scrambling the rest. The network of tunnels forked again and again, but the two Familiars each time chose a fork that led further downward. Twice as they passed a fork, Julian sensed shuffling movements in the tunnel: creatures were retreating away from them, but not in fear because Julian could feel menace radiating from them.

And Rafir's sharp ears could hear faint, distant, growling noises from other forks.

In the deepest part of the Grey Witch's kingdom, they found a broad cave, with several small streams running through channels in the cave's floor. Julian held them back and used his staff to flash light over the cavern. The three looked down studying the cave floor: where the floor was stone, they could see only streaks of mud, but where mosses grew, they could see footprints. Creatures both large and small had come here to take water from the streams.

Julian took a deep breath and began to trace the streams, trying to see if there was a way out for Sebastian or Rafir. Closing his eyes, Julian *reached*. Other caverns in surrounding limestone rock were nearby, but none could be reached from these streambeds — unless — *What sort of magic was the Grey Witch using to force her way through earth and stone? Could that magic be learned?*

The three knelt and drank deeply. After cleaning dust and stains of battle from themselves, they ate a small portion of their food. Some of the threats of the Grey Witch's kingdom seemed to fade, as though washed away by streams of clear, cold water.

"Could you hear them, Julian?" Rafir asked. Julian interrupted the fox by putting his finger to his lips and shaking his head: it was better not to talk, not just now.

They hesitated before leaving the cave and its flowing streams; the air inside the chamber was cooler and clearer because of the fresh, running water. Back in the labyrinth, the glowing darkness of the tunnels made every step seem heavier, and the air harder to breathe. Spiders stared at the Apprentice and his Familiars as they walked past their tangled, dusty webs, and beetles scurried into dark corners to avoid their feet.

Then in the distance came the sounds of grunting and growling noises, followed by the flapping of many wings. As they pressed against the tunnel sides, hundreds of bats flew by, racing away in a panic.

"That's what I was saying," Rafir said softly. "I could hear *things* in those passages. I don't think they were expecting us to go downward, looking for water."

"I could sense something, too," Sebastian added. "I knew then that we weren't alone with this Grey Witch." Julian reached out to touch them, then spoke into their minds:

It would take large things, large clumsy things, to scare all those bats. What I think is this: the Witch is preparing to test us against a number of creatures, large and small. It feels as though she has been studying the three of us for some time. Why she is testing us is a mystery. If we can solve that mystery, we might live to fight other battles.

· ✕ ·

They explored the labyrinth for hours. It felt as though the Grey Witch had been digging — likely helped by teams of goblin miners — for many, many years. Tunnels branched and came together again without any obvious plan. Julian could sense that storerooms and other dark, long-lost chambers had been sealed off for many years. What had the Witch been collecting? What would she want to hide?

As they passed hidden chambers, Julian began to *reach*, trying to sense what lay beyond the earth of the tunnel. Some chambers were the burial grounds of dead things where the skeletons of goblins and gnome creatures lay still in the darkness — in these, the earth of the burial chambers gave out no light. *Many diggers and burrowers died while building tunnels,* Julian thought. In others, rusting machines were stored, perhaps going back to a time when the diggers of tunnels had used mechanical devices instead of hand tools or magic.

At last, Julian found one hidden chamber that gave off an aura of magic and mystery. Julian stopped and studied the wall's surface. Using signals and whispered words, he told Sebastian and Rafir that they needed to dig — and dig quickly.

Julian and Sebastian used their hands to tear at the web of roots covering the lower wall. Rafir began to dig frantically with his paws. Growling sounds could be heard in the tunnel systems as creatures stirred. From the Grey Witch came a blast of hatred:

What are you doing, you little worms!?!

They dug furiously. Growling sounds grew louder. Finally, with booted feet, Julian kicked through the last layer of earth. Bending down, Julian pushed through the low entrance and entered the dark, hidden chamber. Sebastian and Rafir followed closely behind him.

Julian's staff flashed light and they stared up at the chamber's high ceilings. Outside in the tunnels, they could hear heavy feet *thumping* toward them. They turned their faces back from the high ceilings to the chamber's lower entrance. Julian readied for battle. Heavy footsteps seemed to hesitate, then retreat. The three stood frozen for a moment until a dark quiet settled again over the Grey Witch's kingdom.

Sebastian sighed, then took a deep breath. *So, the Grey Witch has decided to let us live — at least for now.*

As the stress left them, they began again to study the chamber. It was large, nearly fifty paces by fifty paces, and overhead, its ceiling was the height of three men. Many years had obviously passed since it was sealed off. Thick layers of dusty webs covered its walls. Wooden chests of many different sizes lay heaped in the chamber's center. Some chests were broken, while others lay on their sides, with their contents spilling out. Most of the containers were made of wood, made stronger by ribs of rusting iron.

Light from Julian's staff dimmed then faded out, though the chamber walls continued to glow so that the goods stored within could still be seen clearly. With soft words, Julian called upon his *cone of silence*, so the three could speak openly.

"First this Grey Witch laughs and laughs," Rafir said, "like some crazy person."

"Then she blasts us with hatred," Sebastian added. "For some reason, she didn't want us to be in this room."

Julian nodded, staring at the stacks of chests. "It's as though she turned to some huge servant and said, 'Get rid of these things,' and her giant threw them all in a heap down here, then sealed the chamber up. It doesn't look as though anyone has been down here since that moment."

"Because the Witch doesn't want us here," Sebastian said, hesitating, "I guess we should look inside these chests — unless it's a trap."

"Secrets!" Rafir said. "Hidden weapons! Maybe even amulets or magic potions!"

"For some reason, she's not happy to have us in this chamber," Julian said, shaking his head and smiling, "but we probably won't find magic weapons."

"Clues!" Rafir said, still excited, and he began poking his fox nose into the insides of broken chests. Julian and Sebastian began to search through contents that had spilled out onto the chamber's floor, though they were much more cautious than the fox.

"Clothing," Rafir murmured, turning to another chest. "More clothes and some old boots — I guess you could call them clues, telling us that it hasn't always been warm down here. Moths have been at them, so I guess that means the Witch wasn't going to bother using them again." The fox turned to a third chest, muttering, "And this one has dishes made from baked clay — most of them broken — and a big old metal pot you might place on a wood fire to boil your porridge. Yum yum. I guess that's a clue that the Witch needed to eat. I never thought that a secret chamber could be so boring."

Julian and Sebastian patiently searched through broken chests, finding mostly household goods. A thick leather volume had spilled out from one chest; Julian leafed through it carefully, but it was in a language he couldn't begin to understand — or in a secret handwriting that even a student of strange tongues might take years to decode.

The three turned to several unbroken chests that were sealed by locks. The eyes of Julian and Sebastian glanced together: one small chest had been set closer to the wall, and it had been placed, not thrown. From it, the two could feel a faint touch of magic.

"What?' asked the fox. Julian shook his head, gently. Though his *cone of silence* still blocked the Witch's hearing, there were spies and other ways to sense events from a distance. Julian placed his staff's base against one of the larger, sealed containers and whispered spell words. The lock sprang open, and they stared inside — and the Apprentice straightened in surprise. In this chest were dolls made of cloth and other carved wooden toys: one was some largish Ogre; another was the smaller figure of a Dragon.

"Now, we've got some real clues," Rafir muttered, "but clues to what?" Julian shook his head and unsealed another chest, one that was filled with the clothes of a small child. Other chests held sheets and bedding, and like the clothing, moths had feasted on them so that they were filled with small holes.

Finally, they turned to the small chest that seemed touched by magic. The wood of this chest was carefully carved, decorated more completely, and its metal ribs had never rusted. With some care, Julian used magic to spring its lock, then slowly opened its lid. The three stared down at its contents.

"Powders and potions!" Rafir exclaimed. "And a wand, a real magic wand! What's inside that pouch of velvet? It's round — and it must be, it has to be — a crystal ball! By all the Nine Billion Gods, a crystal ball! And to think that I called this chamber boring!"

"Rafir, be calm," Sebastian whispered.

"All the power has long ago passed from these things," Julian said softly. "Think of them as clues, but clues that are very strange." Julian sat on one unopened chest and stared into the distance. Overhead, spiders were weaving their webs, and the sharp eyes of Rafir could see that crumbling mothwings were still trapped in ancient webs.

"Children's clothing," Sebastian said slowly, "and children's toys. Could these have belonged to the Grey Witch when she was young?"

"A feeling of great sadness," Julian said, "a sense of loss, hangs over this chamber."

Rafir nodded thoughtfully, his small, enchanted mind racing. "So, do we think that this Grey Witch at one time had a child?"

"Dolls and the clothing container had dresses," Sebastian added, "so it was probably a daughter."

"A daughter who died young," Julian said. "I think if we kept searching, we might find a small grave. This chamber seems to be touched by ghosts."

"So how would this Grey Witch get to be so evil?" Rafir asked, "and so partly dead?"

"Maybe she searched for healing power from one of the Great Dark Gods," Julian said, "to fight her daughter's illness — and her own. Then she gained enough strength to struggle against her own disease — partly. But then lost her daughter. In her struggle, she became the Grey Witch of the North, an evil and powerful being who no longer needed a humble Witch's tools. All her old life was cast into this chamber, then sealed away. A terrible price can be paid when bargaining for power with the great Dark Gods!"

"Even *I* knew that," Rafir said, yawning, suddenly tired.

Julian stared upward. The Sight was strong within him, and beyond the tunnel system and all the dark mysteries of the Grey Witch's underground kingdom, he could sense in the distance overhead that stars were shining brightly, and that their search had taken them well past midnight.

He stood and began pushing storage chests over to the low entrance to the chamber. Sebastian could see that Julian was blocking the entrance, so no one could enter without making noise. Suddenly, Sebastian felt completely tired: they had been exploring for hours after a battle, and a morning's fast march. It was late, and now they would sleep in the chamber where all the history of the Grey Witch's old life was stored. Hopefully, no haunting would wake them. They pulled bedding from broken trunks, and without making plans for the next day, the Apprentice and his Familiars gathered moth-eaten blankets around themselves and slept.

· X ·

Once again in dreams, Julian reached for the link with his parents. He knew that joining them or visiting with them was not possible, but he hoped to hear their voices, passing him hints about the Grey Witch and her powers.

A whisper, he thought, no more than a whisper.

Instead, he found himself seated back in the tower room — no longer a place of dreams where he had once spoken with his parents. Now the tower belonged to the Grey Witch's underground kingdom. She sat in front of Julian with a grim smile frozen on her grey skinned face.

"You have been a naughty boy, Apprentice," the Grey Witch said softly, *"pushing your little nose into my secret rooms."*

"We felt sorrow in that chamber," Julian said. *"I cannot imagine what it would be like to lose a child."* As he spoke, Julian's eyes glanced over the tower: in a fit of rage, the Witch had smashed and scattered the scarecrow dummies of his parents. Little was left of them but scraps of cloth and bits of straw.

Anger flashed across the face of the Grey Witch. "You know so little, and you will pass into the everlasting darkness understanding almost nothing of me. But I will drink deeply from you and learn everything you ever knew."

"There is still time for you," Julian said. *"Release me and I will seek help for you. The Wizards are strong and wise. Though they cannot bring back your child, they might still help you to heal."*

"*Heal me?*" the Grey Witch leaned back, touched her grey skin, and cackled. "*Undo these beauty marks? You can see that I had a little struggle with slippery old Master Death. Why would I hide that transformation, a change that is the source of all my power?*"

And the Gift within Julian whispered to him: **This is the first of the Witch's outright lies.**

"*But you, dear, sweet, lovely little boy,*" she continued. "*Such a sweet, lovely, tasty little boy.*" *In the tower of their dream, she rose and approached Julian, whispering,* "*So sweet, just a taste of you, a little taste.*"

"*Nothing,*" Julian said, *rising and grasping his staff with both hands.* "*You will taste nothing — except the doom that you have chosen for yourself.*"

The Witch felt resistance but pressed closer. She was stronger than Julian, much stronger.

But with his own inner reserves of strength Julian burst the dream link. As he vanished from the tower, the Witch cried out loud in frustration.

·)(·

Julian came suddenly awake. Sebastian and Rafir were beside him; Sebastian was shaking him, while Rafir tugged at his cloak with his small, sharp teeth.

"You were calling out in your sleep," Sebastian murmured, staring at Julian in surprise and alarm.

Julian stood, still breathing hard. "This Grey Witch has been invading my sleep. I need to set a spell-guard over my dreaming mind. It may be that I can never again in my short life reach through the Dreamways for my parents." The Apprentice bowed his head in grief.

Julian would weep, Sebastian thought, but he is afraid to show too much of his sorrow to us. We must all become stronger. It seems that much worse is yet to come.

Chapter Ten

Hobgoblins and Hag Wraiths

ITH HIS HEAD STILL bowed, Julian forced his breathing to slow, and struggled for calm. For years he had used his powers to reach his parents through dream links, and now they were cut off — perhaps forever. But now he had to rally his small allies and fight their way out of this Labyrinth, their prison. He looked up, glancing at Sebastian as though reading his Familiar's thoughts.

"Worse things than bad dreams are yet to come," Julian said softly. "Before we leave this chamber, though, let's make certain we can find our way back here."

Sebastian studied Julian's sea-grey eyes. "You've seen some part of the future, haven't you?"

"Something connected to this chamber of mysteries?" Rafir asked, perking up. "What did you see?"

"A battle," Julian said quietly, and then he added, even more softly. "And something like a ghost."

"If it's something like a ghost," Rafir whispered, "then I'm going to vanish and see if the eyes of the dead can follow me."

Placing his finger to his lips, Julian signaled for silence. Then he began covering up half of their food supplies beneath the clothing and household goods buried deep in the chamber by the Grey Witch. Sebastian nodded: if they were going to return here, they might as well hide some of their supplies for the future. Rafir pulled one packet of food — his least favorite — and pushed it under their moth-eaten bedding.

Then Julian began pulling storage chests away from the entrance. "So far we've been through only the lower part of the Witch's kingdom; now we'll head upward. Both of you should keep your senses alert. Rafir, stay invisible, and scout for us. Walk in my old footprints when you can, to hide your own trail. Sebastian, when trouble comes, I want you up high — use your wings. Don't forget that the sneezing powders you used against the crows can be tried against anything that breathes air."

The three pushed through the Chamber's low entrance and passed into the Labyrinth of the Grey Witch. The glowing light and dark quiet of the Labyrinth were the same, but Sebastian shivered: it was colder than yesterday, and the air was different; it smelled of decay, of dying and dead things.

"I thought you said," Rafir whispered, "that we explored all of the lower Labyrinth. Some other creatures were down there — beings that smell really nasty — and now they are coming to the surface."

"I never said *all* the lower tunnels," Julian murmured. "I guess that the Witch blocked off some deeper passages, and now they've been opened up."

"Tunnels to burial chambers?" Sebastian asked. "Places filled with dead things?"

"Live things," Julian replied, "and they are coming up for us. We should head back to the upper passages; we can explore while I try to find out exactly what's coming up from below. Let's go."

They moved quickly back through the Labyrinth. Before, they had chosen all the tunnel passages leading down; now they picked the tunnels leading up. As they went higher, bad air followed them upwards, and they began to hear soft shuffling sounds: whatever creatures were coming after them, they were not heavy, but there were a lot of them.

As they moved, Julian continued to brush the sides of the tunnel with his staff, *reaching* for the contents of hidden chambers. Behind them, the sounds of many shuffling feet were growing louder. Julian began to jog forward, darting from side to side so he could touch the walls of the Labyrinth and use his Sight to see within side chambers.

"What are you *doing?*" Rafir panted.

"For some reason," Julian said, "one of these chambers will give us a place of safety." He sped forward, touching each side. "I have no idea which it is, but we're getting close to it. Let's see what's following us."

They came to a halt and turned back, panting. Shuffling sounds grew louder, then from around the corner came the first ranks of beings who were half human height holding spears. Their furry bodies were caked in soil, and even from a distance, Rafir could see that earthworms, mealy bugs, and woodlice were living in the caked earth surrounding their bodies. More creatures followed, pressing forward, filling the tunnel. Their eyes glowed yellowy green and were lined with heavy red colored veins. The tunnel was crowded with many of them, and their short wooden spears ended in sharp metal.

Then the smell reached Julian and his Familiars, and they gagged.

"What are these?" Rafir asked, "Some kind of Goblins?"

"Worse — I think they're Hobgoblins," Sebastian muttered.

"Hobgoblins, yes, but something is wrong with them," Julian said quietly. "They shuffle like creatures controlled by magic, not under their own power. The Witch is forcing them to give battle. Let's get away from them."

They raced forward, Julian darting from side to side, while behind them a force of Hobgoblins stumbled forward like doomed zombies — and now Julian could sense magic behind them. Some small, strange Hobgoblin Magician was helping the Witch by pushing his fellow Hobgoblins into battle. Julian would be forced to destroy slaves, not fighters. Anger at the Witch flared inside him.

Suddenly Julian stopped. On the left-hand side of the Labyrinth, some mystery lay buried in a sealed chamber beyond the wall of earth — it wasn't magic, but it hinted of power. They needed to get through. How had the Witch created her digging magic?

Julian reached deep inside himself for the deep well of magic that sometimes surprised him. Nothing came for a moment. He began digging by hand. Rafir and Sebastian began scratching and scraping at the tunnel sides. They would not get through in time; and so, they would need to run for their lives. He glanced up: Hobgoblin spears were now within hurling range. Hobgoblin smells were making him gag. Shuffling sounds grew louder, and in the distance, they could hear the laughter of the Grey Witch.

Like a small flash of lightning, understanding raced through Julian's mind.

"Back," Julian said quietly. "Get back." When Sebastian and Rafir moved away, he placed his staff against the earthen sides and whispered a *surge of ruin* against the soil. In seconds, the soil became lifeless, grey, then began falling away from the side, until a pool of dust formed on the tunnel floor and a small opening was forced into the chamber. Apprentice and Familiars pushed through the gap and left the Labyrinth.

They entered a large, gloomy burial chamber — and came to a complete halt. In the chamber's center lay the dead body of a giant. They stared at the corpse for a moment, then were forced to turn back to the entrance. Hobgoblin noises were getting louder, and they needed to seal the entrance they forced opened. Rafir and Sebastian pushed earth back into the gap. Julian's lips whispered spell words. Magic to strengthen the walls came much more easily to Julian than his spell of ruin.

Out in the Labyrinth, Hobgoblins began to moan. Light from Julian's staff flared in the burial chamber and they stared at the giant's corpse: the creature was huge, with heavy goblin-like features, thick trunk legs, and powerful shoulders. It lay with its hands folded in peace on a low, flat bed, surrounded by trinkets, bits of metal and scraps of paper.

"I had no idea that I would find this here," Julian said softly.

"Find what?" Rafir said. "Every chamber has a new and different mystery."

"I think," Sebastian said quietly, "that we've found the burial chamber of the Hobgoblin's God."

"Or Demigod," Julian added. "We should respect these gifts, or offerings, but look how different they are." He touched trinkets carefully with his staff. "Some of these seem to be made from the bones of mice, while others are jewelry made of finely crafted metal, and still others have prayers written on bits of parchment."

"More than one underground race has left these," Sebastian said. "Hobgoblins normally live in the deepest parts of the earth."

"With Goblins in the middle passages," Julian added, "though they will mine deep down into the depths of the earth."

"And Gnomes in the upper caves," Rafir said. "I remember now. Gnomes even go out in the darkness, to hunt by starlight."

"Most food comes from sunlit lands or tidal waters," Julian said, "so all three races will have to hunt at night — unless the Grey Witch finds food for them."

New sounds stopped them. Out in the Labyrinth, the sounds of moaning Hobgoblins had halted, and they could hear many scraping and thumping sounds as spear points stabbed into tunnel walls.

"We *were* safe here," Sebastian whispered, "but safety only lasted for a few minutes."

"Wait, wait, wait," Julian muttered. "We need to think carefully. This chamber is sealed, but three races visit this holy place all the time." Dust was beginning to enter the chamber, and thumping sounds grew louder.

"Gnomes are scribes," Sebastian said, "writers — maybe writers of prayers. Did they leave these notes with prayers on them?" Rafir sniffed at one message, then another, and then a third. He began to follow the smell of Gnomes and their tracks. In a far corner, the fox began to dig down. Julian and Sebastian also began to clear the soil where the fox dug.

Beneath a thick covering of dry dirt was a metal plate, with a large metal ring as a handle. Julian wrenched it up, and the three stared down into a dark, narrow passage. A tunnel passage led straight down and was built solidly of stone and mortar, with metal rungs made for climbing down its long, dark shaft. If the Labyrinth had been constructed by the Witch of soil from forests and magical root systems, this passage had been made by Gnomes or Goblin miners of stone and iron.

Noise and dust made them look up from the shaft: they could see flashes of metal as spearpoints broke through the wall.

Julian hesitated. "We could stay here," he murmured, "and fight them off."

"Kill zombie slaves?" Sebastian said softly. "Maybe we'll have to do that later — but not today." The Apprentice passed his staff to Sebastian, and it flashed light. They climbed down carefully, Rafir on Julian's shoulder, while Sebastian, even with one hand holding a heavy staff, had no problems with the climb. Julian carried a sack of provisions in one hand and used the other to ease his way down, rung by rung.

A few feet down, Julian took his staff back and whispered spell words, so that the metal plate above them closed, and a small mound of dust settled over its surface so that the Gnome tunnel was hidden once again. They climbed down, then further down, while above them, they could hear the voices of Hobgoblins, moaning prayers to their dead God, a gigantic Goblin mummy.

Julian stared up, listening to the voices of Hobgoblins. From the Grey Witch, Julian could feel a sense of great satisfaction, as though she had accomplished all that she wanted. What in the name of all the Nine Billion Gods was she trying to do?

About forty feet down the shaft made by Gnomes forked: one passage continued deeper, while the second leveled out then headed higher, leading back to places beneath the Labyrinth. Inside Julian the Gift *reached*: the closer they kept to the Labyrinth, the more they would learn — but it was also much more dangerous.

Sighing, Julian led them into the level shaft: it was much smaller than any Labyrinth tunnel, not as wide, and with a ceiling so low that Julian had to bend down periodically. Rafir was happy, though: it was like being in the huge den of a fox. Rafir raced on ahead, tail flashing back and forth.

After a few hundred paces, Julian halted, set down his things, and called up a *cone of silence* so they could speak together. Sebastian took Julian's sack and pulled out a small portion of food for each of them.

"You know," Rafir said, mouth partly full, "those Hobgoblins didn't seem that keen to die."

"Or even to kill anybody," Sebastian added. "Julian, wasn't there some kind of Hobgoblin Sorcerer leading them? Or rather, forcing them from behind?"

"Some kind of Mage," Julian replied. "Somehow, he wasn't eager to have his Hobgoblins die either — and he seemed to have little interest in fighting the three of us."

"This is all getting so strange," Rafir muttered. "What's going to happen next? Am I going to be transformed into a bunny rabbit? Or something worse?"

"Something much worse," Sebastian said, smiling. "So, what exactly have we learned about this Grey Witch?"

"It does seem that she lost a daughter," Rafir said uncertainly.

"And around that time," Sebastian added, "she changed from a simple witch into this Grey Witch of the North."

"After the change," Julian continued the thought, "I'm guessing that her servant, the Giant Goblin, was told to throw her old things into Rafir's 'Chamber of Mysteries,' and seal the chamber up."

"Later, that Giant died," Rafir said, "and became a Demigod for Hobgoblins."

"A Demigod worshipped also by Gnomes, and Goblins," Julian said. "The Gnomes, at least, have separate passageways. The other beings may also have secret paths leading in and out of the Labyrinth — I suspect that they do, so let's keep watch for any of those signs. Also..." Julian hesitated. "Sebastian, you reminded me that it was not good to kill slaves. Thank you for that — I can't let myself become a killing machine, where taking lives comes too easily."

Sebastian touched Julian's hand in reassurance, then came a pause, while each of the three thought their separate thoughts. Finally, Rafir blurted out, "So what exactly does this Grey Witch want?"

Julian sighed. "The Great Gods study other Gods, and Wizards, and Sorcerers, and Creatures of the Darkness, and any other beings of magic trying to learn from them and gain power. The Wizards do the same. This Grey Witch is studying us, watching what we do in different kinds of encounters."

Sebastian shivered, and not just from the cold. "We must have something that she wants badly."

·))(·

None of the Witch's magic lit the Gnome passages, so Julian's staff provided their only source of light. Through the late morning and early afternoon, they explored gloomy, dark tunnels made of stone, looking for intersections where they could return to the main Labyrinth, or even find links to different Goblin sections.

For a time, they could find nothing. No hint of living creatures could be seen — except all the passages had been kept completely clean, with only traces of dust left in a few sections that seemed to have been little used. In the early afternoon, they came to a halt and shared a brief meal. Already the sack holding their food felt lighter to Julian.

"Just so I understand," Rafir said, "from what I saw, Hobgoblins are about half human height — do I have that right?"

Sebastian nodded. "Goblins are maybe a head and a half taller than Hobgoblins, heavier, and much more warlike."

"And Gnomes are just a little shorter than humans," Julian added, "but thinner, more ghostly pale creatures. In old village stories, Gnomes are funny creatures, pudgy things that hide in forests by day, then sneak through gardens in the darkness. Real Gnomes are very secret creatures — they like being left alone and will avoid humans whenever they can."

"There's no smell of Hobgoblin in these passages," Sebastian said. "Maybe a trace of Goblin — as though they entered, looked around quickly, then left. The rest of the smells are all from Gnome creatures. What do you think, Rafir?"

"I smell the same things that you do," Rafir said, "except...the air is getting wetter. I can't be sure, but at the edge of my hearing I wonder if I'm hearing the sounds of rushing water."

"A second source of water would be good," Julian said, standing.

With a goal of finding water, they moved more quickly, but only after another long hour could all three of them hear the rush of underground streams. The Gnomes' passages dipped down, and they reached another fork: one passage continued, while the second led to a broad, low door made of grey ironwood, reinforced by rusting metal. Loud sounds of rushing water could be heard beyond the chamber's door.

Cautiously, Julian pushed the door open; its hinges were oiled, as though it had been used often. They entered a wide chamber. Light flared from Julian's staff. Julian could stand easily, though he could touch the chamber's low roof with his staff. Water sounds were loud, but they were echoes, coming from a distance. In the chamber's center was a wide well made of stone, its width wider than a tall man, protected by a partial wall that came up to Julian's waist.

Julian leaned over, flashing light down the well. Only a hint of dark water could be seen, far down in the well's depths. Sebastian and Rafir leaped up on the wall and stared down. Part of the young Rafir wanted to call down into the depths of the well and hear his own echo, but he forced himself to keep quiet and think.

"I don't see any bucket," the fox said in hushed tones, "so, it's not a place where you bring up water from a well."

"Maybe it's a place where you dump things," Sebastian added grimly, "when you want to get rid of them."

"The Grey Witch rules her own small underground city," Julian said. "Like every city, it needs a source of water and a way of disposing of waste.

Give me a minute, and maybe I can sense more." Sebastian and Rafir were quiet for a moment, listening to the rushing sounds of the underground river while the Apprentice closed his eyes and *reached*.

"I didn't have it quite right," Julian said. "I had forgotten about cities needing to dispose of their dead. Dead things go down this chute. Strange fish are waiting at the bottom — blind creatures transformed by magic, so they will consume everything, even the bones of Goblins, even the matted fur of Hobgoblins."

Sebastian and Rafir glanced at Julian, then stared down into the distant, dark waters, wondering if their own dead bodies would one day be dropped down the Grey Witch's disposal chute.

· X ·

They left the gloomy chamber with its somber well and continued to explore the stone tunnels of the Gnomes. All those tunnels were dark and quiet, clear of spiders and beetles — and all other living things. Only once did Rafir hesitate, sniffing at the base of a low wall, while Sebastian looked around for clues.

"Something died here," Sebastian explained to Julian.

"A mouse," Julian asked, "or something larger?"

"Something with wings, worse smelling than a mouse," Rafir said, sniffing. "That's it, one of those bats."

"One of those bats from the Labyrinth tried to escape and found its way down here," Sebastian said, small face grim. "After it died, a Gnome probably dropped its body down that well, so it could be eaten by blind, sightless fish."

They continued to investigate, beginning to feel the weariness of the day's search. Outside, the sun had set long ago, and Julian sensed cloudy skies, with the rain of early fall beginning to pelt down on the forests and fields. The underground river would soon begin to rush much harder.

Finally, just as Julian was considering sleeping in the dark Gnome passages, they found a second chamber, with a door much smaller than the one opening to the well. This door was sealed, but Julian pressed his staff against the lock, whispering soft words, and the lock unbolted without a whisper of sound.

Julian had to bend down to enter, and he stayed hunched because parts of the ceiling were low. His staff flashed light. This chamber was much smaller than the one housing the well. On the chamber floor stood an even dozen stones. Each stone was tall, like small statues that came up to Julian's waist. Surrounding each stone were scraps of parchment — Gnome prayers.

"We have entered a temple," Sebastian said in a hushed voice.

"And these stones are statues," Rafir said, "of the Gods of Gnomes. They come here to pray to blocks of stones. I asked if this adventure could get any stranger, and suddenly, it's weirder than ever."

"We are supposed to rest here," Julian said in a distant voice, "and then the nightmares will come for us."

Sebastian shook his head, while Rafir blurted, "Nightmares! Then let's get out of here!"

"Nightmares, but not death," Julian said in the same distant voice. "Death lurks outside in the Gnome tunnels of the Labyrinth, but in this chamber, we will face only evil dreams."

They had a brief, quiet meal, then Julian whispered *words*, blocking the Witch from his dreaming mind. With his cloak folded under his head as a pillow, Julian closed off all his fears and sorrows, and he slept.

Rafir paced and sniffed and muttered through the dark chamber, but he too finally curled up beside Julian and slept. Sebastian was the last awake, sitting in the darkness, unwilling to let the nightmares come, though finally, his tired eyes closed.

And Sebastian found himself in a small underground chamber filled with a pale grey light. He was standing before a creature, a furry creature, half human height with the face of a small Goblin: a Hobgoblin. In his right hand, the Hobgoblin held a slender wand — but it was pointed away from Sebastian.

"Where is the Apprentice?" the Mage asked in a whisper. *"I was trying to link with the Apprentice through the Dreamways."*

"The Hobgoblin Mage," Sebastian muttered to himself, then he spoke up: *"Julian has blocked his dreams, so the Grey Witch can no longer reach him. Are you the Nightmare sent by the Grey Witch?"*

"The Witch, always the Witch!" the Hobgoblin Mage snarled. *"No, I am not your Nightmare — that is coming next. I wanted to speak with the Apprentice, and yet perhaps you can answer my question. Why didn't the Wizards send a Wizard to deal with the Grey Witch? Why did they send only this partly trained Apprentice?"*

"A Great Dark God threatens the Wizards to the South," Sebastian said. *"They thought that all three Wizards were needed to deal with him. Julian was the one that they could spare. They didn't realize how powerful the Witch had become."*

"The fools!" the Mage muttered.

"Merlin was fooled," Sebastian said, surprised to hear the words coming from his mouth. *"For my master, the Apprentice, may I ask a question?"*

The Hobgoblin grunted — a low sound like a dog's growl.

"I see that you are the Hobgoblin Mage," Sebastian said. *"Is there also a Goblin Mage? A Gnome Mage?"*

"Dead, both dead," the Mage muttered. *"The Witch killed them. Then she forced her greatest servant, the Goblin Giant, to lie down and die in silence*

in his tomb — or she would have him chopped up, still living, and fed him piece by piece to the sightless fish monsters at the base of her Well of Death. I am alive because I hide in the lower passages and will do the Witch's bidding when forced to."

The Hobgoblin Mage hesitated before speaking. "I see that I am wasting my time with you, and only giving the Witch another excuse to hunt me down. Yet I will say this: Nightmares are coming for you, not from any of the three races underground, but from the Witch and her brutal, cruel, evil, and twisted mind."

Sebastian started to speak again, but he found himself awake, staring into the darkness of the Gnomes' small temple. Over the Gnomes' prayer stones, pale lights were beginning to swirl. At Sebastian's side, Julian stirred. Grey, cloudy smoke was pouring from the stone monuments in the temple. Sebastian's wings flared. Julian sat up, suddenly wide awake. Rafir's eyes blinked open.

From the cloudy smoke, images began to form. The first of them was that of an old woman, hunched and weeping, and her smoky form drifted closer to Rafir.

"Granny!" Rafir whispered.

"Rafir," the old woman, Rafir's patroness, murmured. "Rafir, I am so cold, so cold and lost. You should never have left me. Why did you ever go away?" The fox bowed his head and began to weep quietly.

A second figure took shape and drifted toward Sebastian. The ghostly figure was Julian's height, but much older stooped and bearded.

"Merlin," Sebastian said, though he knew it was not Merlin.

"Sebastian," the Wraith whispered. "Why have you not guided your master into safety? Why did you not protect him? How did you let him fall into this doomed Labyrinth? He will become a dead thing, and so you will die, too."

Two Wraith figures took shape and drew closer to Julian. They were taller than Julian, just turning grey, though age had left them untouched.

"My mother," Julian whispered, "and my father, as they stand today in the halls of some distant Power."

"Julian," the Wraith in his mother's form whispered. "Why did you not follow us when we crossed the river at the ford? Why did you leave us to our fate? Had you not left us, we would be together today, happy, in peace, with the sun shining down upon us, and bound in love forever."

Julian bowed his head and said nothing. To his own surprise, Sebastian was the first to react. He went over and touched Rafir's fur, then spoke to the Granny-like Wraith that kept coming closer to the fox.

"Get back, Witch-sending," Sebastian said, "I was there when Rafir's companion helped him join Julian. Granny was happy for Rafir and his new adventures, and she would never, never attack him like this. If she watched Rafir from a distance, waves of love — not bitter sorrow — would flow toward us."

Sebastian turned toward the image of Merlin. "And you, Witch-sending with the shape of Merlin, the Wizard would never entrust to me the safety of Julian the Apprentice. I am a lesser being, and Julian is too important. Merlin is wise, perhaps even brilliant, and you will hear from him yet."

Julian grasped his staff with both hands. "Grey Witch of the North, you have been clever in peering into our minds and seeing our fears. Yet you were not there at the ford when I was five and my grandmother and I with several others had crossed the ford, while the rest, including my parents, were taken by our foes. You could never have heard their last words to me, when they called on me to escape, then build my strength, and live a brilliant life, with or without them. It does not feel to me that you ever understood love, or kindness, or ever wished happiness for another being."

From far away, the three could feel the rage of the Grey Witch as it boiled over. Her Wraith figures began to change their shapes, to become Hag Wraiths, tall, grey floating witch creatures made of heavy dark smoke and metal, with fingers like daggers, and sharp, jagged grey teeth, and eyes that gleamed yellow in the darkness.

Hag Wraiths drifted toward Julian and his Familiars. As the three backed against the wall farthest from the chamber door, Julian wove a cocoon of rainbow light around them. Hag Wraiths ripped at Julian's shielding with dagger-like hands and pounded at the three with fists made heavy by metal. No longer able to form words, their mouths howled and shrieked, so that even the stone statues in the chamber shook.

Under this attack, Sebastian and Rafir closed their eyes against the nightmares and held their ears to keep down the pain of the nightmares' shrieking noises.

Within their protective cocoon, Julian shook with anger, but he whispered, "Stay strong. This cannot last forever."

But it *did* seem to last forever: all the ripping and pounding and shrieking kept on through the rest of the long dark night. Finally, as the dawn rose over the meadows above the Labyrinth, the Hag Wraiths faded, and the three sank down to the chamber's floor and fell into a deep sleep of exhaustion.

· X ·

Some distance above the three sleepers, the Grey Witch whispered to herself, "'Never understood love,' said that whiney, whimpering Apprentice. Let us see how much love they have left when I am done with them." She stared into the darkness and tightening and untightening her twisted, clawed fingers, struggling to control her enormous rage.

Chapter Eleven
Uraks — and a Ghost

THE *THUDDING* SOUNDS OF tumbling stones woke the three sleepers. Julian forced his eyes open, and even in the darkness, he could see that a wall of stones had been pushed down just ten paces to the left of the chamber's entrance. Beyond the fallen stones was a metal door, and now its handle was turning. Julian stood, with his staff flashing light. Sebastian and Rafir came awake, eyes blinking from the light cast by Julian's staff.

Then the metal door swung open, creaking as though it hadn't been used in years. Gnome soldiers entered the chamber, spears pointed at Julian and his allies. They were an inch or two shorter than the Apprentice, grey and thin, with dark cloaks covering armor made from light chain mail. If they smelled much better than the Hobgoblins, these Gnomes seemed much more willing to use their weapons than their smaller brethren.

"Hear me," Julian said, backing away. "We are captives of the Grey Witch, controlled by her, as she tests us, step by step through her Labyrinth. Now we are trapped in the Labyrinth's Gnome regions. If you wish us out of Gnomeland, simply show us back to the Labyrinth."

Gnomes advanced, spears pointed not just at Julian, but also at Sebastian and Rafir. The fox vanished, while Sebastian took flight; but with the low ceilings, he had no place to hide.

Julian's staff hurled a jagged black bolt of force at the roof. The stone of the temple trembled, a smell of burning hung in the air, and the Gnomes hesitated.

"Why would you wish to die?" Julian asked. "The Witch would thank you by feeding your dead bodies to the sightless fish of the dark river that runs beneath us. I say again: show us out. Perhaps then we can deal with this Grey Witch that you love so much."

Gnomes wavered. None seemed willing to lead. Finally, one lowered his spear, then one by one Gnome soldiers let the points of their spears drift to the ground. Sebastian counted twelve of them, with twelve spears — one for each of the dozen stone monuments.

After a moment of hesitation, one Gnome led Julian, Sebastian, and Rafir back through the metal door. All the menace seemed to have left their encounter, though Julian cautiously reached into their minds, testing them to make certain none would attack from behind as they left the chamber.

One Gnome alone led them through a series of stone tunnels. With his fox senses, Rafir could feel that they were rising to Labyrinth height, then higher. The Gnome took them through a side passage then up a long shaft with metal rungs set into stone; Julian climbed slowly, with Rafir on his shoulder, and Sebastian holding his staff. Finally, the Gnome reached a dark passage hiding a rusting metal door, unsealed it, then pulled it open. Beyond was a mat of roots that gleamed with the same pale lights as those of the Witch's Labyrinth.

With one forceful hand, the Gnome pushed Julian through the mat of roots and into the pale lights of the Witch's kingdom. After Sebastian and Rafir followed Julian, the metal door slammed shut behind them and locked. Without a whisper of sound, the roots of the mat behind them wove itself back to the wall and the opening vanished.

They had been forced back into the Labyrinth — by Gnomes who had spoken not a single word to their intruders.

· X ·

Rafir sniffed the air. The smell of dying things was mostly gone, but now there were heavier, darker smells, stronger and more filled with danger.

"Oh no," Sebastian whispered.

Julian took a deep breath. "Uraks," he said. "I know where this test is going."

"Uraks," Rafir said. "I was trained to smell them by my patroness, Granny. The three sisters were worried about them and asked me to warn them if I smelled them. But why Uraks, why now?"

"They were the third of the creatures created to challenge mankind," Sebastian explained. "The Witch has seen us tested against Carags, the shapeshifters. Then she saw how we fought with fire and archers against Vorrs, the beast monsters of the fields and forests. Now she wants to see how we handle Uraks, the powerful warriors created to destroy human armies. All three of those creatures tried to wipe out the League ages ago."

"It was long before my time," Julian said, "but the League survived."

"They are coming," Sebastian said, "but first I need to speak to you." And Sebastian's hands made a cone shape, asking Julian to seal them away from the ears of the Witch.

After Julian called upon his *cone of silence*, Sebastian said quickly, "Julian, that Hobgoblin Mage tried to contact you in dreams. He was only able to reach me to tell us that the Witch was sending the Hag Wraiths. I don't think he cares whether we live or die, but he hates the Witch, really hates her. I don't thank that will help us against the Uraks, but maybe there's something we can do later."

"Tiny Hobgoblins against enormous Uraks," Julian said softly, staring down the length of the Labyrinth. "That's no contest. Rafir, where are we? We need to get back to your 'Chamber of Mysteries'."

Now they could hear the first sounds of heavy bodies moving — clanking sounds of armored fighters. And they were coming from down below.

"That Chamber is about three levels below us," Rafir said, "and somewhere off that way." The fox's head nodded to his left.

"Those Gnomes," Julian muttered, "may have no love for the Witch, but they would never disobey her, and so they let us out in the worst possible place." Julian closed his eyes and *reached*. Sebastian and Rafir stared back down into the lower passages of the Labyrinth, as the sounds of approaching Uraks grew louder.

"I can feel the Labyrinth," Julian murmured, "almost like a living thing, ready to swallow us up. But not now, not yet. Our first plan was to seek Rafir's Chamber of Mysteries, but we've been blocked by Uraks. So, the second plan is to find Goblin passages. Rafir, Sebastian, we need to smell and sense for Goblins, even if we are moving farther from the Chamber. Let's go."

They sped higher, Rafir sniffing along the base of the Labyrinth, while Sebastian flew from side to side, searching for Goblin traces. Julian glanced back: the first of the Urak warriors could be seen. They were completely armored in black metal, moving toward the three in heavy steps that were filled with menace. They stood two heads taller than Julian and much wider than the Apprentice. In their right hands, they held heavy axes, while in their left were long shields, metal covered by the thick hides of lizards. He could not see to count them all.

"Of course, of course," Julian muttered, "Shielding against my fire, and axes against...." He turned to see that Sebastian and Rafir had stopped searching and were staring at the Uraks with wide eyes.

"Don't stop," Julian said, "find us an exit!"

"It's here," Sebastian said, touching the wall, "if it's anywhere." Rafir and Sebastian began ripping at the roots and earth on the right-hand side of the Labyrinth. Julian spoke *words*: a small section of the Labyrinth's wall began to collapse into a mound of dust.

Another metal door lay beyond the Labyrinth's woven soil. Uraks began to growl, almost chanting as they clanked forward, preparing for the kill. Julian twisted the door's handle; it would not open. He pressed his staff to it, murmuring more spell words. Nothing. Julian called fire against it. The door smoked, but even after Julian smashed it with a booted foot, the door would not open. In the distance, he could sense but not quite hear the laughter of the Grey Witch.

"The Witch has sealed us away from the Goblin passages," Julian muttered. "It must be time for a third plan." Only the distant Witch took note of the blue fire that raced across Julian's eyes.

The Apprentice turned to his Familiars and spoke one word: "Run."

The three turned and raced into the upper levels of the Labyrinth, away from the Uraks, farther from Rafir's "Chamber of Mysteries." From an even greater distance, Julian could feel the malice of the Grey Witch, and her pleasure in his flight. Behind the three, clanking metal sounds grew louder as armored Urak warriors began to jog toward them.

Finally, Julian came to a halt and turned to face their foes, staff in hand.

"Here, somewhere near here," the Apprentice whispered to himself, "a place where tunnels join."

Rafir's wide eyes darted away from the Uraks, to a place in the air where an enormous red tongue was coming out of nothingness.

"Kath," Sebastian murmured, as the great serpent spilled out from a hole in the air.

"Here is the place and now is the time," Julian whispered, "when the Witch plans to kill mighty Kath with the axes of Uraks. Do not fight them, Kath. We will destroy many, but not here, not now." Julian pointed his staff downward, calling out *words*. The floor of the Labyrinth began to fill with dust. Uraks sped forward, though they were slowed by the weight of their clanking dark metal armor.

"Now, Kath, strike downward!" Julian called out. "Free us from this deathtrap!"

The head of Kath raised in the air then smashed downward with enormous power. The floor of the Labyrinth trembled. Dust spread through the air. With his third thrust, Kath broke through the Labyrinth's earthen floor.

Rafir was the first to drop down to the level below. Sebastian flapped down, trailing grey dust, only a second behind the fox. Julian grasped a great coil of Kath's body and the two slid down to the next level. Dust was spreading in all directions. The four of them raced through powdery clouds, heading down toward the Chamber where the Witch had stored her belongings.

Above them, Uraks had gathered around the hole in the Labyrinth's floor, staring down into cloudy confusion — but then the rage of the Grey Witch sent pain flaring through their bodies. Urak warriors cried aloud, then turned, and began jogging back down to the lower Labyrinth to reach the Apprentice and his followers. Now they had orders not just to smash the Apprentice and kill their giant snake ally, but to destroy all four of the intruders.

Julian led the four as they raced down the length of the Labyrinth, Kath thrashing through the tunnel, Sebastian flapping overhead, and Rafir panting to keep up with their snake ally. Julian raced down, though he kept a sharp eye out for openings into the Labyrinth — he could sense that Goblins were stirring.

Then to their left the root and earth mesh of the Labyrinth was shoved aside, and dazed Goblin soldiers, confused and only partly armed, began scrambling from their narrow passageways into the much larger tunnel of the Labyrinth.

"Brush them aside, Kath!" Julian called out, "But do not kill them!" Bolts of force from Julian's staff stunned the nearest Goblins. The massive coils of Kath swept others aside. Swords lashed at Kath but could not bite through his thick snake's skin.

As they ran, the Grey Witch of the North blasted a shout of hatred into their minds:

This game is coming to an end, you stinking little worms and maggots!

Julian staggered as though struck by a blow, while the others stumbled before continuing to race downward.

Panting, they reached the storage chamber where the Witch had cast aside all her old belongings. Julian used his staff to outline a small portal at the base of the Labyrinth wall. He whispered spell words and watched as roots and soil turned to dust. Then Kath struck, and a low portal was opened into the Chamber.

The three scrambled through, with Kath following quickly behind. Light flared from Julian's staff, then he closed his eyes and chanted the most powerful magic at his command. First, he sealed them from the Witch's sight with a force of magic greater than any *cone*. Outside, Uraks were clanking closer, the sounds of their death chants beginning to vibrate through the chamber's walls.

"Now," Julian said, turning to Sebastian, "with the most careful hands, find that crystal globe of the Witch. Find it, take it gently from its storage chest, hold it, guard it as though it was your heart's desire. Rafir, search for Goblin or Gnome or even Hobgoblin passages. We cannot let ourselves be surprised and trapped. Kath, stay at my side."

Again, Julian began to chant. Lines of blue force raced up and down the wall leading back to the Labyrinth. Its substance of soil and roots began to firm, to harden, to become as strong as the poured stone once used to form the foundations of fortresses.

Rafir sniffed and sniffed again, but only traces of underworld people could be sensed. In one far corner, he smelled a slight hint of death, the death of a small one. Had he found the hidden grave of the Witch's child? He looked up, ready to call to Julian, but he could see that the Apprentice was preparing the chamber for battle. Already, the wall leading to the Labyrinth had turned from dark brown to the greyish white color of stone fortifications.

Rafir left the hidden grave and stood uncertainly, tail flashing back and forth. *A fortress, we're in a fortress. But they're going to break through, sooner or later. Where will we go then? Maybe this isn't a fortress, maybe it's a tomb.* Rafir turned to Sebastian; the little Familiar was crouched, holding the Witch's small crystal with two careful hands. *If that crystal ball was going to save us,* thought the fox, *it would be glowing with magic. I guess we need —*

SMASH! The Chamber wall began to shiver as the axes of Uraks battered it with heavy blades made of dark steel. More axes hammered at the wall. Cracks began to run in all directions over Julian's fortress wall — like the web of a gigantic spider. Magic or not, the barrier would last only a few moments longer. Julian stood for a moment, watching the cracks spread, as though frozen in hesitation.

"Julian," Sebastian murmured, "you are not the killing machine. The killing machines — the Uraks — are out in the Labyrinth."

Julian nodded slowly, then turned to Kath and whispered, "Come." The two raced to the farthest right of the Chamber, and Julian whispered spell words at the base of the wall. Dust poured from its base. Kath's tail thrashed, ready for battle. They were going back into the Labyrinth — but *behind* the force of Uraks that were smashing at the wall.

Kath's head pulled back. Then with an almost silent jab, the way was opened back to the Labyrinth. Julian scrambled through. Uraks had set aside their shields to hammer at the wall. Their axes had almost broken through. Julian clenched his staff with both hands. Kath began spilling back into the Labyrinth.

Then Julian raised his staff and sent fire surging toward the Uraks, and the first rank burned, shrieking, and falling to the ground. Others dropped axes and reached for shields to protect them from fire.

"Strike, Kath, strike!" Julian called out. "But watch for axes! I will deal with their axes!" Julian sent jagged black bolts of power against the knees and feet of those completely armored. They began groaning and toppling.

Kath smashed at others. Each blow crushed a single Urak, one at a time. As Kath drew back and smashed, he caught first those with shields only. Julian's staff struck at the hands of Uraks holding axes.

Kath smashed again, aiming at the center of their shields. More fire from Julian blazed at the Uraks. Lightning bolts blasted at axes. Finally, the remaining Uraks fled — some groaning with wounds, while others sobbed in great pain because now the Grey Witch was lashing at their minds with a force that left them howling in agony.

The Witch filled the Labyrinth with a wave of hatred. Julian recoiled in pain, holding his head with both hands. Teeth clenched, he forced the hatred of the Witch from his mind. Then he turned to Kath, checking the body of his serpent ally; Kath had suffered only light wounds.

"Kath, mighty Kath," Julian murmured. "Again, I can never repay you for this moment. One day, though, one day, there might be something I could do...now, Kath, guard this passageway, for I must deal with a matter inside the Witch's Chamber."

Out in the Labyrinth, Kath watched the bodies of dying Uraks twitch and moan. As he stood guard, his great tail thrashed back and forth, and his forked tongue tasted not just the air but also the emotions of the Witch's Kingdom: her Labyrinth was filled with shock, and pain and death. If his serpent's mouth had been more flexible, Kath might have smiled.

Back inside the Chamber, it was dark again, then even darker as Julian resealed the portal leading to the gleaming Labyrinth. Sebastian and Rafir waited in dark silence until the Apprentice finished his spells.

"You won again," Rafir finally breathed out.

Julian's staff flared with light. "The Grey Witch and I can almost read each other's minds. She saw Kath help us defeat the Emissary, and so she planned for him, arming Uraks with heavy axes, and shielding against my fire."

"It feels as though now she's finally ready to kill us," Sebastian said softly. "I think she's learned enough from us, and now she wants to feed us to her blind fishes."

"Perhaps not quite yet," Julian said. "When she calms, she might wish for one other test, at least. Here...." Awkwardly, Sebastian and Julian exchanged the Crystal and Julian's staff, so that light flared from the staff clutched by Sebastian while Julian held the Crystal Ball with both hands.

"You know," Julian said, staring down into the Crystal's depths, "when I first touched this device, I could feel only dead magic. But later, when I thought back to that moment, I wondered if the magic was only completely dead to the Witch's touch, and maybe there was a spark of something else, still alive. Let us see...."

"Oh, oh," Rafir muttered, "here comes that ghost you were talking about."

"Here comes the ghost — maybe," Julian said, and he began to whisper soft *words*. Nothing happened for a time, except that the chamber's air grew more still and tense, and every sound seemed to become louder. Rafir thought that he could almost hear moth maggots chewing on the castoff clothing of the Witch.

Finally, the Crystal grew warm in Julian's hands. When he could no longer hold it, Julian placed the globe on the chamber's earthen floor. Then a grey smoke began pouring out from the globe's depths. Like a slow ghost, it began to take shape.

That shape belonged to the Grey Witch of the North. An astonished Rafir blinked out of sight.

"Do not," the ghost whispered, "try to speak with this ghostly sending, for it cannot respond to you. I am only a warning, a warning and a recording of my own death. I am, or was, The Grey Witch of the North, a lesser weaver of magic, who lived in the northern wilderness of the League.

"Why would any lesser wielder of magic wish to join with the three Wizards who ruled in the south of the League? Great Dark Gods watched them with malice and would one day destroy them. So, I hid from the Wizards and wove my spells below ground. One day I felt the distant touch of the Mind of Merlin, and so I concealed myself further, digging down deeper with the aid of my Goblin allies.

"All was peaceful for a time, and I and my daughter, Madhya, used to leave our tunnel fortress so we could walk in the sunlight. I remember how we laughed together as butterflies fluttered over the meadows. Then, when Madhya was just seven, she became gravely ill. None of my potions or spells could heal her. I should have taken her south, and sought the mercy of the Wizards, who were powerful and remote but far from cruel.

"I sought healers from the Mid-World. Several came, but Madhya could not be made well. It was then that I made my second and greatest mistake. A woman named Zathura came to my aid. She seemed older than me, like a crone, kindly and wise. For a time, Madhya was better, but always she fell back into her old illness. Zathura was called again and again so that this so called 'healer' came to live with us below ground.

"I understood, only dimly, that Zathura was studying me. Was there harm in that, I asked myself? All beings of power learn matters of magic from others, seeking to build their own strength. I did not guess until later, that Zathura was able to change her form, that she wished not just to learn from me, but to *become* me.

"When I finally understood her dark designs, I tried to take my daughter and escape, to seek aid from the Wizards, but I found that all exits were barred to me. Even the Goblin Mage would no longer listen to me. I then put forth all my strength to discover the purposes of Zathura, but I could not penetrate her mind. I only learned that she was far more powerful than I was — and that she was not human. She was nothing close to human.

"Take heed if you hear me from beyond my grave. Beware of the being who is seeking to replace me. I go now into battle with Zathura. I do not think I will survive, and I do not think that little Madhya will live long after I die. Pray that the Maker, who sits at the Heart of the Universe, at the

Center of All Understanding, pray that the Maker will take pity on the 'true' Grey Witch of the North and her daughter, at the End of Time. Farewell."

The grey ghost image slowly faded. The light from Julian's staff died down until they were in almost total darkness.

"So, this cruel and evil Grey Witch of the North," Sebastian breathed out, "is not really the original, real Grey Witch — that Witch is dead. The current one is a fake Witch and not even a mortal human."

"A Carag?" Rafir asked. "Were there ever Carag Mages?"

"There were Carag Mages," Julian replied. "In the early days of the League, two Carag Mages joined Sorcerers to wage war against the Wizards."

"A shapeshifting Carag Mage," Sebastian murmured.

But then the small voice that spoke so rarely into Julian's mind whispered: *The Grey Witch of the North is not human, and she is certainly not a Carag Mage. Remember, Rafir can smell Carags.*

Chapter Twelve

Storm Giants Overhead

MERLIN DREAMED AGAIN OF *a far, distant future time when the sorcerous energies of the Mid-World had almost exhausted themselves. Two talismans remained: one was a sword named Excalibur while the second was a cup of great beauty and power known as the Holy Grail. Why were these dreams taking him so far into the future and so frequently? Was it possible that this distant land represented a future that was growing more likely, even probable, with every passing dream?*

And so, a troubled Merlin welcomed the interruption of his dreams by his fellow Wizards when they reached out to him. Like the meeting of soft ice flows in a frosty ocean, the thoughts of the Wizards joined silently in the darkness, and then they spoke mind-to-mind.

Thorian: *War fleets gather in the ocean depths ready to advance upon Stone Mountain, and yet we are now prepared. So, I must now recognize the concerns of Balardi, my ally and fellow Wizard, who fears for Julian the Apprentice.*

Balardi: *I know that you both feel that I treat Julian as something greater than an Apprentice and ally — perhaps even as a foster son. But the treachery of those known as "Dark Gods" is legendary. So, it may be that the* *warfare on our shores is a focussed diversion, and the real target of our foes is our Apprentice, Julian.*

Merlin: *The thought has also grown in my mind that we have been deceived, that the attacks on our shores are part of a three-pronged strike, with the real threat coming from the North. And so, while you two guard our shores, I will now attempt to discover the truth of this matter.*

· X ·

Far from the Wizards' League, far from Julian's struggle with the Grey Witch, the Benja was troubled. His sisters, Kayal, Naith, and Issah were uncertain about their futures, and so they quarreled, or walked alone at night, glancing up to the stars for inspiration. Each of the three was partly in love with Julian, sometimes believing they had made a mistake when they left the Apprentice.

Only one good thing had happened since their return to the Sorcerous domain of the Mistress of Illusions: Bluescent, Julian's mare had been returned to Sea's Edge and the Halls of Merlin. The Benja understood that Bluescent had nothing like the wisdom and intellect of Sebastian or Rafir, but when separated from Julian she had been the saddest steed the Benja had ever encountered. The three sisters had fed Bluescent by hand, patting and reassuring her, but Bluescent always looked beyond them, hoping for Julian's return.

Meanwhile, the Mistress of Illusions was watching the three sisters and the Benja closely, sensing that their service was coming to an end. Soon they would leave her magical kingdom within the Mid-World, and return to the solid earth of Alantéa, the source of all magic. Where would they go? What would they do?

When the Benja was troubled, he floated high in the night sky, watching starlight shining brightly over the lake's surface. This lake lay at the center of the magical kingdom created by the Mistress of Illusions, and it was the Benja's favorite place. He had to remind himself that the lake was only partly real. Even if fish with silvery skin swam happily through its waters, the lake was made more of magic than of water.

The Benja's troubled mind relaxed as he studied the magic of the lake. But then a voice reached to him out of the darkness: *"You, too, are also made of magic, at least partially formed of Sorcery."*

"What?!?" the Benja called out, and his floating gold body dropped down fifty feet closer to the lake's surface.

"Do not be afraid," said the voice, *"This intrusion comes only from the Mind of Merlin, speaking to you from a great distance. It is dark here in my place of power at Sea's Edge, and I sit with eyes closed so I can watch from afar as the stars shine over your magical, gleaming lake. I have two things to say to you: the first is about your future, the second is a question."*

"Our future!" the Benja said. "Where do we go, and what will we do?"

"Those things are not yet known because your sisters have not yet agreed upon them. But when I search your future, I see how your powers will change: in greatest need, a dagger will form in your hand, colored gold, but formed from a metal that is as strong as steel, reinforced by magic, and then you will be able to take shape and fight beside your sisters."

"Fight beside them!" the Benja breathed out. "I never believed it possible, and I would defend them to the death — but, Wizard, you also had a question for me. What could I possibly know that you do not?"

"There was a moment, a time of great danger when the Fates met at the border of the League and the Witch's underground kingdom, when your own enchanted mind brushed against the mind of the Grey Witch of the North. What can you tell me about that encounter?"

"You want me to relive that moment?" the Benja asked.

"That is why the mind of Merlin reaches to you, Benja."

"So much was happening," the Benja murmured into the night sky. "Vorrs were leaping through the inner fortress, while hawks raged down on Carags and Vorrs...then as we began to overcome those creatures, the Great Emissary attacked us. My sisters buried arrows in its wound, and then Kath was called, and Julian's servant shattered the Emissary's frame. Your Apprentice fought like a Demigod, not just a low-level wielder of magic.

"It was after that battle that the ground opened up and swallowed Julian and his small allies the Familiars. The sun was shining down on our moment of triumph for one brief second, then suddenly they were gone. My senses followed the Apprentice down below where he lay beneath the ground, but then a cold and cruel and far greater power brushed me aside."

"Think about this carefully, Benja. This 'cold and cruel greater power,' was it human? Or was it something other than human?"

"I know so little about these things," the Benja said, hesitating. "I am only a lesser force, so young...and yet as I think about it, I had never met a mind like that of the Witch's. I would have thought the Witch's mind would be something like the mind of the Mistress of Illusions, powerful and clear, but human. And yet the Witch's mind was not anything like that — now, as I think about the Witch, I do not believe she was anything resembling a human."

"I feared that you would speak those words," Merlin replied, and the distant Wizard seemed to sigh. *"You have touched the minds of shapeshifting Carags. Could this Grey Witch of the North have been some sort of Carag Mage?"*

"When I reached into the minds of Carags," the Benja said, "It was like touching a jumble of worms and centipedes. The mind of the Grey Witch was colder, stronger, much more horrible and twisted even than those Carags."

"*Then I have made a terrible mistake,*" whispered the distant voice of the Mind of Merlin.

The Grey Witch, once mortally afraid of Merlin, had almost completely forgotten about the Wizard. She sat in her place of power, staring with only a part of her mind at a large image, a vision screen that showed the Apprentice fighting off a band of Goblins. The reach of her magic allowed her to see and hear things inside her small kingdom, though sometimes the Apprentice was able to close off her hearing. She watched, mind churning with dark thoughts.

Kath, no longer needed, had vanished. Goblins were harassing Julian by throwing sharp metal darts at him, trying to wound both Apprentice and Familiars, but not kill them, not yet. Goblins kept on missing, while the Apprentice was trying hard not to even injure a single one of them. In their own strange ways, the Apprentice and her Goblin servants were working together.

Anger stirred in the Witch, but it was a waste of time getting angry with the Goblins. One day she would have servants worthy of her power, and then all the Goblins could be fed to the blind fish at the bottom of the well. The little sightless monsters would bite and chew and gobble, while the Goblins would squeal and shriek and promise to love the Witch forever. Too late, Goblins! The Witch laughed.

Anyway, what she was watching was only a game, one of the last few scenes before the end of this incredibly stupid story. Was there much left to learn from Julian before she replaced the Apprentice? She was almost there, almost ready to take his form... and **become** *Julian the Apprentice, Destiny's Darling.*

She turned from the vision screen showing the Goblins and the Apprentice as they pretended to fight, then walked down a narrow hall. She passed the false tower constructed to capture the dreaming mind of the Apprentice. Beyond the chapel dedicated to her Great Dark God, she turned a corner and entered a separate chamber, a broad room with a high ceiling. This chamber was made of six blocks of mirrors — one mirror for each wall and one each for floor and ceiling.

Once in the chamber's center, her body began to squirm and shake as she twisted out of her shape as Grey Witch of the North, taking the shape of Julian the Apprentice, the Child of Destiny.

In her right hand, she held a staff identical to Julian's — but it let out only a string of tiny black sparks. Laughing quietly to herself, she curled her left claw-like hand, copying Julian's use of a Sorcerer's power. Frowning in worry, she let a blue fire race across her eyes. Studying herself and all her reflections in her hall of mirrors, she decided that she had almost settled into her next form. She was well on her way to becoming Julian the Apprentice.

Now was the time to make up a new story for the Apprentice. Her false face of Julian trembled, and a terrible dark scar formed over the left side of Julian's face. The scarred side of his face was burned as though damaged by fire in battle, and the left eye peering out of the scarred side was grey as though tormented by evil visions. Clearing her throat, she began again to practice Julian's quiet young voice:

"After the death of Sebastian and Rafir — the dear, sweet little ones — I could not return to the Halls of Merlin with this blackened face. And Kath would no longer come when I called...." The Witch in the form of Julian hesitated. It would be better to destroy Big Coils — Kath — along with Little Pests — the Familiars. Perhaps a powerful and obedient slave could be created, a Sending that would track down Kath and kill him quietly in his deep, dark, sorcerous burrow.

"Even now," the Witch-Julian continued, "far from the Wizards and their League, as I await my destiny, I still must weep for the little ones." Once again, the Witch tried to weep and again, she stamped her foot in frustration — this time one of "Julian's" eyes produced a stream of tiny green tears, while a single glob of yellow pus slipped down from the other.

She cursed loudly in a language no human voice had ever used, then muttered in the common tongue of Alantéa, "Practice, practice, practice."

Julian's left hand curled with power and the dart heading for his shoulder went flying overhead, burying itself in the matted roots of the Labyrinth.

"Rafir!" Julian called out. "Stop! Don't pull at them!" The invisible fox had been trying to help by tugging at the sleeves of Goblin dart throwers. But the Goblins were trying hard to miss Julian, not to wound him — and the fox, by spoiling their aim, was making the encounter more dangerous than it should have been.

Rafir pulled back but stumbled against another Goblin, changing its aim. This time, the dart went dangerously close to Sebastian, who was flying overhead. The little Familiar responded by hurling a handful of his crow fighting powder down at the ranks of Goblin sentries.

Goblins began to sneeze. Rafir sneezed, and a second later Julian did too. Coughing, they backed away from Goblin sentries, down deeper into the Labyrinth, back toward the caverns where water ran freely over stone floors. Goblins followed them slowly, half heartedly, and they were beginning to stare into different sections of the Labyrinth as though other problems were drawing them away.

"Sorry," Rafir murmured.

"I'm sorry, too," Sebastian said, and then the little Familiar also sneezed.

"We're just trying to stay alive," Julian said, "but we should be —" The Apprentice halted because Sebastian's hands were making a cone's shape, asking Julian to protect them from the Grey Witch's sight and hearing.

Julian spoke *words*, then turned back to Sebastian, "What's happening?"

"It's the Hobgoblin Mage," Sebastian whispered. "After he reached for your dreaming mind and couldn't link with you, I think he's started to work through me. He's sent a key to the tunnel systems into my mind, so I can see...like tiny, flickering lights...entrances to Hobgoblin passages. We can escape from these Goblins."

"Ugh," Rafir muttered, "Hobgoblin tunnels — smelly, dark places, filled with worms and centipedes, and maybe small nasty things that bite."

"But better than dying," Julian said, watching the Goblins, who were retreating into side passages, leaving the three intruders alone for the moment. "Hold those images, Sebastian. I don't think we need them just now. Something's coming. I can feel the night sky trembling far above us. The Labyrinth is hunching down as though getting ready for battle. Gnomes, Goblins, and Hobgoblins are beginning to hide in their deepest tunnels. And from the Witch, I can feel something that is close to...fear."

· ☾ ·

Back in her shape as a Witch, the Grey Witch walked back and forth in her place of power, watching screens powered by magic that showed the world above her underground kingdom. It was dark night above, with grey clouds only partly blocking a bright half moon. In the north, stars were shining brightly, but from the south masses of clouds were racing toward her Labyrinth. A force of Sorcery was coming for her — the magic of the most powerful of Wizards.

"*Merlin,*" she snarled, "*you squinty faced little puffed-up human Magician. So, you think you are mighty because you have lived more than two hundred years and have aged only a few days over the last fifty years. Merlin, you have the life of an insect! For every breath you have ever taken, I have taken ten thousand! And I will take a hundred billion more breaths after your miserable, stinking, short life is over!*"

While the Grey Witch was snarling her feet were dancing nervously over the floor, and her hands twitched, preparing to call upon her own magic. What sort of power would Merlin's Sending have? What kind of force was racing through the skies toward her? Her vision panels could only show events close by, and so she began mumbling spell words in an ancient dark language never spoken by the voice of any human.

Images began to form on the wall in front of her, showing the ocean at the shore of Sea's Edge where Merlin ruled. The water was almost completely white with stormy foam. Enormous waves were smashing down, pounding the shoreline. Then, as the Witch watched on, huge, bearded heads began to rise from the ocean floor, followed by chests, then bodies, then enormous arms and feet. There were two of them. Locks of hair, thick as human bodies and white as seafoam, stuck out in all directions as though sea salt had stiffened it. Each of their foreheads was matted with seaweed, while their wild eyes were made from hundreds of broken seashells. Lightning trembled at the edges of their enormous fingers.

"*Storm Giants!*" she cried out. "*A Great Spell has been launched at me! Great Dark God whom I serve, this was not part of our plan!*" *No response came to her cries. The wall before her showed two Storm Giants striding north — toward her kingdom! Clouds boiled overhead, seeming to lift the two more quickly to their destination. Lightning flared in the sky.*

And she could see that above the storm clouds, above the Storm Giants, the eagle, the Eye of Merlin, was flying overhead as though directing their attack. Under glowing moonlight, the eagle seemed driven by powerful magic, flying faster than any winged creature of Alantéa had ever flown. They were coming so quickly! There was so little time to prepare!

Filled with rage and fear, the Grey Witch left her place of power, scrambling down a narrow hall into the place she had created to trap the dreaming mind of Julian — the tower.

As she passed through the tower of dreams, she muttered, *"I need to rid myself of this place, for the Apprentice, Destiny's Doomed Darling, will never live to come here again."*

In a smaller room next to the tower was the chapel where she pretended to worship her ally, the Great Dark God, whose aid she now sought. Casting herself before the altar, she murmured, *"Great One, Majestic One, help me now for the Wizard is striking at the heart of my kingdom."* No answer came just as no response had come the last six — no, seven times.

As the Witch rose, she whispered in much different tones, *"If you think that I will die quietly, pass into Death's Dream Kingdom without telling anyone about your role in killing the Apprentice, you are greatly mistaken." There, she felt a response, a quiver, a hint of concern. At least now both she and the Great Dark God were afraid — the God would not be afraid of Merlin, but other Gods were watching.*

The Great Dark God will respond, the Witch decided, likely by drawing away our foes. There was another ally she could call upon from long ago, but that being was far, far away, and had not responded in more than a hundred years. She was on her own for the moment.

The Witch scurried away, calling upon all the power at her command.

· ✕ ·

Other Great Gods watched events from a distance. Sitting in his place of power, surrounded by glowing lights and bands of smoke that rose through his dark kingdom, the Great God Wotan allowed himself a grim smile.

"At last," Wotan murmured, "the Wizard Merlin sees the danger to his lesser servants and sends aid. It was rash of me to promise aid to the Apprentice, for it would likely mean only the death of a second mortal hero. Now, I am freed from my promise, as long as the Wizard emerges victorious."

Wotan had little love for the Wizards, though he tried to aid many of the heroes of Alantéa the Forerunner as long as his interference was hidden, and there was no threat to his own power.

· ℳ ·

"What's happening to this place?" Rafir wondered out loud. Now that the bands of Goblins were gone, the Labyrinth had grown completely quiet, and free of movement, as though Gnomes and Goblins and Hobgoblins had never lived in the Witch's kingdom or built their own tunnel systems beside the great Labyrinth. It was also getting darker. Light from the glowing earth that covered the sides of the Labyrinth was slowly dying down, like a setting sun.

"The Witch is drawing all her strength back to her place of power," Julian said softly, "and I guess that some of her magic had been lighting the Labyrinth." Julian's staff flashed light and they began moving slowly up the Labyrinth, watching tunnel sides and ceilings for any sign of movement. Only shadows moved on the walls of the Labyrinth, and everything was quiet, except that Rafir thought he could hear rumbles of thunder in the distance.

"I can feel it now," Sebastian whispered, "war is coming to the Grey Witch and her kingdom."

"We need to get higher," Julian said. "Even though it seems so unlikely, there might be a chance for us to escape." Julian began jogging upward, with Rafir running easily beside him, while Sebastian flapped overhead.

Then came the first lightning strike.

WHAMMM!!! The Labyrinth shook, and Julian was knocked to the ground. He knelt but stayed off his feet as a second strike shook the Labyrinth. Instead of standing, Julian knelt, closed his eyes, and *reached*.

"Storm Giants are raging overhead," he whispered, eyes still closed. "Very powerful magic is coming from Merlin. "Let me think, let me see what I can see...."

Images came into Julian's mind. He could see Storm Giants overhead, enormous creatures made of cloudy matter and seafoam and magic. Lightning bolts were raging down at the Grey Witch of the North and her kingdom. Above the Storm Giants, clouds blocked the night sky, but the eagle, the Eye of Merlin, had flown below the cloud cover and was croaking defiance and anger at the Witch.

SMASH!!!

As more lightning crashed down, other images reached Julian's mind: they came from the ocean's edge at Stone Mountain to the east where Thorian ruled. Landing boats with many armed men were racing toward the beaches, and out in the deepest waters of the ocean, warships were speeding toward the Wizards and their League.

So that was the Witch's answer! She had called upon her ally, that unnamed Great Dark God, to attack the Wizards. While the Wizards fought off the assault, she would find some way to hold back Merlin's Storm Giants. He could feel her magic striking back at the Giants.

Julian's mind reached out into the night, watching the battle from a distance: the Grey Witch was strong enough to fight off the Storm Giants and still keep Julian and his Familiars captive. They could not escape. After the battle, she would kill both Apprentice and Familiars, and then...then she would become Julian!

Julian knelt, frozen by his discovery. Become me? But why? What could she hope to do by becoming me? There had to be an answer to that riddle! And there had to be some way out! He took a deep breath; he could not show his fear to his small allies.

Julian opened his eyes and stared at his shaken Familiars. "I need to sleep," he said. "I need to dream."

Rafir's eyes were wide in astonishment. "What!?!"

"His parents," Sebastian said quietly. "The Grey Witch is too busy to interfere with his dreams. Julian needs to speak with his parents."

·){ ·

SMASH!!! Down came more lightning. Thunder rattled the ceiling above the Witch's head. Parts of the Labyrinth were collapsing under the pounding, and dust filled every passage. The Grey Witch was shaken, but she could feel her own strength building.

"Careful, now, careful, Wizard," she murmured. "You wouldn't want to bury your wonderful Destiny's Darling along with the sweet little Grey Witch of the North, would you?" More lightning smashed down.

"And then again," the Witch muttered, "you whiny little mortal Wizard, you might just want to bury all of us." It was time to start repairs to the Labyrinth, so she sent pain surging through every part of her kingdom. She could hear her subjects moaning. From a distance, she could feel the

Apprentice and his Familiars also wince, and she smiled. But her workers — Gnomes, Goblins, and Hobgoblins began filling the Labyrinth, digging through broken tunnel sections, bracing sagging walls and roofs.

Some of the workers wore masks to deal with the dust. Some had tools. Some were dazed with fear and pain. Some would die as sections of the Labyrinth collapsed. The Grey Witch shrugged. There would always be enough of them to carry out her wishes until she could find better slaves.

Dark, grim words poured out of her mouth; power surged through her kingdom. As the Labyrinth slowly healed itself and grew stronger, she turned her attention to the creatures attacking her underground kingdom.

First, she would deal with the eagle: how would the Eye of Merlin enjoy becoming a moth? Her greyish dark skin pulsed with power. Transforming magic leaped out into the night. She watched the encounter from a distance, a cruel smile flashed over her face.

"Even," she muttered to the distant eagle, "even if I can't change your size, and you become a *giant* moth, no Storm Giant would obey you, and after that, the hawks of the sky would shred your shiny wings and send you crashing to the earth...." She fell silent, watching intently as her grey magic smashed at the eagle in mid flight — and white light flashed in the sky as the Eye of Merlin's protective spells drove off her own magic.

With a snarl, she turned her powers on the Storm Giants.

"Fire!" she muttered as her dark skin pulsed again with power. "Fire will burn the two of you into smoke!" Flames raced up through the night sky. With a wave of huge, cloud filled hands, the Storm Giants countered: heavy rains and stormy winds swept every last flicker of fire out of the night sky. More lightning, even stronger blasts, pounded down, and the Grey Witch was hurled to the ground. The cavern with its deep well collapsed, killing hundreds of the blind, monstrous fish beneath it.

Grimly, the Witch rose to her feet, and again her grey skin pulsed with power. A deep chill, a winter frost surged out into the night — and Storm Giants washed it away with warm rain. For the first time in hundreds of years, the Grey Witch felt tired.

"But I am still strong," she whispered. "Over thousands of years, there have been times when I took different forms and moved to new dwellings. But I have never been defeated. I will never be defeated."

Through the long, stormy night the Grey Witch and the Storm Giants fought with magic, while more lightning smashed down, and the kingdom of the Grey Witch began to collapse, tunnel by tunnel.

·)(·

Julian's dreams took him to a dark place where he could see nothing. He was lying on soft ground while the earth shook around him. Far above him, lightning pounded down again and again at the upper Labyrinth. His dreams hadn't taken him back to the tower, but he was somewhere inside the kingdom of the Grey Witch.

In the darkness, a soft voice whispered, "Julian." He struggled to his feet. Light flared from his staff. Julian found himself standing only ten feet from his parents — the real dreaming minds of his own parents and not just images he had made up for himself. They were older, but time had not yet bent them with age. Their faces were smiling with joy, though their eyes were wet with tears.

"My mother, my father," Julian whispered. "I never thought I would see you again, even in dreams."

"We are here," his father said, "because our master, though he has no great love for mortal mankind, still has a sense of justice."

"*Come to us, child,*" his mother said. *Three dreaming images came together like clouds meeting. Julian's head bowed, and he wept. But to be with them at all, even in dreams, was better than nothing. It was so much better than nothing.*

They drifted back from one another. Julian could see that now they were in the chamber where the possessions of the real Grey Witch of the North had been stored.

"*This Witch Creature has made the tower of your dreams part of her own underground empire and a trap for you,*" his mother explained. "*Anyway, that place is far too close to her own place of power, where she is now fighting Merlin's Storm Giants.*"

"*Look around you, Julian,*" his father added. "*This chamber still holds secrets. In some strange way, it still has power beyond the crystal.*"

Julian's mother nodded in the dim light. "*What sort of power remains here we do not know, but we have been permitted to study this Grey Witch of the North. We do not believe that she is human.*"

"*She is a shapeshifter,*" his father said, "*and so we guessed she was a Carag Mage. But she is no Carag Mage. When we used the limited force of magic allowed to us, when spells were cast to search for her past, it seemed that she was ancient, incredibly old, before the Carags were created as nightmare enemies for humans.*"

"*Some sort of lesser God?*" Julian asked. *Both his mother and father shook their heads.*

"*Before even the Gods were born,*" his father said softly.

"*I know so little of that history!*" Julian said. "*But all the Ancient Powers are gone, except....*"

"*Except the Creatures of the Darkness,*" his mother said softly. "*Julian, the Grey Witch of the North is a Creature of the Darkness, from the line of Demons and Dragons.*"

"*But all those beings have been no more than clumsy monsters,*" Julian said, shaking his head.

"*Not all,*" his father replied.

"*A few were more powerful than many of the Gods,*" his mother added, "*while others with much less power were able to form complex thoughts — including magic spells. That Creature of the Darkness with lesser power but able to perform magic at a high level is your Grey Witch of the North.*"

"*What the Creatures had in common was magic, a force of sorcery and great physical power,*" his father said. "*I know that the Wizards have not taught you well — they were trying to protect you, I suppose. But somewhere, somehow, there is information inside or around you that will help you fight this thing.*"

His mother lowered her voice, whispering, "*Julian, some other Power watches over you. There is aid that might come to you, help at the right time, under the right circumstances.*"

"*I have sensed something, too,*" Julian whispered back, "*though it is another mystery.*"

His parents stood back, preparing to withdraw from his dreams.

"*We have told you all that we know,*" his father said. *The faces of his parents were shining with love, but tears were streaming down their faces.*

"*Do you weep,*" Julian asked, "*because I am doomed? Because I will soon be dead?*"

"*You may die, but you are not doomed,*" his father said. "*You have at least a fighting chance. Fight, and do not let the Darkness drag you down! For some reason, your destiny has always been linked to the Creatures of the Darkness. We see now how they have always watched you from a distance. Our master tells us that the wisest of the Creatures speak of a mortal who will come to end their nightmare lives. Most call him 'The Destroyer,' while a few refer to him as, 'The Redeemer.' Perhaps your destiny is to become a transformer of the Creatures of Darkness, the light that sweeps away nightmares.*"

"*I'm a lesser Apprentice,*" said Julian, "*not suited for such an enormous task. You should not weep because monsters exchange unlikely rumors.*"

"*You have been disguised as an Apprentice,*" his mother said, struggling with her tears, "*while you have the power of a full-fledged Magician. We weep only because these are our last moments together.*"

As his parents slowly faded from his dreams, the small voice in Julian's mind that spoke seldom to him murmured, **This separation will not be permitted to stand. I will not permit it to stand.**

· ꠸ ·

Late into the stormy night, with much of her kingdom in ruins, the Grey Witch finally found an answer to the power of the Storm Giants. Her blasts of fire had been drowned by water, and her deep frosts had been washed away by warm rain. Dust storms had been blown into distant forests.

Black sorcery had not worked. She had created creatures out of her darkest dreams and sent them against the Storm Giants — who had simply crushed them with enormous feet. Her transforming magic had failed; all the dark, pulsing energy had been turned aside by counter spells that gleamed white in the darkness.

Finally, she had sent Hag Wraiths against Storm Giants. Like the Giants, Hag Wraiths were built from smoke, magic, and traces of real matter — for the Storm Giants it was seafoam, and for the Hag Wraiths it was metal. Hag Wraiths floated in the air, attacking Storm Giants with fingers like daggers, and sharp grey teeth.

If the Wraiths were tiny compared to the Giants, there were too many of them for the Giants to pull away and destroy. As four or five Wraiths were torn apart or smashed to the ground, hundreds of other Hag Wraiths ripped and chewed at the legs of Storm Giants. After a time, the Giants could no longer stand; they fell to their knees. Their cloudy hands were tearing at Hag Wraiths, and they were slowly losing.

When the Storm Giants were clawed to the ground, their magic would leave them, and the winds would take them.

"No more lightning, Smokey Ones?" the Witch asked, though she could only manage a whisper, and she was so exhausted that she was leaning against a wall.

Above the Storm Giants, the Eye of Merlin croaked out a cry of rage and frustration.

"And you," the Witch said to the distant eagle, barely able to whisper, "you stinking little flapper, you should go back home to your busy, busy master. War has come. There's no time for little flapping insects to play anymore with the lovely Grey Witch of the North."

But now, with her struggle finally won, she was losing control over her body. The Witch sent one last burst of magic into her empire so that neither victims nor slaves could escape. Then she slumped to the ground in exhaustion, losing her shape as the Grey Witch of the North, changing into a form no human would ever have recognized.

· X ·

In his place of power, Wotan sat back with a grim face and considered the Witch's victory.

"I admired the strength and wisdom of the young Apprentice," the Great God murmured, "and so I promised him aid. That pledge was a grave miscalculation, for if I keep my word, a second hero will die. What should be done? And how did this Witch Creature become so powerful?"

Chapter Thirteen

A Battle That Could Never Be Won

"**J**REACHED MY PARENTS," JULIAN said softly, "this one last time. They told me that they will probably never again be able to speak to me in this life. When they left me, their eyes were shining with tears. But I will not go away; I will never stop trying to free them." Julian trailed off, staring into the distance.

"And this Grey Witch who is not the real witch?" Sebastian prompted.

"I'm sorry," Julian said. "What I learned is that this Grey Witch of the North is not a real witch. Nor is she a shapeshifting Carag Mage. Instead, to my astonishment, she is a Creature of the Darkness, a very strange monster in disguise."

The three of them had retreated through broken sections of the Labyrinth, back to Rafir's "Chamber of Mysteries," where the crystal of the real Grey Witch had been stored. This chamber was mostly unharmed, although clumps of earth had fallen from the ceiling, and layers of dust covered almost every square inch of the chamber. After entering the chamber, they pulled their stored foodstuffs from hiding and then had a brief morning meal. Several levels above them, an exhausted Grey Witch still slept.

Rafir saw the two glancing up from time to time and guessed that they were wondering how long the Witch would sleep.

"So, it's not really a Witch," Rafir said. "What do we call it now?"

"'Grey Witch' will have to do for now," Julian said, "at least until we know more about what sort of Creature we're dealing with."

"That's what's bothering me," Sebastian muttered. "The Wizards have been so careful to keep us ignorant. The only Creature we knew anything about was that Dark Emissary, and only then because you and Galad had to fight the thing!"

"And that Creature is gone," Julian said. "One less out of many thousands."

"I can...." Rafir started hesitantly, but then Sebastian stood up, and began pacing through the dust. The little Familiar, normally so even tempered, had finally become angry.

"All of those explosions! Storm Giants overhead! Tunnels collapsing! Hundreds of Gnomes, Goblins, and Hobgoblins dying underground! And all we've learned is that we're fighting a Creature of the Darkness! When do we ask, 'So what kind of a monster is it exactly?' Goodness, nobody really knows, but at least we realize that it's a monster...so, what now?"

"You know...." Rafir tried again.

"What a wonderful outcome!" Sebastian continued, pacing in the dust. "I'm broken and dying or being eaten alive, and my last thoughts are supposed to be, 'I can die at peace now because I know it's a Creature of the Darkness that's going to eat my dead body. Thank goodness I finally learned that! Goodbye, world!'"

"If you could just...." Rafir said, this time a little louder.

"What were the Wizards thinking!?!" Sebastian's voice was raised, and his frustrated feet danced in the dust. "They sent us into this crazy, stupid trap without telling us so many of the things we needed to know!"

"What were the Wizards thinking?" Julian repeated. "Rafir, did you ever hear them talk about the Witch when you were invisible? What were they thinking?"

"I have absolutely no idea," said the fox. "But what I *do* know about is Creatures of the Darkness."

"What?" Sebastian asked. His voice was still raised, but he stopped pacing and stared down at the fox. "You mean Merlin told you things, but deliberately kept Julian and me ignorant?"

"No, wait," Rafir said. "Calm down for a moment. You know that when I was growing up, I was with Granny, the old Sorceress. After she showed me some of your adventures with Julian, she knew that I wanted to leave her and join you, so she tried to keep me entertained. We studied pictures of greater and lesser Gods. Another thing that we did was to watch images of Creatures...." The fox, embarrassed, hesitated. "Sometimes, maybe more than once a month, we would have Monster Night."

Sebastian stared at Rafir in astonishment. "Monster Night. I suppose she fed you milk and cookies while you watched great big images of Creatures of the Darkness gobbling up smaller monsters."

"Actually," the fox said in a low, embarrassed voice, "she made the images small, so they wouldn't be too frightening. And it was tea and biscuits, not milk and cookies."

Julian was suddenly focussed. "That's one of the things my parents told me — that somehow information about the creatures was near us. Rafir, you are that information. See what you can remember."

"Well, first of all," Rafir said hesitantly, "there was this thing called The Nameless. It's so hard to describe, but it ruled deep in the ocean. Some of the big, ancient sea monsters were still swimming around from long, long ago, but the Nameless ate them and...What?"

Julian and Sebastian had been exchanging glances.

"We think we need to *see*," Julian said gently, "not just have these things *described* to us."

"Seeing would be nice," said the fox, a little annoyed.

"Let's try again, Rafir," Julian said, "but this time, try to imagine your time with Granny. Start with something we could see clearly, distinctly."

Julian's right hand stroked the fox's red fur while the lips of the Apprentice whispered soft *words*. Rafir frowned as he tried to concentrate. A small cloud began to form in front of the three of them, but it was so blurry that it could have been a mountain peak — except that it moved.

"Keep going, Rafir," Julian said. "I'm beginning to think like a fox." Unkind words formed in Sebastian's mind, but he clamped his mouth shut. Julian needed to concentrate: he was trying to draw images from the mind of the fox so that all three of them could watch them.

The image slowly cleared until a creature that was as high as a cliff formed. Its four arms were formed of snake extensions, each larger than Kath, while its head was more massive than any lean snake's head, more like an enormous ancient lizard's, and its two stump legs were scaly, with spikes jutting out from them.

"The Lord of Snakes," Rafir whispered. "Way, way too big, and no hint of shapeshifting ability."

"A tall man wouldn't even come up to its knees," Julian added. "So, if we're dealing with a shapeshifting creature, it would need to be smaller."

Rafir sighed. "There was one that changed shapes with a funny name. It was called The One/The Many. Let me see if I can remember...." Images formed in front of the three, cloudy at first, then they slowly grew clearer. A huge creature was trampling through a forest, crushing trees as it moved. An enormous head had one eye in the center of its forehead. Five demonic horns rose from the top of its head. One arm held a huge club, while a second arm smashed trees aside. A massive tail helped to balance its form.

"That's The One," Rafir whispered. "The One can take on many different shapes — but only a single shape each day. In Erivan Forest, the Elf Lords and the Kindreds kept trying to drive it away." The three could see much smaller figures gleaming silver and white, hundreds of them on horseback. Some were launching arrows, while others hurled magic at the creature.

"Whenever The One got in trouble," Rafir whispered, "it would change into The Many." Now the scene grew darker as though night had come. Suddenly the huge monster seemed to fall apart, to shatter into a thousand dark scrawny monsters with small, beady eyes and dark teeth. They were much smaller and faster, so that they raced away into the night, into the depths of the forest where the riders could no longer follow.

"So that's The Many," said Sebastian. "Ugh."

"Good work, Rafir," Julian whispered. "But let's keep going. The Witch still sleeps, but not forever."

"I should start with the strongest," Rafir murmured. "I'll try to remember them with the worst of them coming first. Here's the Nameless, ruling the ocean."

An image formed, showing an enormous shark prowling the ocean depths.

"That's not much of a monster," Sebastian said, shaking his head.

"Wait," the fox said, concentrating. Suddenly, a large shadow passed over the shark. Alarmed, the shark tried to dive down, but before it could flee, an even larger creature with squid-like arms grasped the shark and bit into it with a beaky mouth. The great shark thrashed helplessly then stiffened and died.

"A sea monster," Sebastian breathed out. Rafir shook his head, concentrating. Seconds later, an even larger shadow loomed over the feeder and its feast. With three monstrous heads, each with many eyes and several mouths, the Nameless began to gobble up the other two predators.

"Wow," Sebastian breathed out.

"The next strongest was the hulking Spellweaver," Rafir said, panting a little as though struggling with his memories. Images formed, showing a smoke-filled court, with a massive figure seated on a throne. It had short, stubby arms ending in slender wrists and delicate hands. Powerful spells came from the Spellweaver's lips, and dark energies lifted from its slight fingers, passing through the smoke filled chamber, magic rising to do battle with the Spellweaver's enemies.

"That thing looks very, very powerful," Sebastian murmured. "Is it as strong as a Wizard?"

"It doesn't matter," Rafir said. "Granny told me that the Spellweaver vanished hundreds of years ago, lost in some unknown battle, maybe. Anyway, here are the rest."

Images formed and vanished, replaced by other images, ranging from huge spiders to monsters shaped like giant, dark, twisted Angels. A final scene showed two Creatures of the Darkness, on a frozen mountain top. Each had started to feed on the same dead Stone Giant that lay dead on the peak with ice beginning to cover its yellow skin. One Creature had begun at the Giant's head, the other at its feet. When they met at the middle of the Giant, at its waist, one monster's mouth extended a little wider than the others' and it gobbled up both the Stone Giant and the other Creature of the Darkness.

"Monster night," muttered Sebastian. "Ugh, ugh, and ugh."

"I was much younger then," Rafir said in a small voice. "Now I agree with you: ugh."

"I may never be able to eat again," Sebastian said, "and after watching all those horrible creatures we're no further ahead."

"We've missed something," Julian said. "Meanwhile the Witch is struggling to wake up. We need to go back to the monstrosities quickly. I think that there was something in the background of those images, or in the shadows. I could almost sense it."

They watched again as the Nameless swam through dark oceans. It was completely alone; not even the smallest fish dared to come close to it.

The Lord of Snakes stood by itself, without servants or slaves. Only clouds moved overhead as the Lord of Snakes stared silently into the distance as though inviting battle.

The One/The Many was attacked by the Elf Kindreds in Erivan Forest and no lesser creatures or servants came forward to counsel or defend it.

But in the court of the hulking Spellweaver, two shapes were standing in the shadows surrounded by smoke and incense. Julian's lips whispered *words* and the images brightened and cleared. The two shapes grew more distinct: two robed figures stood, reading aloud from heavy volumes.

"They look like Goblins," Sebastian whispered, "but larger."

"Goblin Mages," Rafir panted with an effort. "Granny said that Goblin Mages served the Spellweaver. I guess that they're supporting it with Goblin magic."

"But look beyond it, over there in the corner," Julian said softly. "There's a third figure, deeper in the shadows, and it's whispering along with the others. It is forming magic from its mind, so it doesn't need a book of spells...."

"And it's larger than the Goblin Mages," Sebastian murmured. "Is it some sort of Goblin Sorcerer?"

"Something is happening to its feet," Julian said, and he straightened, glancing upwards: above them, the Witch was stirring. When he stared again at the image the shadowy being's legs had reformed — to become the thick legs of a giant frog with webbed feet.

Above them Julian could sense the Witch groaning, struggling to wake.

"Could it be the Witch?" Sebastian asked. "But look — the thing's legs are changing again!" Now those legs had become the legs of a goat, ending in hooves.

"I'm guessing that this image is from long ago," Julian added, "when the Witch Creature didn't have complete control over its shapeshifting ability."

"I'm having trouble holding on to this image," the fox panted.

"Just a few seconds longer," Julian whispered, concentrating on the image. "Where's it going now?" The Witch Creature, still chanting, tiptoed with its goat hooves around a curtain. When it returned, its legs were once again those of a larger Goblin, and now its legs no longer wavered.

"Did it find some way to restore itself?" Sebastian asked. "Refresh the shape it picked? Or was it the Spellweaver trying out a new form?"

"No, it wasn't the Spellweaver," Julian muttered. "The Witch was an ally and servant of the Spellweaver's, a powerful Creature of the Darkness itself. Just as Wizards keep Magicians as allies and servants, the Spellweaver kept the Shapeshifter. As to the source and nature of the Witch's strength, we had better learn more about her — and quickly. Or else our time on this planet is going to be very, very short. Get ready because the Witch is awake."

The three shook with pain — the Witch had risen and was sending a blast of white-hot pain shooting through their minds. Then she shrieked down at them:

"You've been poking your rotten noses in the wrong places, you stinking little worms! But your end is coming — right now!"

·)(·

The Witch walked back and forth, her mind flaring in rage — and fear. They had found out about her former master, the Hulking Spellweaver!

They knew she was a Creature Indomitable! But they had no way to get this knowledge to the Wizards, or to any of the Great Gods who might wish to destroy her.

The Grey Witch of the North took a deep breath and cleared her mind.

"Julian the Apprentice," she muttered. "Destiny's Darling. Stronger than he looks, a being with some hidden powers, and a few secrets. All those tricks and secrets will be useful when I *become* Julian. Now's the time to finish them all off: Destiny's Darling, Little Talking Pests, and Big Coils. All of them, dead, dead, and buried deep, or gobbled up in the guts of monsters. Except I will need to keep a bit of flesh, maybe a few fingers from the Darling's magic left hand so that the memory of his form, my next body, will never fade. The time has come. This little game is over."

She took a second deep breath and walked a little unsteadily to her place of power. As she walked, all the fatigue from the last night's battle faded, and she reached with the strength of her magic through every chamber of her kingdom. The Apprentice was preparing for battle. She stopped, leaned back, and laughed gleefully.

· X ·

In Rafir's "Chamber of Mysteries," Sebastian again made a cone shape with his hands. Once sealed from the Witch, Julian looked back to Sebastian.

"That Hobgoblin Mage is calling to me," the little Familiar whispered. "He tells me that the Witch is ready to destroy us — but we can still use Hobgoblin tunnels if we need to get away from here. There's actually one in this chamber. All we need to do is shove aside a few of these chests."

"A final battle is coming," Julian said softly. "If Gnomes or Goblins, or Hobgoblins ever wished to be free of the Witch, perhaps it's time to change sides."

There was a pause, as Sebastian exchanged thoughts with the Mage.

"He says," Sebastian repeated, "that the Witch is far too strong. She was testing you before, but now she's going to kill us all. The mage is sorry that the Witch is so powerful, and that you were not strong enough to defeat her. He tells me that there are passages that the Witch doesn't know about. He is leading his people as far from this place as he can."

Julian shook his head. If the Apprentice failed, he thought that the Hobgoblin Mage was doomed; but he said nothing.

Overhead, the Witch struggled to organize her mind. *Calm, be calm. Has there been anything overlooked? Does Destiny's Darling have any more secrets?*

The Witch had been sitting in her place of power, making her final plans. Now she stood and began walking through the Labyrinth's highest levels. She peered into the Tower of Dreams, where two straw dummies lay broken on the ground. *Little Destiny's Darling, who was so very, very clever, never did find out that there was real magic hidden here, did he?*

She laughed, walking further down the hall until she could peer into her Hall of Mirrors. Her battle with the Storm Giants had left several of them shattered, with broken fragments on the ground. *No sense in bringing in Goblin craftsmen to remake these: I will soon be gone, and all those Goblins will be dead.*

All humor left her as she turned into the chapel alcove where the altar to her patron, the Great Dark God was still covered in dust. None of her slaves were allowed in this place, so it had not yet been cleaned. Absentmindedly, she took a rag from her cloak and dusted the altar. *No sense in burning bridges, is there? But it would be nice, one day, to find a way to destroy this stinking, unreliable, so-called Dark God.*

Will I still need a powerful patron when I become Destiny's Darling? Why not return to the Spellweaver, who has so successfully hidden itself? We never fully trusted each other, but we were allies for all those many years. It's worth thinking about, is it not?

With a sigh, she walked down the ramp from the upper levels and stood listening beside the great doors that led to the Marshalling Gallery. There was silence beyond the doors. Carefully, quietly she pulled them open, hoping to surprise sleeping guards.

Inside the chamber, Gnomes and Goblins came to attention, saluting the Witch, then bowing. Twenty Gnomes and twenty Goblins were always on guard, though the Marshalling Gallery had space for almost a thousand. The great hall had many entrances, lighting on all sides and high ceilings. The Witch saw that spiderwebs were gathering in several patches, but she didn't bother with her usual punishment.

Silly slaves, soon you will all be dead. She returned to the upper Labyrinth, letting the guards seal the door behind her. Walking up the long ramp, she returned to her place of power and turned to her next task.

Destiny's Darling, your final moment is coming. For my first step, I need to rub my hands in glee and then laugh, that's what Witches are supposed to do.

She did rub her clawed hands together and she did laugh; the laughter was real: she had a real ally, one that could be counted on much more than any of the remote Dark Gods. Taking a deep breath, the Witch spoke words that no human had ever spoken or even heard. A wall of mist formed before her, and in the darkness beyond the mist, large forms shuffled, waiting to be called over into the Witch's underground kingdom.

At their forefront, a large, powerfully muscled creature stood covered in light armor made of chain mail. The creature's helmet was off and batlike ears jutted out from the sides of a bald head. It seemed to have been born with scars, deep lines on either side of its dark green face. A long sword was sheathed at its side, leaving its hands free. Both those hands were turned, palms upward, and coils of smoke curled from them as though a force of magic was at its command.

The Witch laughed to herself. *My Ogre Mage! Leading a band of Stone Golems! When they're done with the Apprentice, they might as well kill off the rest of my underground slaves, so that nothing will be left of the Kingdom of the Grey Witch when I am gone! Then let the Wizards destroy the Ogre Mage. Nothing, not even a trace, will then be left of the Grey Witch of the North!*

"It is time," the Witch said. *"Repeat to me your instructions. Begin with the great serpent, Kath."*

"Stone Golems," said the rumbling voice of the Ogre Mage, *"will tear the serpent into ten thousand bits of scale and flesh and bone so that no magic will ever make it whole again."*

The Witch nodded. *"Now, much more importantly, what of the Apprentice and his servants?"*

"The Apprentice and his Familiars are to be destroyed," said the Ogre Mage in a rumbling, low voice, *"and then consumed. I will eat them myself, bloody piece by bloody piece."*

"Except?" the Witch prompted.

"Except for three fingers from the left hand of the Apprentice," the Mage replied. *"Those are to be given to you."*

What the Witch loved most about dealing with the Ogre Mage was that she could read his mind. While all his responses were correct, and he bowed in obedience, his mind was muttering, *Get out of my way, you Old Hag!* The Witch tittered with laughter.

"Come through then," the Witch said. *"As agreed, you will be the next ruler of this kingdom, when I depart for other tasks."* The Witch stepped aside, and the Ogre Mage passed through the wall of mists into the Witch's kingdom.

As he passed her, she could hear his mind muttering, *Finally! What was the Old Hag doing, playing so long with that feeble little human and his tiny allies?*

Behind him, seven figures followed, zombie-like, lurching forward with heavy feet behind their master. Stone Golems were made of brown granite stone with polished surfaces that glowed even in the dim light of the Witch's underground kingdom. Not a single thought passed from the Stone Golems to the Witch; their minds were filled only with their master's will, and they had no separate lives.

The Witch's eyes gleamed: there were only seven Stone Golems, but they were stronger than many hundreds of human warriors — at the end of a battle with humans in armor, more than a hundred humans would lie dead or dying, while the Golems would lose only a few chips of stone.

The Witch tittered at the image of broken humans, then grew thoughtful. The Stone Golems were so heavy that she wondered if they would fall through the flooring of the Labyrinth. But then the Witch shrugged: soon she would become Destiny's Darling, and none of the problems of her little kingdom would trouble her, ever again.

In the chamber where the belongings of the real Grey Witch were stored, Julian again prepared for battle. *Words* passed from his lips, and the walls stiffened, growing greyish white as the earth of the Labyrinth grew strong as stone. More *words* followed, and the tongue of Kath could be seen, a slash of red darting out from a hole in the air.

"But Julian," Sebastian said, "the Witch knows us, knows our strength. Why wouldn't we try the Hobgoblin passages? I've been shown all the passages leading from this chamber. All we need to do is push aside a few storage chests. The Hobgoblin Mage thinks that the Witch has no idea where they lead."

"We can't be sure what she really knows," Julian murmured, then he knelt beside Sebastian and Rafir. "Listen. There's a force of destiny still in this chamber. I don't know exactly what it is, but it's still here. I —"
He was interrupted by the distant shout of surprise and cries of pain. Julian stood and stared with his farsight through the walls of the Labyrinth.

"Tell us," said the fox. "At least tell *me*, because Sebastian can see things, too."

"A Mage," Julian said, "a huge being with powerful magic is coming for us...some sort of Troll or Ogre Mage. Behind him, beings of stone follow. They are coming for us, but when they see Gnomes or Goblins, they are killing them, too. The Hobgoblins have fled, trying to hide in secret tunnels, though I don't think they will survive for long."

Julian knelt again. "Listen to me. If the battle goes against us, you must escape through Hobgoblin passages, and seek the Wizards."

"We will never leave you," Sebastian said, shaking his head.

"You *must* leave me," Julian said. "It's the job of Familiars to survive and warn others."

"Would the Eye of Merlin flee?" Sebastian challenged.

"I'm not going to —" the fox started, but he was interrupted by more shrieking sounds as Gnomes and Goblins died in pain. Those sounds were followed by the heavy, pounding footsteps of their enemies. As the ground shook, bits of earth from the ceiling tumbled down.

Julian stood, and through a wall of stone regarded the Ogre Mage: the creature's body seemed incredibly strong, and it was armed with powerful magic.

Then suddenly in a pulse of five seconds, the Gift inside Julian sent a surge of thoughts and images racing through his mind.

Scaly bits of flesh and pieces of broken bone were lying on the chamber floor. Kath would die, torn into a thousand pieces by Stone Golems! He couldn't call on Kath! Kath go far from this place!

He could read the mind of the Ogre Mage! He was so tuned to the mind of the Witch that if she could read the creature's mind, he could, too! The Mage intended to eat his flesh but save three fingers. Why? Because the Witch needed to keep a bit of his substance, so she could maintain the shape of Julian!

He stared wildly around him: this Chamber was important to the Witch because she needed a piece of the real Witch to hold her Witch's shape! Somewhere within this chamber was a substance the Witch needed to hold on to her form....

But it was too late to do anything about that.

And finally, the small voice that spoke so seldom through his mind cried out, and now it was shouting:

We are facing a battle that can never be won! Flee! Flee! Flee! Or die!

Stone Golems smashed at the chamber wall, and it began to shatter. Sebastian leaped onto a heap of three chests, pointing downward. Julian pushed them aside and pulled up a gateway made of wooden planks. They stared down into a dark tunnel. The smell of dead and rotting things rose up from below, and they gagged. But then a section of tunnel wall crashed down, and all their other choices were gone. So, they dropped down a dark, narrow Hobgoblin passage, one that was filled with millipedes, centipedes, masses of earthworms, and tangles of webs made by spiders that lived on small prey.

Behind them, Stone Golems smashed down the chamber wall. Then their stone fists pounded down on the chamber's floor until it began to crumble. Pebbles and clumps of earth pelted down on Julian's head as he fled downward. Peering down into the narrow Hobgoblin passage, the Ogre Mage began chanting. Power in the form of grey mists began to gather to his palms.

Chapter Fourteen

The Distant Power of a Great God

FAR FROM JULIAN, FAR from the Grey Witch, far from the Wizards and their League, the Great God Wotan sat in his underground throne room, a dark cavern that was lit dimly by eight glowing, smoky fires. He leaned forward, lost in contemplation: a moment of decision had been forced upon him and his face was grim.

Two ravens flew through the upper air of the cavern, flapping through mist and smoke, sending images and sounds from the world outside down to the Great God Wotan.

I cannot see the Apprentice, sent the Raven named Thought, *for he is far below the surface of the earth, trapped in the underground kingdom of the Grey Witch of the North. Yet from a distance, I can sense his danger. The doom of the Apprentice is almost upon him.*

Great One, sent the Raven named Memory, *recall how you promised the Apprentice aid at the last. That moment is coming.*

Great Lord, sent the Raven named Thought, *you have known that if you keep your pledge, you will likely only send another hero to his own doom, without truly aiding the Apprentice.*

"The death of another hero would be added to those of the Apprentice and his two small allies," murmured Wotan. "Can this action be justified?"

The Great God rose and stepped down from his throne. Less than a hundred paces to the left of his throne, a huge stone carving was hung on the cavern wall, a carving showing an enormous face. As Wotan walked toward this face, even the Great God seemed small before the face of Mímir, Wotan's farseeing though lifeless advisor. Into this stone carving, Wotan had fed all the wisdom he had gained during his many travels throughout Alantéa and the Far Lands.

"Old Stone Face," Wotan said, "is it a proper act to send a second hero to his death, only to keep a promise made by a Great God to aid a first hero?'

Huge stone eyelids lifted, and eyes formed of blue granite stared down at Wotan. "Of what use is it to be a Great God," murmured the great stone lips, "if a Great God does not keep his promises? And is the doom of that Apprentice named Julian truly upon him? Then let all the Gods and Powers, Hidden and Unhidden, and Creatures of the Darkness beware, for their own destinies are ensnared with his."

Wotan nodded somberly, turning away and murmuring, "So be it."

Julian coughed as he pushed his way down through the Hobgoblins' narrow passageway. The air was filled with the smell of death and decay so that he could barely breathe. Magic from above was reaching for him, trying to clutch him, prevent him from fleeing. He couldn't see it in the darkness, but it felt like a rope, a living, magic rope, a force that would hold him still so Stone Golems could tear him apart, and then the Ogre Mage would consume his dead body, bit by bit.

His staff surged with power. Magic flared from his curled left palm. Julian groaned with the strain — and finally, he broke free.

Now, where were Sebastian and Rafir? He turned back up the tunnel's shaft. Light flashed from his staff. His two Familiars were only twenty feet above him — but they were trapped. Grey lines of power were binding themselves around the two, magic coils of a living rope. And the rope's binding was thicker, heavier than the cord Julian had struggled with: it had held them longer, becoming stronger with every passing second.

"Julian," Sebastian whispered, "this thing has us. Get away. Get out of this place while you can."

"Make this Grey Witch pay," Rafir muttered, still trying to squirm free. "Get help from the Wizards and make her pay."

Their words were brave, but their voices were shaky, and their small eyes were filled with fear. Julian climbed back toward them. Overhead, the pounding of Stone Golems was sending pebbles and soil showering down on all three of them, like a small landslide.

When Julian reached them, he whispered, "I've been able to hear the Witch's thoughts for some time now — it's like a small dark voice coming from a distant room. She calls me 'Destiny's Darling,' and she wants to become Julian the Apprentice and replace me. What she *doesn't* know is that all three of us are part of that same destiny. When we three are together, we become stronger."

Julian reached out to Sebastian and Rafir, touching each of them. "Now, be part of that destiny. Close your eyes. Think of magic as a small spark. Then let it burst into flame inside of you."

Moments later the grey coils of living rope fell away from the two Familiars, and the three scrambled further down into dark Hobgoblin tunnels that smelled so strongly of decay and death.

Above them, the Ogre Mage roared in frustration, then he smashed down with both fists against the chamber's earth flooring. Stone Golems battered downward with their own massive fists until the flooring made of packed earth finally gave way and they tumbled down to the level below.

Several levels overhead, the Grey Witch nodded to herself. "Interesting that Destiny's Darling had one last little secret, but I think that's the last surprise for the lovely Grey Witch of the North."

· X ·

Why was the Sword moaning? All the fighting was over, wasn't it? Galad was walking along the shoreline at Stone Mountain, while a soft rain drizzled down over his bare head. Behind Galad, the great fortress of Thorian was perched on top of Stone Mountain. Everything was still and quiet; even the wind had died down.

The only motion Galad could see came from the shore, where the ocean's breaking waves continued to push and pull dead bodies along the sandy beaches.

Galad walked through the rain, watching the dead men with a cool pity. They were soldiers and sailors, serving one of the Great Dark Gods. But really, they had only been pawns, part of a complicated game played by one of the Great Dark Gods, a game to keep the Wizards busy, while one of that Dark Gods' allies — the Grey Witch of the North — lured Julian into a trap. Now was the time for the Wizards to deal with the Witch, but there were still warships headed toward the League, and so the Wizards were being kept busy.

Galad shook his head: the Wizards would always be trapped defending their great fortresses. He stared back up at Stone Mountain, the fortress of Thorian, while at the League's center was Gravengate, and farthest west were the Halls of Merlin at Sea's Edge. Were any of those fortresses worth the loss of Julian the Apprentice? Galad didn't think so. Shaking his head, he walked slowly through the rain over sandy beaches.

Once again, the Sword moaned, and Galad finally drew it from its sheath. The Tarnished Sword was made of a mixture of metals and several different forces of magic. To an outsider, it looked more like a rusty mistake that would shatter at first contact. But the Sword did all the shattering and was never even scratched.

"All right, what is it?" Galad asked the blade. And the Sword darted and stabbed in several directions as though confused. Then it moaned again, sensing danger while not able to discover its source.

"That's not much help," Galad muttered.

Then suddenly, a chill swept over him, and he shivered. Seagulls, suddenly surprised, began flapping out to sea, calling out their harsh gull cries. They were flying desperately away from something.

Galad turned, facing the great fortress on the peak of Stone Mountain. Bits of metal were flying down toward him, surging through the air. What were metal pieces doing in midair, and what sort of things were they? They even looked something like...his own armor. Yes, that was his helm, and his light chain mail and his own shield speeding toward him as though carried by invisible ghosts.

Galad laughed. Was he going to be attacked by his own armor? Was an invisible ghost going to put on Galad's armor and force him to fight himself? It was hard to tell, but the metal flying through the air seemed to lack a weapon, even a pike or a dagger. Maybe the ghosts flying down with the armor had grown so old that they were beginning to forget things.

"Get ready to slash metal," he muttered to the Sword. "It's my own armor coming after me — that's all right because I'm not inside it." But instead of getting ready to defend Galad, the Sword sheathed itself firmly at Galad's side.

Then hands, invisible, powerful hands, swept over Galad, pulling corselets of metal over his body, arming him for battle. Galad, too, was extremely strong, and he forced his right hand down to his Sword hilt — but the Tarnished Sword would not draw, it would not obey Galad.

"What!?!" Galad cried to the Sword. "You're not going to help me? You're not even going to fight?"

The Sword gave out a moaning cry, of sorrows mixed with the beginnings of its battle cry. It was getting ready to slash magic and metal — very soon.

Galad stood, forced into armor by a force far greater than his own strength, greater even than the might of magic that the Wizards possessed. Winds and mists gathered around him, and he could hear the croaking sounds of large birds — crows or ravens.

From Stone Mountain came radiances of blue and gold, magic leaping from Thorian's place of power. The air around Galad grew dark, but before he was swept away, he could see the Eye of Merlin raging toward him, crying out in fury.

The Eagle was too late. Thorian's magic with its blue and gold magic rays was brushed aside. Galad was swept away from the shoreline of Stone Mountain, perhaps never to return to the Wizards and their League.

· ꓧ ·

As the Ogre Mage and his Stone Golems crashed down through the chamber's flooring, the Hobgoblin tunnel systems began to collapse around Julian and his Familiars. Pressed by soft soil that reeked of decay and death, they squirmed downward a few more feet, then Sebastian led them sideways until they broke into a larger passage, one that had air that was easier to breathe.

Sebastian had led them into a Gnome passage where the tunnel's earth was reinforced by stone. This tunnel shook, and stones fell from its roof, but it wasn't collapsing — not yet, anyway.

"Where next?" Sebastian asked, taking a deep breath. "Are we going to run or fight?"

"Both," Julian replied, "but nothing we can do leads to victory. And yet we have to try everything. I can read some of the Witch's mind: she wants the Ogre Mage and his Golems to kill everyone, first the three of us — and then all the other underground dwellers. Then the Wizards are supposed to destroy the Ogre Mage and his Stone Golems.

"Nothing will be left of this Witch Creature and her kingdom once she takes my form. Does this Ogre Mage understand his own danger? Do the underground tribes have any idea that they are doomed? How can we show them? How can we break these alliances? Think, Julian, think."

Julian called on the small voice inside him, but it had no answers. Shudders shook the Gnome tunnel as Stone Golems battered their way toward the Apprentice and his Familiars.

"Let's try it," Julian whispered. "Let's try it, but not die in the attempt."

"Try what?" Rafir asked. "You know I'm getting so angry that part of me just wants to bite this Witch Creature. At least get one bite of her before we're done."

"Maybe later," Julian said, then he turned to Sebastian, "We need to go back up to the burial chamber where the Hobgoblin Giant lies. Can you get us there?"

"I think so, yes," Sebastian said, and now his mind was seeing other passages as the Hobgoblin Mage guided him. "I have to take us through the well system where the blind fish feed, then up."

"That's good," Julian murmured. "Stone Golems will follow, smashing everything in their paths. Let all the underground tribes see that the Ogre and his Stone Golems are their real enemies, and not us. Let's go."

Julian's staff flashed light as they climbed up through the Gnome tunnels. When the tunnel's surface became more level, Julian broke into a run. The air was getting much better. Behind them, Stone Golems had smashed their way into larger Gnome passages, and Julian could feel the ground shudder as they lurched their way toward him.

Magic was reaching for them...but the Ogre Mage was too late because just in front of them was the broad, low door made of grey ironwood that led to the well system and the blind fish creatures that swam in the river below. They pushed through the door, then carefully sealed and barred it behind them.

Sounds of rushing water still greeted them, but most of the well system had been ruined. The well's stone walls had toppled over into the river beneath them. Cautiously, Julian peered down into the rushing water, *reaching*...most of the blind fish had been killed during the Witch's battle with Storm Giants. If the Witch succeeded in becoming Julian, the rest of the fish would be doomed because no one would be left to feed them.

Rafir had stayed beside the door, sniffing the air, feeling the ground tremble as Stone Golems lurched closer. Panting, the fox turned back to Julian and the broken well system and looked at the Apprentice with big, questioning eyes.

"I know," Julian said, taking a deep breath. "They are almost here. Where next, Sebastian?"

"Back through Hobgoblin tunnels," Sebastian muttered. "That smell is going to stick to me forever."

"Smelling bad is better than being dead," Julian said. "I know that's not much of a choice for heroes, large or small, but let's go."

They gagged again as they entered the upper Hobgoblin passages — if anything the smell of rot and ruin had grown stronger. Behind them, Stone Golems smashed down the door to the well system and began pounding down the chamber's stone walls, toppling them into the well below. More blind fish died and were carried away by the powerful currents of the underground river.

Sebastian led them through dark, narrow passages that curled to their left then led higher. As Stone Golems smashed through Hobgoblin passages the narrow tunnels began to fall apart. Damp soil pressed against them. Sebastian and Rafir felt their fur crawl with worms, centipedes, and spiders. They squirmed upward, gagging from the smells around them.

Finally, the Hobgoblin passage ended; overhead was a roof of wooden planking. Above them, Julian sensed that the Great Goblin Demigod lay in his burial chamber, surrounded by charms and bits of paper with prayers written on them. Julian tried to shoulder the planking aside, but too much weight had been placed on it. He raised his staff, whispering a *surge of ruin* against the barrier. Dust and soft soil and charms left by the underground tribes collapsed over them.

Coughing, they climbed up into the burial chamber. Julian's staff flared with light. More dust and earth had fallen in the chamber, but underground dwellers had carefully dusted the Goblin Demigod free of dirt. The dead Giant lay with his arms folded as though sleeping in peace. The number of charms and scrolls of prayers around him seemed to have doubled since the first time they passed through the burial chamber.

"Many have passed through this place," Julian whispered. "I guess that in times of trouble more of the underground dwellers come to pray to their Giant."

"And he couldn't save a single life," Sebastian finished. "Julian, those Golem things have broken back into the Labyrinth. We have only a moment before they come here, so do what you have to do. Then we'll run...again...until there's no place left to go."

"The underground tribes seem doomed," Julian murmured, "but every being should be allowed to fight one last battle...."

Julian raised his voice, calling so that all around him could hear: "They are coming to kill us — the captives of the Witch — then destroy all of the underground tribes! All of you will die! You must rise and defend yourselves!"

Then magic filled his voice, and now when Julian called out, his words shook the Labyrinth:

"Rise and defend yourselves!"

No response came from the underground peoples; all they could hear were the *thumping* sounds of Stone Golems pounding their way through the Labyrinth. As Sebastian led them back into Goblin passageways, Stone Golems reached the door to the Giant's Burial Chamber. Massive stone fists battered the door down. After smashing the Giant's broken dead body to the ground, Stone Golems followed Julian into Goblin passages, pounding, always pounding. As Julian raced through the underground passages, he sent a thought into the mind of the Ogre Mage:

The Witch wants you dead, too, Mage. She knows that after she has left her kingdom, the Wizards will destroy you. Then nothing will be left either of the Grey Witch of the North or the Ogre Mage serving her. There is nothing for you in this place and you should leave this doomed kingdom.

I will feast on your dead flesh, replied the Ogre Mage, *and after, I will be Master of this underground kingdom!*

I will have become the most bitter of meals, Julian sent, *and both you and your Stone Golems will be dust and ashes soon after.*

"I have no words that will stop them," Julian murmured as he hunched forward, staying low to avoid smashing his head on the low ceilings of the

Goblin tunnels. "And nothing we say or do seems able to turn Gnomes, or Goblins, or Hobgoblins against the Witch."

"I see what you were trying to do," Sebastian panted. "You were hoping that Gnomes or Goblins would rise and defend the Burial Chamber of their Demigod. But they couldn't, and so we run, run, run until we wear out or come to the end of the Labyrinth and all its smaller tunnels."

They were headed back to the main Labyrinth through twisting Goblin side tunnels when a *shudder* passed through Julian. He stopped and straightened, nearly thumping his head on the low ceiling. Then he listened carefully to the small voice that spoke so rarely inside his mind: **Matters have changed. We may now be allowed a fighting chance to remain alive.**

"Sebastian," he whispered, "can you find a way for us down to the depths, to the bottom caverns where water slides over stone floors? There's a chance — if only a tiny one — that we might be able to escape from this Grey Witch of the North."

· ⅀ ·

They paused at the end of the Goblin tunnel. Moisture, a shallow puddle was seeping underneath the door. When they pushed the creaking door open, more water slid into the Goblin tunnel.

As they stepped into the bottom cavern, the dim light in the cavern was filled with shadows, but they could see that another human, larger and armed for battle was kneeling on the cavern's far side, face turned to the cavern wall.

"Galad," Julian whispered.

"Hello, Julian," Galad said, still kneeling.

Chapter Fifteen

The Ogre Mage and His Stone Golems

RAFIR BLINKED OUT OF sight and crept toward Galad while still invisible. Was Galad only an illusion? Or was the warrior a Carag in disguise? He didn't *smell* like one. Through their magic, Julian and Sebastian could hear the Tarnished Sword humming at his side, so they knew that Galad was as he seemed. But why was the warrior still kneeling on the cavern floor? Why hadn't he turned and faced them? Cautiously, they walked slowly over the cavern's damp floor until they stood at Galad's side.

"By all the Nine Billion Gods," Julian murmured, "how did you come to this place?"

"I have no idea," Galad said softly. He still knelt. Just in front of him, two Gnome soldiers lay propped up against the cavern wall, bleeding from their mouths. Their bodies shook as they struggled to breathe.

"These drew weapons against me," Galad explained. "The Sword would have slashed them dead in seconds, but I would not draw it. I only used my shield to smash them back. But I used strength enough to disarm humans — and these Gnomes turned out to be smaller and lighter than humans. Can you help them?"

Kneeling beside Galad, Julian called on his healing arts. Whispered *words* echoed through the cavern, mixing with the sounds of running water washing over stone floors. Moments later, the breathing of the Gnomes steadied, and they slipped into healing sleeps. Galad and Julian stood and studied each other with searching eyes.

"I'm glad that they live," Galad said quietly. "Because of the Tarnished Sword, death is always around me, though there is never a good reason to slay simple sentries. Now, moments ago you called upon the Nine Billion Gods, asking how I came to this place. I must guess that one of those many Gods, a very powerful one, captured me as I walked along the beaches at Stone Mountain, and then sent me to your aid."

"Earlier in this strange adventure one of the Powers gave me information and advice," Julian said, searching his mind, "but he would not let me recall that God's name. Did that God send you here? Or has some other Power simply balanced this contest for his or her own amusement?"

"That we may never know," Galad replied. "Meanwhile the Sword is beginning to hum its blood song. Where is this Grey Witch?"

"She can't be happy that you have entered her kingdom," Julian said quietly, glancing overhead. "Something is happening above us, in the upper part of the Grey Witch's kingdom. Where, indeed, is the Grey Witch?"

· X ·

Many levels above them, the Grey Witch exploded in rage. She left her place of power, sweeping through a long corridor until she stood before the altar of the Great Dark God.

Then she shrieked: "What have you done to me?!? In our pact, you promised protection! Yes, you drew off the Wizards, but now you've let some other meddling God send help to Destiny's Darling! What are you going to do now?"

As before, no answer came from the Witch's ally, and so she turned, snarling, "I suppose that now is the best time to let your identity become known. I will send word out so that all the Nine Billion Gods, and other Powers, and Creatures Indomitable, and Magicians will know how you plotted against the Wizards and their League — and were so feeble that you could not force your will upon them."

This time a response came: from a shadowy, midair space above the Dark God's altar, an enormous black hand shot out. This hand was formed of six fingers, covered in dark scales and they leapt at the throat of the Grey Witch and began to squeeze.

"Ugh," groaned the Witch as she was lifted off the ground, choking.

·)(·

"The Grey Witch is distracted," Julian muttered. "Meanwhile, we have other, much more pressing problems. Listen." In the silence of the underground cavern, they could hear not only the sounds of water sliding over stone surfaces but now the *thud, thud, thud* of Stone Golems was growing louder as they pounded their way downward.

Rafir blinked back into view. "Stone Golems are coming."

"Led by an Ogre Mage," Sebastian added, "much stronger even than Julian. Thank the Maker you are here."

"One day," Galad murmured, "I will meet a force greater than I and the Sword can handle. I understand that I will never die in bed. Now do not take offence, but normally I would embrace each of you, but you are somewhat gamey, covered with a nasty, slimy mix of decay and death."

Julian laughed. "If you spend too much time in Hobgoblin tunnels, you will smell like us. Anyway, it's too late to wash. Stone Golems are coming." As he spoke the Sword began to sing, and its strange song finally woke the fallen Gnome Soldiers. Still bleeding from grey mouths, they staggered to their feet and began backing away from Galad and Julian.

"Battle and death are coming," Julian said quietly to them. "Tell your leaders and your peoples that they can die fighting, or they can die trying to hide. If we defeat the Witch, you can all live in peace, but if the Witch triumphs, all the Goblins, Gnomes and Hobgoblins will become as dead as your Goblin Demigod. For your own peace of mind in life or death, the underground tribes should rise, form an alliance, and give battle."

While one Gnome sentry fumbled with a hidden doorway, the other glanced back and forth to the humans — and to a section of cavern wall that was beginning to crack from the pounding of stone fists. As the two Gnomes scurried into a tunnel's side passage, the cavern's limestone wall shattered, and the first of seven Stone Golems entered the cavern.

"Maker's Touch!" Galad muttered, watching as a second then a third massive creature entered. "Are these things as powerful as they look?"

"Stronger," Julian replied.

"But not swift and agile, I hope?" Galad asked.

"Not swift. I will save magic for the Mage," Julian said.

"Then it's time to reduce their numbers," Galad muttered, then he called out to the Stone Golems, "So it's lurchy, lurchy, lurchy, hey lads! Maybe it's time for all of you to have a bit of a sleepy time."

Galad skipped forward, shield set aside, swinging the Tarnished Sword with both hands. He hewed at the first of the Stone Golems.

Clang!

The Tarnished Sword bounced off the Golem's stone surface, then the blade howled in frustration. Only the smallest stone chip fell from the Golem's body to the cavern floor. In the meantime, a fourth and fifth Golem entered the cavern and began lurching toward Galad and Julian with their arms extended, like slow moving horrors in a nightmare.

"That's it!?!" Galad called to the Sword. "*Clang!* And that's all you can manage?" The Sword howled again.

Sebastian's mouth sagged open in surprise. *Clang? Some God uses incredibly powerful magic to send Galad to our aid, and he can't help so we're all going to die anyway? That makes no sense at all!*

Stone hands were groping for Galad, but the warrior edged away, then slipped under another Golem's reach, and hewed at a third.

Clunk!

And now when the Sword rebounded from the Golem's stone surface it had smashed a chunk of stony shoulder from the Golem. As the stone of the shoulder struck the cavern floor, it fell apart, dissolving into dust.

"You're learning, Sword!" Galad cried. "Though maybe not fast enough!" Galad slashed a third time.

Whine!

Again, the Sword met resistance, but now it finished its cut, and a stone hand fell to the cavern floor and became a small mound of dust. The wounded Golem lifted what was left of its stone arm to its face and studied it with a puzzled look. Other Golems were lurching toward Julian...who backed away from them, while his lips whispered spell words. No magic came from the Apprentice — not yet.

"Finish your spell!" Sebastian hissed.

"Not yet," Julian murmured, then he raised his voice. "Get back, Galad! You need your shield. The Mage is upon us!" Galad turned, leapt, and rolled, coming to stand beside the Apprentice, now with a shield in his left hand, and the Sword, still snarling in frustration, in his right.

And then the Ogre Mage stepped into the cavern, both hands with palms open, surging with power.

Black magic leapt from the Mage — but at Galad, not at Julian.

"Down!" Julian called out, and he stepped in front of Galad. A shielding of white light blazed before the Apprentice.

Galad dove forward, squeezing through the legs of one Golem, then as he rolled, he chopped at the legs of a second creature of stone.

Smash! And now the Sword exploded with sound and flashed with light. With one leg severed, the Stone Golem toppled slowly to the ground — but then it began crawling, arms extended, groping for Julian. Galad rolled, then slashed again, severing the Golem's other leg at the hip...and still, it crawled toward the Apprentice.

Julian was backing away, his shielding of white light beaten and battered by the more powerful Ogre Mage. Galad was rolling and scrambling over the cavern floor, while the fists and feet of Stone Golems smashed down, trying to crush him. Sebastian hovered in the air just behind Julian, while an invisible Rafir hid in the shadows, glancing at the cavern ceiling where stalactites shuttered in the air in the air like a force of doom.

It would be nice, thought the fox, *to have those huge stone columns drop down on the Mage and his Golems. Go ahead, drop, fall...though it probably wouldn't hurt any of those creatures.*

"I am your master," the Ogre Mage snarled at Julian, "and I will still consume your flesh, though the carcass of your larger mailed ally will feed the blind fish in the underground river, for I do not need his flesh...."

Galad was up, darting toward Stone Golems, but now they stood together in a tight row, arms extended, reaching for Galad — six of them remained standing while the seventh crawled slowly over the cavern floor toward Julian.

As the last strands of Julian's white shielding gave way, the Apprentice cried out, "Now, Kath, now!"

The serpent's huge head leapt out from midair, smashing the Ogre Mage from his feet. Then the snake's head pulled back and vanished, leaving only a shadow in the air.

With the Mage down, Julian started his spell again, still backing from lurching Stone Golems. Galad dodged backwards, and with one stroke severed the head of the crippled Stone Golem. The creature's head became dust, but the rest of its body kept crawling toward the Apprentice.

"It's too stupid to die," Galad muttered, but then he used a mailed foot to shove the fallen Golem away from Julian. The headless Golem kept crawling over the damp cavern floor, though now it was headed away from them, far to their right, toward the darkest part of the cavern where shallow pools of water were forming on stone floors.

"One done," Galad said grimly, "six left." Then as the Sword moaned, Galad turned to Julian. The Apprentice had finished his spell. Hands made of grey stone were rising from the cavern floor...and those grey hands reached for the brown stone ankles of Stone Golems and held them fast.

Other stone hands reached for the fallen Ogre Mage and pinned him to the floor.

"That's magic fit for a Wizard," Galad muttered. "Now where's this silly so-called Witch?"

"Too soon for the Witch," Julian said through clenched teeth. "This struggle is far from over."

On the floor of the cavern, the Ogre Mage snarled — something between anger and laughter. His own spell words were harsh and brief: larger stone hands than those summoned by Julian rose from the cavern floor, and these were blacker than the darkest night. Black hands crushed grey hands into powder and the Ogre Mage rose from the floor. Stone Golems, suddenly freed, lurched again toward Galad.

"You are stronger than you seemed, Apprentice," the Ogre Mage muttered, "and your serpent ally was nicely concealed. I think I should deal with Big Coils first." And the Mage reached with his huge right arm into the shadowy midair circle where Kath had disappeared and groped for the serpent.

"Galad..." Julian whispered. But the warrior was already moving. Slipping as fast as lightning outside the reach of Stone Golems, he leapt forward and slashed at the Ogre Mage with his Tarnished Sword.

Light and sound exploded through the cavern as enchanted metal met enchanted flesh. The Sword whined in fury, then the huge left arm of the Mage thudded to the cavern floor...and the Ogre Mage groaned.

Galad dove away, circling back toward Julian, rolling once then crouching — and he chopped once again, this time at the brown stone leg of the nearest Golem...and missing one leg, a second Stone Golem toppled over.

The Sword then began its victory song. Julian was quiet, watching the Mage carefully. No blood was spurting from the Mage's fallen arm, or from its shoulder. Snarling in pain, the Mage called upon the power of his cupped remaining right hand. The severed arm on the floor twitched, then it leapt into the air...and attached itself again to the Mage's shoulder.

The only sign that the Mage had been wounded was a break in its chain mail armor. No blood was left on the floor, not even a trace of its dark flesh.

Galad's face tightened: half a smile and half a snarl. *Next time let the Sword slash its head off. Let's see how well the Ogre's magic works when it has no head.*

"This Tarnished Sword has some power," the Mage murmured. "It will become my own weapon when I stand over your dead bodies."

"The Sword would never serve you," Galad said, his voice completely unafraid. "And I have been in many battles, Mage — I can sense the stroke and counter stroke of each clash. I do not believe that you will stand over our dead bodies. I think we will stand over yours, while your Stone Golems become powder on the ground, damp and wet and wasted."

"You should listen closely to Galad's words," Julian said quietly. "This fight is becoming much more complicated. Use your strength as a Mage to look into the future to behold your own destiny."

The Ogre Mage stared into the distance. "A rabble of Hobgoblins is coming to your aid. These creatures are small, soft, and fearful. Why should I be concerned?"

"They are many, and they come with ropes and snares and cloths," Julian replied. "Even Stone Golems move poorly when bound by many coils of rope and blinded by cloth hoods."

"And you have your warrior with his enchanted sword, and your powerful serpent ally," the Mage snarled, "and your own slippery, treacherous, partly-hidden strength. But these matters have never troubled me before." The Ogre Mage again cupped his hands. Smoke and magic gathered to his palms.

"Wait just for a moment," Julian said softly. "A thought, a vision of the future lies just at the edge of your Sorcerous reach. Let that vision enter fully into your mind."

The Ogre hesitated, staring into the distance, and then he murmured, *"Battle is renewed. We are too evenly matched so that I cannot quickly prevail. Again, the sword slashes a limb from me, and this time the serpent emerges from nothingness, and gathers the limb with him. My arm passes forever into regions unknown to me. I become a cripple, and the last vision I see before death is the Tarnished Sword, smoking and moaning as it arcs toward my eyes, and then I become a dead thing...."*

The Mage then raised his voice, calling out, "Grey Witch of the North! Come aid me now or I will leave this place! You have lied to me, and even planned to leave me to die in the lost world of your dark tunnels! Make these things right or I will be gone!"

In the silence that followed, an invisible Rafir forced himself to breathe quietly; but his small heart was pounding.

"It seems," Julian said in the same quiet voice, "as though she is busy, perhaps dealing with some other conflict. If you leave now with your Golem servants, we will let you go in peace. If you stay, either you will die, or I will die. No other choices will be left to us."

"Then I am gone," the Mage said grimly, "and I will take my servants with me." As he turned away from Julian, his mouth spoke harsh, forbidding spell words. A curtain of dark mist formed before the Mage. Stone Golems — five of those remaining — began lurching toward the Mage and the wall of dark mists that were gathering in front of him.

The Ogre Mage hesitated before departing, but then he turned to Julian.

"This contest is not over," the Mage said to the Apprentice. "I have never been defeated; I will never be defeated. If you survive the Witch, I foresee that we will meet again...at the Goblin Market in Far Avalon. And when we meet there, no Tarnished Sword will come to your aid."

The Mage passed through his enchanted curtain into a land filled with dark mists and was gone. Five Stone Golems followed and also vanished. One crippled Golem was crawling slowly toward the dark curtain when the magic gateway disappeared. The lost, one-legged Golem stiffened suddenly, then it became a pile of dust on the damp cavern floor. Finally, the last of the Golems, headless and blind, stopped crawling through the darkness when it was also transformed into dust. Then shallow streams of water carried the dust of all Golems deep underground.

"Very, very nice," Galad muttered. "It's wonderful to see how Ogre Mages treat their loyal servants. And I thought the Wizards were sometimes indifferent and uncaring! Enough. What is your lovely Grey Witch up to?"

"What could the Witch be doing?" Julian asked softly. "At times I can sense some of the Witch's thoughts, yet now her mind is hidden, so I have no idea what she's doing."

·)(·

The Grey Witch was struggling to breathe. In a few seconds, the Witch would have to give up its form, showing itself to be a shapeshifting Creature of the Darkness. The Great Dark God holding her might have suspected her true form, and then it would know. All her future plans would become worthless.

But then the hand around the throat of the Witch relaxed just enough that the Witch could breathe and speak — a little.

"Great Lord," the Witch croaked, "I have made a terrible mistake. You in your majesty have helped me always, and then I threatened you, something that should never have happened."

Scaled fingers squeezed again, then slowly relaxed.

"I understand that words are not enough," the Witch croaked. "Let me make matters right. I will destroy the intruders. Then I will feed all the underground peoples to the sightless fish. After, I will vanish into the Mid-World. Not a trace of my underground empire will be left, and none will ever know how the Wizards' two greatest servants, this slippery Julian, and this clumsy Galad, were destroyed. The Wizards will be fatally weakened, and none will know how you — with the slightest twitch of your fingers — began the destruction of the Wizards and their League."

The hand let more air into the Witch, though her voice still croaked: "Release me and I will send a flood of pain against all those in this underground kingdom. Then I will destroy them all." Hesitating, the hand relaxed a little more — then it finally vanished.

"Humans do have a saying," the Witch muttered, rubbing her throat. "If a task must be done, then do it yourself. Enough of allies. Enough of servants. Death is coming for you, Destiny's Darling."

Chapter Sixteen

The Transformation
of the Grey Witch

"TELL ME ABOUT THIS Grey Witch," Galad said, sheathing the Tarnished Sword.

"There was once a real Grey Witch," Julian replied, "but she was overcome by a hidden monstrosity, a shape-shifting Creature —"

Then pain swept over all of them, and they hunched down. Groaning sounds echoed into the cavern: Gnomes and Goblins and Hobgoblins were all moaning in pain.

"Come," Julian whispered to Sebastian and Rafir, and the two Familiars stood beside Julian, each touching one of his legs. Julian reached out to Galad, and the warrior extended his own hand.

As they linked, the pain lessened, although it did not vanish.

"The Witch calls me 'Destiny's Darling'," Julian said quietly. "We've found that Sebastian and Rafir are part of that destiny — when we touch one another, we become stronger. This time, when you joined us, the pain grew even less, so here in this underground kingdom we learn that you, Galad, are part of that shared destiny."

"'Destiny' is too big a word for me," Galad muttered. "One step at a time. Let's deal with this Witch first. You called her a shapeshifter, a Creature of the Darkness. Not one single legend even whispers about such a being."

"The Wizards tried to protect us," Sebastian said, his old anger at the Wizards stirring. "Instead, they left us ignorant and weak."

"In fairness," Julian said, "this particular Creature of the Darkness has kept itself very carefully hidden, seldom changing shape, always taking on the form of some living thing or person, then disposing of the original being so that not even a trace was left. The monster now wearing the form of the Grey Witch of the North wants to discard its old form and become Julian the Apprentice with his strange 'Destiny,' whatever that might be."

"Let's see," Galad said grimly, "how many different shapes this Creature of the Darkness can take after the Sword has chopped it into small pieces."

·))(·

Hundreds of feet above Galad, the Witch heard the warrior's words, and she began muttering, "Your stinking little sword will never touch me, never come close to the lovely Grey Witch. And yet on second thought, the Sword may have its uses. Killing off all these scurrying undergrounders is going to be busy, busy work. Let the Sword do some of the slaughter, while the Apprentice wastes his magic destroying Goblins and Gnomes."

She laughed as she sent another wave of pain through her kingdom, then she cried to her subjects in a great voice that reached through every inch of her underground empire:

"Arm yourselves! Form battle lines! Destroy the Intruders!"

Julian stared upward, nodding grimly. "Chopping up the Witch has just become more complicated. She is going to force us to fight through the

underground tribes before we can get to her. There may be a thousand or
more beings underground, and the Witch wants us to kill all of them before
she destroys us herself."

Still linked, Julian spoke silently into their minds:

*I've been thinking about one way to weaken the Witch. Gnomes, Goblins
and Hobgoblins may no longer follow the Grey Witch of the North if she loses
her Witch shape. We think she needs a link to the original Witch to be able to
keep her form. We know that fact because she planned to keep three fingers of
my left hand, so she would always be able to maintain my Apprentice shape.
Sebastian, can you get us back to Rafir's "Chamber of Mysteries?" If any part of
the real Witch remains, it will be in that Chamber.*

"First back through Goblin tunnels," Sebastian muttered, "and then
upward through Hobgoblin passages."

At Galad's side, the Sword whined faintly.

"For once, I agree with the Tarnished Sword," Galad said. "The Sword
and I have no idea where we are, or where we're going."

"We're at the base of the Labyrinth," Sebastian said. "At the next level,
an underground river runs through the Witch's kingdom, a place to dispose
of dead things. A little higher —"

"Words are nice," Galad interrupted, "but not all that helpful. I don't
suppose the Witch left you a map, did she?"

"There *is* no map," Julian said, "but Sebastian and I can show you what
the Labyrinth looks like. Sebastian is linked to a Hobgoblin Mage, who
wants badly to have the Witch disposed of, as long as he's not in any danger
himself. Sebastian?"

As Julian whispered spell words, he and Sebastian touched. On the
floor of the cavern, images grew.

"Here we are at the base of the Labyrinth," Julian said, "while above
us are the middle passages, with their underground river, and a place

where Gnomes honor their dead. At the next level is Rafir's 'Chamber of Mysteries,' and another great room where the Demigod of the underground tribes, a giant being lies, surrounded by the written prayers of his followers. This is as far as we've gotten, but above that level is the Witch's Marshalling Gallery, and at the very peak is the Witch's place of power, a place I have only visited when the Witch invaded my dreams." As Julian spoke, each of the levels glowed, showing the complexity of the Labyrinth, then finally all the many passages filled out, a honeycomb of many tunnel systems intertwined.

"By all the Nine Billion Gods," Galad muttered, "here's an empire right under the noses of the Wizards and they had almost no idea what was happening. What do these different colors mean?"

"I let the main Labyrinth gleam with gold," Julian said, "as hopefully, it will one day lead out of here. Red marks the Goblin passages, while the Gnome tunnels are blue-grey, and those smaller burrows coloured green were made by Hobgoblins."

Galad rubbed his face, trying to remember his old lessons. "What were we taught? Gnomes in the upper passages, Goblins somewhat lower, and Hobgoblins at the lowest levels. Each tribe has a passage at each level. How, or why did the Witch let them get so jumbled up?"

"I don't think she cared," Rafir said. "She was concentrated on becoming Julian, 'Destiny's Darling,' but feel free to ask her yourself. I'm not going to bother."

"All right, that's a start," Galad said, patting the Sword, which was beginning to whimper at his side. "You said something about Hobgoblin tunnels. Does that mean I'm going to smell like you three?"

"Probably worse," Rafir added, with a touch of malice. "We're smaller and can slip around narrow passages. You're much bigger and will need to squish your way through."

"'Squish' sounds really nasty," Galad said, "but let's go before the Sword starts to complain again."

Sebastian led them back into Goblin tunnels, then up through narrower Hobgoblin passages. The smells of rot and ruin were worse than Galad had ever imagined; even the Sword was silent as though holding its breath. Finally, they squeezed out from Hobgoblin passages into the main section of the Labyrinth.

Galad let himself take a deep breath, then he muttered "I can do 'ugly,' but that was really disgusting —" He was suddenly quiet, listening to rustling sounds. One moment the Labyrinth was empty, then in the next moment bands of Gnome soldiers were pouring out of side passages. They filled the passageway, forming a tight formation that stood five Gnomes deep, spears extended in front of them.

"I am *not* happy about this," Galad said.

"Sebastian," Julian called out, "is there a way around them, through different tunnels?"

The Familiar shook his head: no. "If we can just get beyond them, we can be out of the main Labyrinth in a few seconds."

"What must be done," Galad said, drawing the Tarnished Sword, "will be done." The Sword began moaning. Small trails of smoke began lifting from its surface.

"Wait!" Julian called out, raising his staff. "Shield your eyes!"

Light flashed from his staff, blinding the Gnomes. Galad sheathed his Sword and leapt forward, smashing the spears, and mailed bodies of the Gnomes aside with his shield. Julian was behind him, Rafir on his shoulder, while Sebastian flew overhead.

Once through Gnome battle-lines, Julian turned back and light from his staff flared again, blinding the Gnomes a second time. Then

Sebastian led them forward until they were able to slide left into a Goblin passageway.

"Very neat work," Galad muttered, as they raced forward. "Why have the Wizards kept you at the Apprentice level? Are they afraid that you might one day become an Adept or even a Sorcerer and leave their service?"

"You should ask Merlin that question," Rafir panted. The fox was scrambling along an uneven surface. Part of the roof of this section of the tunnels had fallen and the fox was leaping over stones and clumps of earth.

"One day I might reach the Adept level, and become a Magician," Julian added. "I will never rise higher than that."

Inside Julian, his inner voice whispered, *But the Sight is strong within us, and will grow stronger than any Adept's Sight — if we survive.*

"We need to sneak a truth potion into Merlin's goblet," Galad said, "so he will be forced to tell us what's really going on in his mind. Where —" Galad halted. Moments before, Gnomes had been forced to fight them, and now Goblins were leaping out of side-passages. Bands of Goblins surged out, armed with bows and arrows, and there was a fire in their eyes, lit by the Witch and the pain she lashed them with.

"Wait!" Julian cried out. "Do not —" The first volley of arrows leapt at them. Most were waved aside by Julian. Three fell away from Galad's armor. One gouged Rafir's side and the fox cried aloud.

"Now there's no help for it," Galad snarled. He slid his visor down and drew the Tarnished Sword. The Sword moaned.

"Cold," Julian muttered, "a deep chill. Goblins are the most warm-blooded of the underground tribes." Waves of chilled air leapt from Julian's staff. Dark Goblin bodies became suddenly white with frost. Some slid to the ground. Others backed away, seeking escape into side tunnels. A few tried to draw a second volley of arrows, but their fingers were frozen, and bows slipped from their hands.

"Rafir, Rafir," Julian said, rubbing his hands over the bloody fur of the fox, "please don't die and leave us." Spell words raced from Julian's lips, and the fox shuddered, then drew a deep breath.

Sebastian said nothing, though sorrow and fear surged through his body, while his mind whispered, *Rafir, please don't die and leave us.*

"That hurt," the fox whispered. "Just a little bit lower and you would have needed a new Familiar." The fox took a few steps, circling as though checking his tail. "But now I'm feeling stronger. Let's go."

Half-frozen Goblins were pushed aside. The Witch punished her servants with even greater pain so that all the Goblins still standing held their heads with frozen hands. Wincing in pain, Sebastian fluttered up to Galad's mailed shoulder, while Rafir crawled up to Julian's. When Julian and Galad touched the four were again linked and their pain could be managed.

As they pushed on through the Labyrinth, bands of Goblins and Gnomes tried to block them, but their efforts were half-hearted, as though they realized that the Witch would punish them whether they won or lost. Many had now fallen to the floor of the Labyrinth, wrapping their heads with heavy, damp cloths as though that would prevent the Witch from delivering pain to them.

"Just think," Sebastian panted, scrambling over the tunnel floor. "This Labyrinth is part of the Wizards' League. It's too bad they never bothered to visit this place themselves."

"They defend their fortresses and the coast," Galad said. "If I hadn't learned about this underground Labyrinth, I would probably have made the same decision. Oh no...." Sebastian had come to a corner of the Goblin tunnel and was scratching at a lower wall: they were re-entering the messy, tainted Hobgoblin passages.

"One more section," Sebastian murmured, pushing his way through a mass of soft soil that teemed with earthworms and millipedes. "Then we're through." Overhead, dusty spider-webs hung down, and they were forced to push through them.

Far above them, the Witch finally realized their destination, and shouted out in rage:

"Stay away from there, you stinking little maggots! Or...."

"Or what?" Rafir muttered. "Or you'll try to hurt us? Or you'll try to kill us? That would be a surprise, a real shock, wouldn't it?"

Then all four of them were silent as they pushed through dark, soft passages while brushing webs from their faces. Galad tried holding his breath, but after a few minutes, he had to gulp air that was filled with rot, ruin, and the decay of small, dead creatures.

Finally, they were through the Hobgoblin section, re-entering the main passage of the Labyrinth. Scattered Gnome and Goblin soldiers were leaning against the walls of the tunnel system, while some lay on its floor. The Witch had weakened them with so much pain, that none could even reach for weapons.

"Good work, Witch," Galad muttered. "It would be nice if all the enemies of the Wizards had the same talent for leadership."

They neared Rafir's "Chamber of Mysteries." As they came around a corner, Julian could still sense a trace of magic from the storage chamber of the Witch. The walls that Uraks and Kath had destroyed had been partially repaired, but a few gaps remained, and they slipped inside, though Galad was forced to shoulder his way through.

Inside, Galad stood in silence for a moment, staring up at ceilings covered by dusty webs. Then he glanced at storage chests, many now broken open with all their clothes and toys and housewares and moth-eaten clothing spilled onto the ground.

"So, these," Galad said, "are the things of the original Grey Witch. Somewhere in here is the Creature's link to the Witch of old, maybe a dried bit of flesh — but how are we supposed to find that?"

"We would have trouble," Julian said, shoving a chest to the chamber's centre, "finding a small piece of the original Witch. That means we need to destroy everything. Help me." Galad began lifting then hurling chests into the chamber's centre. More strongboxes broke open. China shattered, framed pictures were smashed, and metal containers broke apart. Old spell scrolls and slips of paper scattered onto the ground.

Overhead, the Witch shrieked. Their sense of pain vanished, as the Witch lowered the pain levels for the underground tribes, hoping to rally them to battle once again.

"The Witch never liked us being here," Julian said, panting. "Now, we understand why. Sebastian, Rafir, find everything you can. Work together — Sebastian, if you use magic to sniff, Rafir can dig down where you point. What we are looking for might be small, or it might be large."

"I found a grave before," Rafir said in a small voice, "but it was a child's grave."

"I sensed it too," Julian said, "and it's not the Creature's link to the Witch. It's just another of this Creature's evil deeds. Pile stuff onto this mound. Work. Dig."

They located the last of their provisions and tried to eat some of them while working. Galad accepted only water.

Sebastian and Rafir found the crystal ball belonging to the original Witch and placed it in the centre of the mound that Galad and Julian were building. To Sebastian's senses, it was now a dead thing, without a trace of its original magic.

Galad was sweating now. Dark smears from the tunnels ran over his hands and forehead and he wondered if he would ever get clean before he died. "So, what kind of magic," he asked Julian, "are you going to use to make all this stuff vanish?'

"My powers aren't strong enough," Julian replied. "We will need to use fire."

Galad let the strongbox he was holding slip to the ground. "Fire?" he asked. "Then everyone underground will die from the smoke, except for a few creatures that seal themselves in side-passages or can escape into the meadows overhead."

"No one will die if I can help it." Julian stopped, staring toward the main Labyrinth. Goblins, lashed by pain and given false promises of freedom, were assembling outside. Galad picked up the fallen strongbox and hurled it on the mound. More goods followed: large chests from Galad, anything hinting of magic from Julian, and smaller items from the Familiars.

"That's almost all of it," Julian murmured, then he raised his voice: "Now, Witch Creature, let everyone see you as you really are! Your old links will be broken by fire! Fire will cleanse this chamber!" He raised his staff, calling out spell words, and the mound burst into flames.

Smoke rose swiftly to the chamber's ceiling, and they began to cough. Holding his breath, Julian pointed his staff toward the chamber's ceiling and spoke spell words, calling upon *a surge of ruin*. Debris from the roof fell back into the chamber. A hole in the chamber's roof formed, then smoke surged upward.

"I can vent more smoke later," Julian muttered, coughing, then he peered into a gap in the wall leading to the main Labyrinth: Goblins were choking, backing away, though there was still some menace in their eyes.

"They won't give way without a fight," Julian murmured, then he whispered soft *words,* and the smoke in the chamber lessened, swirling upward. But now with flames surging through the chamber, heat was becoming a problem. Tangled spider-webs were burning and even bits of wood that lay some distance from the bonfire were bursting into flames.

"Julian," Sebastian said, tugging at the cloak of the Apprentice. "We need to go. Where next?"

"Up to the Witch Creature's place of power," Julian said. "We saw that she has a place just below the upper Labyrinth. She calls it her Marshalling Gallery. But first...." Julian turned and raised both his hands as though dealing with a greater power. "Grey Witch, the real, human Grey Witch of the North, hear me now! If there is any part of your magic still alive, know that we now go to confront the monster who betrayed you. We will destroy this Creature if we can, so be comforted. Rest in peace as you sleep the Long Sleep. Farewell."

"Nice to take time," Galad muttered, "to say goodbye to a ghost. How far up is this 'Marshalling Gallery'?" Sheets of sweat were running down Galad's body, with the heat made greater by the chain mail he wore.

"It's just below the peak of this underground kingdom," Julian said. "Sebastian, we can't use the main Labyrinth — or the Goblin sections. Can you get us higher?"

"Yes," the little Familiar said softly, and his mind whispered, *Witch, here we come.*

· X ·

The Witch Creature stood in her place of power, calling on the underground tribes to gather in the great Marshalling Gallery that lay just below her place of power. The Goblins were obeying her, while the Gnomes moved slowly, reluctantly. Hobgoblins, as always, were slowest to respond. None of her slaves seemed to have much hope. She prepared another blast of hatred, but then she smelled burning and saw that traces of smoke had risen even to the highest level of her kingdom.

"All my plans will come to nothing," she muttered, "if everyone, including Destiny's Darling, chokes to death, then burns." She began murmuring *words* that no human had heard before or would ever understand. Hidden tunnel shafts opened, and smoke began escaping into the air above her kingdom. In the fields and forests overhead, the fall wind and rains swept the smoke west until it mixed with autumn mists.

Then the Witch felt the first *shudder*: the hidden bits of the real Grey Witch were beginning to burn, and the Creature was losing its hold over its Witch form.

"Destiny's Darling," the Witch snarled, "filled with so many nasty little tricks. But the lovely Grey Witch has a few tricks of her own. Did the Ogre Mage speak of meeting the Apprentice in the Goblin Market? The Apprentice will never leave here, but the Witch has been to the Goblin Market, where potions are sold, and powerful forces of magic bartered. Better to forget how she got to the Market, or what she was forced to do there. But now is the time for those potions from the Goblin Market to be used."

She turned from her place of power, walking down the hall into the false tower she had created to trap the sleeping mind of the Apprentice. Straw figures — dummies created to mock the parents of the Apprentice — had long since been broken apart and lay like litter on the floors.

"It would have been so much easier," the Witch Creature muttered, kicking the straw aside, "if the Apprentice had lost hold of his dreaming mind up in this tower. I would have become Destiny's Darling, and that young human would be so very, very, dead."

On the third shelf just behind the books that were not really books, the Witch took three hidden packets of powder and carefully opened them.

With some disgust, she noticed that her left hand had lost its human shape, becoming a confused mess of scales and snake-like extensions..

She stared down at the packets and their contents. For unknown reasons, Goblin Mages coded their magic by colour. One packet contained a powder that was green-black, while the second was reddish black. The third had a dark powder so black that light had trouble reaching it. Very carefully, the Witch Creature poured each of the three packets into her mouth and swallowed their contents.

In seconds, she could feel enormous forces surging through her body. Her hands became again human, though still dead-looking. More important than her hands, both her mind and her magic were growing steadily stronger.

"Twice the strength!" she cried. "I will need more of these potions. Perhaps Julian the Apprentice will meet the Ogre Mage in the Goblin Market — except that it won't be the old Destiny's Darling, it will be the new version. Maybe I will let the Mage know this fact before he dies in great pain." She laughed, then suddenly her mood darkened.

"Why those little double-dealing Hobgoblins with the souls of stinking rats!" she snarled. With her magic grown stronger, she could sense that the Hobgoblins were slipping through the vents she had opened to let the smoke escape.

She sent a blast of pain and hatred at their fleeing forms. A few of those closest to her stiffened and fell dead, but many had already escaped into the fields and forests and other Hobgoblins were scurrying up through the vents, leaving the Witch's kingdom forever.

"Ah...." With her mind growing more powerful, she could see now how the Hobgoblin Mage had planned the escape of his tribe over the years. First, he had obeyed her when forced to, waiting for his chance, all the time using smells that would drive her away. Hobgoblins had used the smell of decay and death to protect themselves! Why had she not understood that earlier?

She walked out of the chamber, kicking the straw of dead dummies in disgust. Now would come battle, the death of her enemies, and the beginnings of her new life. Suddenly, she stopped and straightened. Her mind was still racing with all three magic potions surging through her body.

She might lose the coming fight! There was a chance, although a very small chance, that she might lose! Down the hall was the altar she had built to worship the Great Dark God who had been her hidden ally. She walked silently down the hall until she stood before the altar, thinking hard.

Would the Dark God help me win the coming battle? No, he would destroy me in an instant, whenever he had the chance. If I died, no one would ever know how he conspired against the Wizards and their League. There is no one for me even to tell, no one to aid me...unless...I turn to the Spellweaver, my patron of old, from so many long years ago...greatest of those left of the Creatures Indomitable, more powerful than most of those beings calling themselves Gods...in the past I whispered to him, but never really tried to reach him. Now I am stronger....

The power of the potions had made her more powerful and wiser — but also more cautious, and so she moved some distance from the altar to her former patron. Let the Dark God believe that she still worshipped him. Back in her place of power, she reached again to her master of so many, many years ago.

"Great one," she whispered, *"for so long you have hidden away from me. Yet I know that you still live. I still dream of you, my Master of Old, the Spellweaver, greatest of the Creatures Indomitable. Know that I would still be your servant if I could see you, even if I could hear you...."* Then a thought reached out to her from an enormous distance.

!?!

Spellweaver, I am here! Your shapeshifting ally of old. The Witch, and onetime Creature Indomitable, thought to her old ally.

Never speak of me! Not to anyone!

No, of course not. The Witch was silent for a moment, mind churning. *Yet a time of peril may be coming for me. At the last, if all else fails, may I call upon you?*

From the other side of their link, the Witch felt a surge of strange emotions, carefully concealed thoughts and fears and desires, then finally, a response came.

Call me if you need me. I will help you at the last.

"So that's done," the Witch murmured. "Now for the Apprentice." But in the back of her mind, a small voice was whispering, *The Spellweaver was hiding his true thoughts. What was he really thinking? What did he truly wish? Could the Spellweaver be as untrustworthy an ally as that Great Dark God who must not be named?*

She shook her head, clearing all those strange and confusing thoughts from it. She walked down the ramp that led to her Marshalling Gallery. She pulled open the great door that was made from beams of wood, reinforced by dark metal. The guards were still standing, but hundreds of other listless Goblin and Gnome soldiers struggled to their feet and raised their weapons.

Instead of blasting them with pain, the Witch — with her mind made now wiser by the three powerful potions — cried aloud: "Battle is coming! Victory will be ours! We will feast tonight!"

· 𝕏 ·

Smoke rose with them as they climbed, but it was now only a trace in the air. Most of the grey clouds of ash were escaping through the Witch's vents. An invisible Rafir ran in front of them, while Galad was just behind the fox, holding the Tarnished Sword. As they neared the Marshalling Gallery of the Witch, the enchanted blade began to hum.

Suddenly the fox blinked back into view.

"You should put the Sword away," Rafir said. "That Hobgoblin Mage is just ahead of us, together with a band of Gnomes and a few Goblins. Has this Mage become some sort of ally?"

"If he wishes to be," Julian said. Galad shrugged and sheathed the Sword. Just around the next winding turn of the Labyrinth, the Hobgoblin Mage stood waiting nervously. Behind him, more than twenty Gnome soldiers were armed with slender spears and large shields. A half-dozen Goblins had joined with the Gnomes and were armed with bows. None of them looked truly eager to fight anyone.

When Julian and the Mage met, they reached out and touched each other. Thoughts and images were exchanged.

"It seems that your people have escaped," Julian said. "Why did you not join them?"

"I should have." The Mage looked away nervously. "No doubt I should have. But these," he glanced to the Gnomes and Goblins behind him, "sought me out. They have seen how careful you have been to preserve their lives, while they understand that the Witch cares nothing for them. This underground empire of the Witch has become our nightmare prison, and you are their only real hope to break free. So, on this day, we will fight at your side."

"I had thought," Julian said softly, "that the Witch Creature would lose its witch form so that all the underground tribes could see that they served a monster."

"That has not happened," the Mage murmured. "Do you see the sweat beading on my forehead? Do you see how my hands are shaking as though diseased? I am like that because the Witch's strength has surged, perhaps even doubled. Who might have foreseen this moment? Yet now it's too late to dream of escape. We need to go and give battle. Perhaps there is something beyond defeat, forces greater than death."

"That is not a stirring call to battle," Galad noted. "Julian, I love having allies and wish that we had legions of Gnomes and Goblins. Yet I need to ask this: is it possible that some of these might turn against us when we confront the Witch?"

"That is a very good question," Julian replied. Then he turned, carefully studying the faces of each of their new allies. Finally, one Goblin archer and two Gnome soldiers looked away from Julian. Then, without saying a word, the three put down weapons and left.

Other Gnomes and Goblins fell in behind Julian, as he walked cautiously toward the Witch's Marshalling Gallery, speaking in hushed tones with the Hobgoblin Mage.

The doors to the great hall opened outward into the Labyrinth. As with other major gateways in the kingdom of the Witch, these gates were made of massive beams of treated wood, reinforced by bands of dark steel. Other gates had been the height of a tall man, while these were easily three heads higher than anyone in their party.

Galad came to a halt before the doors then stood back from them. With his right hand, he drew the Tarnished Sword, while in his left hand he held a shield that had been bashed and dented many times, and only partially repaired.

"I have the strongest armor among us," Galad told them. "Pull these gates open and I will be the first through. Let's see how much shapeshifting this Witch Creature can do after the Sword has carved her into small pieces."

Julian shook his head. *You won't face the Witch Creature. She will want you to kill her slaves before you reach her.*

The gates were pulled open, and Galad stepped through.

Shouts and jeers greeted him. Hundreds of Gnome soldiers smashed the metal tips of spears against shields, while Goblin archers stomped the floor of the Marshalling Gallery with mailed feet.

"Shields," Galad called to the Gnomes behind them, and shields were raised. All knelt behind them except Julian. Waves of Goblin arrows lashed at them. Julian waved many away; others fell harmlessly from Gnome shields.

"Now there's no help for it," Galad murmured, and the Tarnished Sword moaned.

"Watch your eyes!" Julian called out. A blinding light flashed from his staff, forcing Gnomes to shield their eyes. Then cold surged from his staff, and Goblin fighters fell back, bows slipping from their frozen fingers.

"Now, Galad," Julian cried. "Carve weapons — but do not carve flesh!"

Galad leapt forward, his body and shield smashing Gnome soldiers aside, while his Sword slashed at spears. Pushed forward by Julian, their own Gnome allies began to guard his flanks.

Gnomes and Goblins fell back. Metal spears were slashed to the ground. Galad was becoming the tip of a dagger, a weapon pointed at the Witch. Julian stood behind Gnomes and Goblins. In a battle of the few against the many, the few were winning.

The Witch responded with a shout that filled the Marshalling Gallery:

"You stinking good-for-nothing rabble! Why can't you even kill each other off and save me the trouble!"

Gnomes and Goblins winced; some held their ears.

"Behold the Witch," the Hobgoblin Mage called out. "She is beginning to take her true form." Rustling sounds rippled through the Chamber. Heads turned. A few Goblin arrows were launched, but Julian waved them away, as one by one, all eyes were drawn to the being they had known as the Grey Witch of the North.

A Witch's head was still there. But now it was just a floppy dying thing on the top of some grey blob-like creature. All the Witch Creature's clothing had been torn into tatters, as her blob form spread out in all directions. As they stared, black tentacles belonging to some sea monster began extending from her blob-like form, reaching across the floor toward Julian and Galad.

"Hee, hee, hee," the Witch Creature tittered. "I suppose I've lost track of my old body. Whatever will happen next?"

Even the head of the old Witch was wrong: it sagged, as though it had once been a sack filled with air, and now all the gases inside it were slipping away.

"I'll tell you what happens now!" the Witch thundered. "I'm going to take on a new form, and then you will all die! Die, die, die!"

A shielding of white light flared in front of Julian. Galad pressed forward, less than ten paces from the Witch. Then he leapt. The Tarnished Sword arced through the air.

And the Witch Creature spoke four harsh words in a language never heard by living mortals.

Everything was frozen for a moment, then Galad fell backwards, so weak that he was barely able to hold onto the Sword. Julian pushed past Galad's bodyguards to stand at his side.

"Destiny's Darling," the Witch said, reaching for Julian with a dark tentacle. More white shielding flashed in front of Julian. Galad staggered to his feet. The Sword, almost moving by itself, slashed at the Witch's tentacle. Goblin arrows began arcing toward the Witch.

The tentacle slithered back before the Sword could reach it.

"Always so difficult," the Witch Creature murmured, then the Witch spoke spell words again, this time five harsh words. Every being — except for the Witch Creature — stood frozen in the Marshalling Gallery. They stood frozen by a force of magic that was so powerful that none of them could move.

The sagging head of the Witch Creature breathed a deep sigh of satisfaction. "So that all of you know," the head muttered, "I'm making a little game of this. The weakest will die first, not the weakest in strength, but the weakest in willpower. I wonder who will be standing at the last, before finally falling dead to the ground."

The sagging puffy head of the Witch laughed. "Will this big, grim hero of a warrior be the last one standing? Will it be Destiny's Darling gasping for breath? Could the Tarnished Sword be the last thing to die? Hah! There goes the first of them!"

At the rear of the Chamber, a cluster of Gnomes had been slipping toward the exit. Now they fell, dying, slowly, gasping for breath.

"See, the weak ones are going first," said the Creature, its witch's head nodding as it sagged. In twos and threes, Gnomes and Goblins were slumping. Some were breathing shallowly while others lay frozen in the first stages of death.

Come on Rafir! The fox shouted to himself. *You're the hero, the invisible fox. At least bite the Creature once before you die!* Rafir stretched and strained, though he was unable to move.

Galad's mind was shouting at the Sword, calling on it to leave his hand and slash the Creature. *You, Sword, you have moved without me before! Rise now and slash the Witch!* Overcome by the Creature's dark magic, the Sword's dreaming sleep grew steadily deeper.

Julian was waiting until the Creature's witchy face turned away from him. Then his mind shouted:

Now, Kath, now!

"No, no, no," the Witch Creature said, almost gently. "I think we have seen the last of Big Coils. Though I wish you and the rest of these squirming, dying things would quiet down. All your thrashing minds are making this much more difficult than it should be."

Galad was frozen, unable to move, but he could hear those words, and he called again on the Sword to strike. And deep inside Julian, the small voice that spoke so rarely in his mind cried out, *Resist! Fight until the end! The Witch is not in complete control!*

Sebastian was hidden, shielded behind Julian, struggling to free himself.

This Creature can't see me, can't sense me. Move a finger first, Sebastian, you weak, silly little Familiar. Then move your hand and free Julian.

Nothing moved; nothing would ever move again. The little Familiar's anger at the Wizards boiled over. *Merlin, you had so much wisdom and you let this happen! How could you ever have been so completely fooled!*

"Stop all this thrashing!" the Witch Creature yelled, and with that burst of temper, in a brief second, hundreds of beings did move, a finger here, a hand there, a mouth slipping open to moan.

Slight sounds rustled through the Chamber then it was again still.

Only the fire of Sebastian's anger allowed him to break free. Still hidden behind Julian, he reached out to the leg of the Apprentice with both of his small hands and shook him — but Julian still stood frozen.

Sebastian tested his wings. The Witch Creature could sense motion but still could not see Sebastian. Still filled with fury, the little Familiar rose in the air and hurled his only weapon down at the Witch Creature.

A packet of sneezing powder.

As the packet struck, Sebastian called down, **"Die, Witch, die!"** Then he hurled a second packet.

And the puffy Witch's head of the Creature sneezed, then it sneezed again.

Galad was suddenly in motion. The Tarnished Sword arced down, slashing at the Creature's blob-like substance. Light flashed, and an explosion burst through the Chamber. Streams of yellow and green fluids discharged like pus from the Creature's wound.

The puffy Witch's head howled in pain. Flames leapt from Julian's staff, setting fire to the Creature's seeping fluids so that it moaned as it turned and fled, trailed by flames.

Gnomes and Goblins rose from the Chamber's floor, calling out in fear and anger. Some fled, while others joined the fight against the Witch Creature. Streams of Goblin arrows arced after the monster. Gnome spears stabbed at its soft substance.

The Witch Creature reached the Chamber's end and found that there was no place left to flee — the doors leading to the Grey Witch's place of power were too narrow for its blob-like shape to squeeze through. Snarling, the Witch Creature turned to give battle.

First, it caused the fire from its wounds to die down, so that it smoked rather than blazed. Then its Witch's head began calling out dark words of great power.

But before it could finish the spell's third word of power, a bolt of jagged black lightning leapt from Julian's staff.

The Witch's puffy "head" exploded. The Creature turned and fled again, moaning for help from deep inside its dark blobby substance.

"The monster calls for aid," Julian muttered, "but help from where?" Then he was silent because assistance was coming — another being of enormous power was suddenly drawing closer.

"Back, Galad, back!" Julian called out. "All of you, get back from the Witch Creature! Stay away from it!"

Gnomes and Goblins stood frozen for a moment, then began backing away. In front of them was the Witch Creature, while behind the Creature an enormous dark curtain was forming, covering the long, broad wall of the Chamber.

"Julian, what is happening?" Galad called out.

"This Creature of the Darkness is calling upon a greater Power," Julian said, "a much, much greater Power." His voice rose. "Get back, all of you stand away from the Creature!"

Galad lowered the Tarnished Sword, though he did not sheathe it. "So, are we doomed? After this long struggle, and after defeating a powerful Creature of the Darkness?"

"Doom is coming," Julian said, still backing from the Witch Creature and the Power it had called up. "Doom, but not necessarily ours."

Now the dark curtain at the Chamber's end faded into smoke.

Beyond it lay a grim fortress, massive dark stones piled on massive dark stones. The sky overhead was cloudless, even airless. Stars burned brightly overhead, though it looked as though no sun had ever existed in that faraway land.

It was as though they were staring at the dark side of the moon.

"The Spellweaver," Julian breathed out. "The shapeshifting Witch Creature has called on its old patron, the hulking Spellweaver."

Now the Witch Creature began moaning in fear, starting to pull back from the dark fortress — though now it was too late.

Huge strands of dark smoke leapt from the fortress. Reaching into the Marshalling Gallery, hundreds of strands gathered around the Witch Creature's blob-shape and began to tug it toward the fortress.

It's like a giant spider, thought Rafir, *dragging a giant worm into its underground lair.*

The Witch Creature struggled, its own powerful tentacles grasping into the Chamber's walls, floors, and ceiling.

Gnomes stabbed at tentacles with spears, while Goblins drew daggers and hacked at the Witch Creature's blob-shape, while all the while the Creature moaned.

"It is calling for help," Julian said softly to his Familiars, "and no one in her old kingdom will even begin to give it aid."

Sobbing with pain and fear, the Creature was pulled from the great hall through the enchanted curtain and into the dark fortress.

And then the being known as the Grey Witch of the North was gone. The dark curtain it had called upon vanished, leaving only the chamber wall. Weapons were lowered. A hushed silence fell over the Marshalling Gallery. Their long, nightmare struggle with the Grey Witch of the North had finally come to an end.

Chapter Seventeen

The Road Back

IN THE DISTANT, ENCHANTED kingdom of the Mistress of Illusions, the three sisters sat glumly around a listless fire that provided more smoke than warmth. They were resting in a small guardhouse cabin, a few hours before sunrise. When dawn came, they would call out the morning watch.

Kayal watched Naith as she half-heartedly poked at their fire, while Issah went to a window so she could stare out into an overcast night sky. Their brother, the Benja, was out in the night, floating through the darkness. As always, whenever the three sisters were unhappy or fought among themselves, the Benja left them. Then he could reach by magic into distant places, or sometimes even see glimpses of the future. Nothing in the night sky or in visions of the future could trouble the Benja like his sisters' disagreements.

Time passed slowly for the three sisters. More smoke rose from their fire and had trouble finding its way out into the night. None of the sisters wanted to be the first to cough.

Then suddenly the smoky gloom of the guardhouse was lit by bright gold: the Benja was back, gleaming with gold light, floating in the middle of the air.

"The Apprentice is alive!" he cried aloud. "And the Grey Witch of the North is dead!"

Their mouths opened in astonishment, then the three sisters glanced at each other, each thinking the same thought: *So, we will meet Julian the Apprentice again! At the Goblin Market in Far Avalon! Where exactly is that place? And when will we meet him?*

·)(·

Julian, Galad and the Familiars stumbled out of the Labyrinth into the early morning light, blinking and laughing, walking away from the Kingdom of the Grey Witch. Deep down, the four of them understood that they would never return to this part of the Wizards' League.

Water from the underground streams had helped to clean their bodies, while the clothes of Julian and Galad had been washed by the underground tribes. Even after being baked dry, their cloaks and shirts were still damp, and they shivered a little as they hiked through the morning sunlight.

The light made all of them blink, even Rafir. Although they had to shield their eyes from the brightness of the sun and were chilled by the cold of late autumn, nothing could keep them from smiling and their steps were light. They were alive, and they had survived the nightmare underground Labyrinth of the Grey Witch. Not one of the four turned to look back to the kingdom of the Grey Witch. Instead, they faced forward to the south, on their way back to Gravengate.

Gnome workers had made canvas backpacks for both Julian and Galad so that the two of them could share the weight of Galad's armor. Julian's backpack also included written treaties, one from each of the underground tribes, promising obedience to the Wizards and their League. Privately, Julian thought that most of the underground peoples would pass back to the north of Alantéa, or into the enchanted kingdoms of the Mid-World.

A whisper of thought reached Julian's mind. He stopped and stared up into the morning sky.

"The Eye of Merlin is coming for us," Julian murmured, "flying, as usual, faster than any winged creature."

"If the Wizards were brilliant," Galad said, "They would send horses to help us with the return journey." He was quiet for a moment, walking steadily south, then Galad finally asked, "How much are we going to tell the eagle?"

"Everything," Julian answered. "The Nine Billion Gods and other Powers have no love for the Wizards and their alliance. The Wizards have focused on their fortresses and the coastline while overlooking other sections of their League. They need to look east, west, and north, as well as to the south. Also, the four of us are their Emissaries, their defenders, and they haven't really prepared us to deal with the many kinds of beings ranged against them."

Galad shook his head and looked away: he doubted that the Wizards would listen to Julian, or to himself.

"Ahem," Sebastian said. "We don't think it's a good idea to correct the Wizards. We think they don't like to be told what to do. From all our dealings with them in the past, we feel that they will need to come to their own conclusions."

Galad smiled. "I suppose this 'we' is you and Rafir. What do the two of you suggest?"

"Tell them everything, but keep the story only to the facts," Sebastian replied. "Don't add your conclusions — let them draw their own. Meanwhile...*we*, Sebastian and Rafir, will take the Eye of Merlin aside, and tell him, Familiar to Familiar, that keeping us ignorant just hasn't protected us at all. Instead, it's made our lives much more dangerous. I think that's more likely to get through to them, than being lectured by their two strongest emissaries."

Galad smiled at the thought. "You know, that actually might work. What do you think, Julian?"

"I like it," Julian said. "Balardi is somewhat approachable, while Thorian is not, and when I speak with Merlin, his mind always seems focussed on the many problems of the Wizards' League, or on future challenges, or he's thinking about the dark events of the past."

"Or about the troubles of a different universe that's far beyond our own sun," Galad added. "All right, it's done. The Familiars will take over, and I'll toast them with a goblet of ale in one hand while the other holds an enormous drumstick."

"When I'm speaking with the Eye," Rafir said, "I'll need to make certain that I understand everything clearly. So, what exactly happened with this 'Transformation of the Grey Witch,' as you and Julian call it?"

Galad looked a little uncomfortable.

"Wait," Sebastian interjected. "Julian and Galad are going to tell us about some unhappy ending that has no place in a fairy tale. Rafir, when you see a smaller creature gobbled up by a predator — like a hawk taking a rabbit, what do you feel?"

"A bit of fear," Rafir said, "and a touch of sadness."

"I feel the same sort of thing," Sebastian said. "Now what would you feel if something bad — really bad — happened to this Grey Witch of the North?"

"You mean," Rafir said in disbelief, "that we've been fighting this crazy old Grey Witch of the North, a Witch that turns out to be a Creature of the

Darkness, a monster that keeps trying to torture then murder us, take over Julian, and become a fake and evil Julian. Now when something horrible happens to this Witch Creature I'm supposed to feel bad about that? I try to be the best little Familiar that I can but, please! I'm sorry, but it's goodbye Witch, and I'll sleep better now that she's gone."

"And that's what I feel," Sebastian added.

"I think," Galad said, glancing at Julian, "that the Witch Creature was 'transformed' — into food. What do you think, Julian?"

"I felt hunger," Julian said, "from the other side of that dark curtain. I think that this enormous Spellweaver was hiding in a place where no other living thing could survive. When it found enchanted flesh, it satisfied its hunger."

"And the Witch Creature," Galad added, "was filled with surprise and fear, the same kind of fear that your rabbit showed when taken by your hawk. So, one Creature of the Darkness gobbled up another monster. That's happened before, and it will happen again. The question I had was this: where was this huge Spellweaver hiding? It looked like it was living on the dark side of the moon."

"What we saw was not the moon as we know it," Julian said. "I think that we will let Merlin worry about the Spellweaver and its hiding place."

"Anyway," Sebastian said, quoting Rafir, "'Goodbye, Witch, and I'll sleep better now that she's gone.'" The little Familiar flapped his wings and lifted into the morning air. Sebastian felt lighter after their long struggle underneath the ground, and he flew higher than he usually did, letting the sunlight warm his wings as he coasted South through the light breezes of early morning.

Galad let a brief smile flash over his face, then he shook his head in dismay. "By all the Nine Billion Gods, I've been in a lot of close battles, but this is the first time I've been saved by sneezing powder. Think about it, Julian: you with all your carefully hidden strength of magic, while I held the Tarnished Sword, and we were saved by sneezing powder!"

Julian laughed ruefully, with little humor in his laughter.

"Wait just a minute," said the fox. "This 'Destiny' of ours is bound to have some close calls and some difficult moments. But think about this: Julian is the most powerful Apprentice who ever lived, stronger than many Adepts. And you, Galad, are there many warriors who might be your equal in Alantéa the Forerunner? Is there even one who could match you? Are there any weapons equal to the Tarnished Sword? I don't think so."

Rafir flicked his tail back and forth, ready to race into the morning sunlight. "And in addition to you two heroes, you have two of the most adorable Familiars on the planet. Never bet against the heroes, especially if they have two extremely cute Familiars helping them." The fox flashed out of view and began racing south, speeding through soft grasses.

Galad threw back his head and laughed the laugh of a hero in his greatest moment of triumph.

Julian smiled and felt some of the stress leave his body. His small family — Rafir and Sebastian — was safe. He was marching south beside Galad, his closest friend and ally. His parents still lived, and one day he would find some way to reach them, some way to free them. He glanced around, freezing images of their return journey forever in his mind.

In the east, the sun had risen, gleaming with a radiance of gold over Alantéa the Forerunner.

Above them, Sebastian was coasting easily through the morning breezes. The sky overhead was so incredibly blue and clear that it seemed that it might not rain again until the storms of late fall battered the coast.

Green grasses lay everywhere around them, while many of the surrounding trees still held clusters of the brown and yellow and red leaves of autumn.

And Rafir ran ahead of them, with finches and robins and horned larks and emerald jays flapping away from the passage of the invisible fox as he raced — without a care in the world — back toward Gravengate.

The Grey Witch of the North is the third of five books.
The Sorcerers and the Marids is the sequel.

·)(·

Manufactured by Amazon.ca
Bolton, ON

24601455R00152